SMALL TOWN EMP

Survive the Chaos

Survive the Aftermath

Survive the Conflict

Cover Design by LJ Mayhem Covers
www.relaypub.com

SMALL TOWN EMP BOOK TWO

SURVIVE
THE AFTERMATH

GRACE HAMILTON

BLURB

The New World Order is at hand.

Civilization has crumbled since the EMP thrust humanity back into the Stone Age, and dangerous factions now scavenge for scarce resources in this terrifying new world.

Austin Merryman wonders what the future holds for his teenaged daughter, and if the madness surrounding them is even worth surviving. For now, the group is safe in his brother's prepper house nestled in the Rockies. But the calm can't last forever. With sixteen people crammed together in the tiny mountain home, tensions are bound to erupt. It doesn't help that his brother's lazy friend gets twisted pleasure from stirring up animosity, pitting brother against brother and daughter against father as battle lines are drawn.

But decisions about who stays and who goes are ripped from their hands as information on the USB drive lays bare pieces of the NWO's plans. Austin realizes the horrifying truth of why he's in their sights, as well as the danger he's brought down on those he loves most. When tragedy again strikes the small group, it will be up to Austin to make the hard choices necessary to ensure their survival.

Until a dying man utters the single word that changes everything…

CONTENTS

1

Austin Merryman walked outside his brother's luxury home, which had been built with the apocalypse in mind. The place was a treasure, given all that had happened, but that didn't stop it from being cramped. Breathing in the fresh air of the outdoors, he took a minute to look around and take stock of who was where. It was tough keeping up with sixteen people. He could hear male voices coming from the right, mingled with the repetitive *thwack* of an ax hitting wood.

Down the driveway, he saw a couple of the women from the revivalist crew. They were carrying plastic grocery bags filled with what looked like weeds. Well, scratch that—they actually were weeds, technically, but the women were using them for some project or another. He couldn't remember what it was.

Thinking he just needed space, he started walking into the trees to find a little peace and quiet. Ever since they'd gotten into the USB the day before and scanned through the litany of files on the thing, his mind had been in overdrive. He'd barely slept at all, thinking about everything he'd seen and trying to make sense of it.

"Hey, is everything okay?" Amanda Patterson asked, her voice coming from behind him.

He turned to look at the woman who'd saved his life and become what he had to think of as one of his best friends. She was stubborn, opinionated, intelligent, a heck of a shot... and very easy on the eyes.

"Everything's fine," he acknowledged, and when she didn't look like she believed him, he moved to sit on a large rock surrounded by tall pine trees, out of sight of the house.

"I wanted a minute to think without being asked what to do next," he explained quietly. She smiled back at him, and he could tell just from her expression that she understood his feelings.

"There's a lot of people who are lost and confused... needing some direction. I guess you're the guy to give it," she said, sitting down beside him and nudging his arm.

"Lucky me," he grumbled.

His eyes moved around the area. It was pretty. A place he would have loved to park his fifth-wheel and hang out for a couple weeks. His brother's property was high up in the mountains north of Denver, Colorado, completely off the grid and off the beaten path—way off. There wasn't a single road that would lead directly to the house. You had to take a series of dirt roads and know the way if you wanted to find it without getting turned around, which made it an ideal hideout in a world gone bad.

It was a safe haven, without a doubt, and he was grateful for the roof over his head, but he didn't know if it was the right choice for a long-term living situation. With all that had happened, though, how could he know what the right choice was? He needed a few minutes to himself, away from the busy household filled with relative strangers. It had been nearly a week since they'd all begun cohabitating, and he'd barely said more than a few words to most of them. He didn't know them and wasn't sure he could blindly trust anyone. They were living in different times that required him to be a lot more careful than he'd once been.

But Amanda was something else. Outside of his brother and his daughter, she was the one among them he felt sure he could trust. After all they'd been through together, he had to trust her.

Beside him, she picked some dry moss from the base of the rock. "Good tinder," she muttered.

He looked down at the moss in her hand. "I suppose."

She frowned back to him. "Come on, Austin, what's the deal? We walked how many miles to get here? We've barely caught our breath! And now that we're here, you're thinking about leaving, aren't you?" she asked.

He couldn't stop the slow grin from spreading over his face. "You think you know me so well."

"I think I know you well enough to see you're feeling a little stir-crazy."

"Do you ever get that feeling that the other shoe's about to drop? I keep looking over my shoulder. All that stuff on that drive..." He stopped talking, shaking his head at the thought of what they'd been caught up in.

"I get it, I do. But let's celebrate our win. You're here, Savannah is here, and the house is solid," she said.

Austin nodded, knowing she had a point. He was happy to be reunited with Savannah, and grateful to the revivalists for keeping her alive and getting her to the house, but he wasn't sure where they went from here. There'd also been no talk of the others moving on since they'd arrived, and that only served to complicate things. He didn't want to be ungrateful, but how long could the house support all of them?

"We have to figure out what happens next," he said. They'd been putting off the conversation, but it had to happen.

"Austin, everyone is recovering from the long journey here. Let's give everybody a minute to figure stuff out."

"If they don't leave in the next couple months, winter will set in and traveling on foot will be impossible. The Loveridge family has a home in Salt Lake City—that was their original destination. Is it still? How do I ask them if they plan on staying or going without sounding like a total jerk?" he asked.

She shrugged, her eyes ranging over the forest around them. "Like I said, give it a few days. Tonya Loveridge is still grieving and recovering from the trip. I don't know if she can make it on her own."

"She has Malachi and the others," Austin pointed out.

"You know what I mean. None of them are ready for that."

He nodded, knowing she was right. "That may be true, but sixteen people in that house all summer is going to be rough."

Summer promised to be hot and miserable in a world without AC. Fortunately, the house was surrounded by trees and lots of shade, but that only went so far, and it was one of the few things they had going for them. The metal walls and roof were great for keeping out unwanted guests, but they promoted the feeling of living inside a steel box. The only opening was the front door, which they'd taken to leaving open all day to allow fresh air into the house.

"It is getting a little stuffy in there," she commented, her eyes moving around the area before she spotted more hanging moss and moved to climb up on another rock to pluck it down. She added it to her little pile of tinder and then crouched to rub some more moss from the rock where they'd been sitting.

He looked down at her, watching her gathering supplies even as they chatted. Looking for supplies had become second nature. Today, her dark hair was pulled back in a ponytail, showcasing her pretty eyes, and she was so easy to look at—watching her had become second nature for him. "Yeah, stuffy is one way to put it. I wish Ennis would have stockpiled deodorant," he muttered.

Amanda chuckled. "I know you're not telling me I stink," she said, nudging his knee.

He smiled. "No, you know what I mean. We need to get better ventilation in there."

"It's only going to get hotter," she replied with a grimace on her face, finally looking back up to meet his eyes.

Austin nodded, staring off into the trees and thinking about the many issues they had to deal with. He felt like they were treading water, barely getting by and not making any real plans for the future.

"It'd be nice to have more blankets or sleeping cots, too."

"Who needs a blanket when it's eighty degrees in the house?" she quipped.

"Sleeping on the hard floor is getting old. It's like we have everything except for comfort. It's better than sleeping outside on the cold, rocky ground, sure, but I think it would be a morale booster if we could all sleep better. Let's face it, almost none of us are spring chicks anymore," he said.

Amanda laughed. "Speak for yourself, buddy. I'm young and spry."

He chuckled in return as she gave up on the moss and sat back down beside him. "I've seen Gretchen weaving pine needles," he told her. "Maybe she can make sleeping mats. She could use grass, maybe, which might be softer if we could find enough. Anything would be better than sleeping directly on the floor. If only we had yarn. I heard one of the other women say she loved to knit."

"I know how to knit," Amanda said casually.

Austin turned to look at her. "Really?"

"Yep. I'm pretty good at it, too."

"I don't think there's anything you're not good at," he offered, making her blush a little.

"What else is running through your mind? Besides knitting, I mean," she joked.

He shrugged. "I don't know. A lot. I'm thinking long-term, just in case we have to stay here. You say the Loveridges aren't ready to travel, and that's fine, but I think we need to know what everyone is planning, and when, or we're going to be caught unprepared. Right now, we're burning through resources pretty fast. We need to be thinking about how to make it all last."

"Like what?"

"The propane, the food, the water—everything," he murmured.

She nodded, looking unsurprised. "The propane is definitely going to be an issue. We can't keep using the stove to heat water. It's wasteful. We should be cooking our meals outside."

"The ladies did build a fire the other day to heat the water," he commented.

"Yes, but we need a stove. It wouldn't be hard to make, what with all the rocks around here. If we're here in the winter, we'll be able to use it then, too, if we build a cover over it," she added.

"Good idea.

Amanda looked off into the trees, lost in thought as she continued and he listened. "We can use foil to make a solar oven and save on using the propane stove, as well. We won't have to worry about building a fire. We can make bread, stews, or even casseroles in it," she said. "And we can use it to boil water."

"You sound very excited about aluminum foil," he teased her, but a smile had come to his own face also—maybe he just needed something to focus on, he thought, to feel like they were doing something instead of treading water.

She all but giggled, knocking her shoulder into his as she replied. "Foil's better than gold in this off-the-grid situation. There are so many ways to use it! If those windows were exposed, we could cover them with foil to block the sun or use it in the winter to keep the heat trapped inside. It's a great way to clean dirty pots and pans, too. Trust me, foil is a big deal," she said.

"All right, I'm going to take your word for it," he told her, and then he caught her hand in his and gave it a squeeze. He didn't need to tell her that part of what she'd offered him that day was simple companionship—a like mind to share the worry. That meant as much as any idea, no matter how valuable.

"I think your idea of weaving a grass mat is good, too, Austin.

It will give Gretchen and the others something to focus on that could really help. I feel like they're always waiting for something, for us to tell them to do something," she added a moment later.

Austin raised an eyebrow. "We've been here a week. Didn't you just tell me to give it some time?"

"Ha. Yeah, fair enough. But in terms of routine, and them looking to us for direction, it sometimes feels like a month," she admitted. "I'm not saying I want them to leave," she quickly added.

"If they are all going to stay, I think we need to build some shelters."

"Like cabins?" she asked.

"Yeah, why not? Ennis has plenty of tools around here. It would make the sleeping arrangements a little more tolerable. Four people to a room is crowded," he pointed out.

"You're not telling me anything I don't already know. That is a good idea, though. The shelters wouldn't have to be big, either —just large enough for a few people to sleep in," she said.

"What about winter?"

She let out a sigh. "One problem at a time."

"Alright, so how about we at least bring it up tonight—test the water, see what people are thinking. And if they're not thinking on the lines of staying or leaving yet, that will get the conversation started."

"Okay," she said, more slowly. "But we won't push anything, right? I still feel like everyone needs more time to adjust and decide what they want. We can give them a few days."

"I agree," he said. "We'll give them a couple days, at least, to decide what they want, but tonight we can start the discussion and make sure everyone's thinking about what the long-term plan is. And, meanwhile, we can get started talking about what arrangements will have to be made to make it all work. If everyone wants to stay, we talk about building small cabins," he said. "In the meantime, I think we really need to drive home the need to conserve resources."

"That'll make everyone understand we're not in more than a temporary holding pattern, too," Amanda said. "It'll help folks make up their minds."

That said, she offered him a grin that suggested she might expect to see one on his own face, but it faltered when he didn't return the expression. Instead, he shrugged and looked back off into the trees, down toward the house. It was good to have a plan, and to have her on his side in being ready to start this conversation... but he didn't feel as optimistic as she apparently did.

"Okay, Austin, come on, what's really got you out here sulking and crawling inside your own head? It isn't the heat because the heat isn't intolerable. Just wait until July."

Austin stared down at the ground littered with little green vines and plenty of dry pine needles. Amanda knew him way too well. He liked it and hated it at the same time. It reminded him of what things had been like with his late wife. Having someone know you better than you knew yourself was comforting. But he wasn't sure he was ready for any of that to come back—not yet.

"I can't get that crap we saw on that drive out of my head," he confessed. "All that information. It was hard to take in, and I don't even understand most of it. Thank God Nash is here. That kid is smart. I hate not being able to know what's happening. I've never been one of those people who can put my head in the sand and hope for the best, but now I'm just confused."

Amanda's soft laugh washed over him. "You're a journalist. By nature, you have to dig. You have to know the how and the why."

"I do! It's how I work, Amanda. I need to know what's coming. I thrive on information. I hate that I can't make heads or tails of that gibberish we saw. It looked like the ravings of a mad man planning for world domination through a series of computer programs and viruses. Is that what you got out of it?"

She wrinkled her nose. "In a nutshell, yes, but maybe we're wrong. Maybe it really is the ravings of some crazy guy with too much money and too much computer know-how."

"Savannah said Zander claimed there was a group of people doing this," he reminded her.

She sighed. "I don't know what to think about any of it. It's overwhelming, but what can we do about it right this very minute? Nash is going over it and looking for anything that might help us or give us an edge, but we're not the ones in control. I know that's a hard pill to swallow—trust me, I get it. I don't like it, either. But we have to focus on the right now."

"It isn't about a lack of control, but more about why? Why would anyone want to do this? I need to know the end game," he admitted, standing up to pace. "The stories I used to cover about various wars and scandals all had an end game. The people were doing what they did because they wanted something. What do these people want—the earth in general?" he demanded. His voice had raised with the frustration, but he couldn't let it go.

"They're crazy, Austin, in the literal sense of the word. You just can't let them drive you crazy," Amanda answered, reasonably enough to make him scowl at her logic as she went on. "They clearly have big egos. You can't ever apply reason and logic to irrational, egotistical fanatics," she said.

He shook his head, running a hand over his stubbled jaw before looking back at her. "The entire world is being affected by their schemes. Who does that? Who wants to destroy an entire world? What, there are like seven billion people on the planet, and we have a couple hundred rich, arrogant jerks who decide their way is the only way? I don't get it. I can't get my head around it. It is insane!" he said, his voice rising more as he gave voice to his thoughts.

He'd been unable to think of practically anything else since they'd opened the files on the USB drive. Austin, along with Amanda, Nash, and Ennis, had decided it was best to keep the information to themselves until they knew what to do with it.

He didn't want Savannah worrying any more than necessary. And Tonya Loveridge, for one, was barely hanging on and certainly didn't need any more stress. As the leader of the revivalists, she'd have been the logical one to share the information with, but all of them knew she wasn't up to shouldering more information.

"Nash said he was working it out," Amanda said in a low, soothing voice. "Let's give him some time to try and make sense of it all."

"We have a single laptop, and we're somehow supposed to be able to use it to bring them down and fix everything. Or at least make it more bearable. Really? How? I'm guessing the whiz kid isn't that smart. I don't know much, if anything, about computers, satellites, or digital technology in general, Amanda—I'm a journalist, not a scientist. This stuff wasn't supposed to come down to me."

Amanda stood up and caught his arm, forcing him to face her before she answered. "Austin, relax. Let's take this one day at a time. Let's focus on what we do have, rather than what we don't. There's enough food to last a few months, assuming everyone stays. The water supply, that could get a little tricky, but we'll figure something out. We have a roof over our heads and, unlike the rest of the world, we still have electricity from the solar panels during the day, and the turbine as back-up, too," she reminded him. "We'll start rationing and thinking about the future. I think that will help bring you some peace. You need a plan, and now we have one for the short-term. We're okay for now."

He smirked. "I used to make so much fun of my brother for spending all that money on the house. One year for Christmas, I gave him a hat made from tin foil. It was pretty funny then, but I guess he's probably the one laughing now."

Amanda's soft laugh filled the area. "If it had been my brother building a house like this, I probably would have done the same thing."

With that, Amanda tugged Austin back to their rock and they sat in silence, listening to the trees rustling in the slight breeze high overhead. He remained silent beside her, thinking they both needed a bit of peace after the productive, if stressful, conversation they'd just had. Above them, a variety of birds were singing their songs as they flew from branch to branch, happy as they could be and not caring a bit that the world was in serious turmoil. Their world was completely unaffected. Austin envied them.

As more moments passed, Austin felt himself calming down and finally just appreciating the peace of the forest. It was nice to have company that didn't require conversation. There was an easy comfort between him and Amanda that allowed them to be near each other without feeling like they had to fill the silence.

Part of his problem lately was that he didn't get enough silence—in his mind, anyway. He'd been thinking a lot about everything he'd seen and heard since the day the world had gone dark. When he'd been looking for Savannah, he hadn't had a lot of time to really think about the why behind the darkness. Since he'd had to confront Zander and had gotten her back, it was all he could think about.

"It feels like a cult," Austin finally blurted out, speaking the thought he'd found himself circling back to. Again.

"What? The revivalists? I thought we already established they're okay," Amanda replied, her face twisted with confusion.

He shook his head. "No, not them. I don't think they're a cult. A little different, but I don't think they're marrying twelve-year-olds to old men or drinking the blood of virgins. I'm talking about these egomaniacs who created this disaster."

"You think they're a cult?" she asked, clearly not following his line of thought.

"Think about it. They've devised this plan to destroy every-one's belief system. They're stripping everything away, leaving the human race almost helpless. Because we're not all completely mindless, insipid fools, they've propagated civil wars, destroying the populous that wants to try and stay strong, to think for themselves. Then, we have these savior guys, the wealthy elite who know better than all of us, ready to swoop in and save the day. They have their rules that all must follow or face death," he explained, his brain moving fast as he compared the facts to his research on other established cults. This was the first time he'd gotten a chance to speak any of these thoughts aloud, and they made more and more sense as he did.

"Now you're kind of creeping me out," Amanda muttered.

"Think about it, Amanda! They want to be the supreme rulers. They think they have all the answers. They're rewriting the laws, beliefs, and trying to control human nature. They didn't like what they saw and decided to change it by eradicating the population like the people were nothing more than a cancer on the earth!"

Amanda put one of her small hands on his thigh, instantly calming him with her touch. "I know it seems bad when you think about it like that, but let's worry about our little corner of the world. They're out there, and we're right here."

What she said made sense, but thinking of all that evil out there, trying to change the world and come down on them... it was hard to ignore. "Is it worth it?" he finally asked, half to himself.

"Is what worth it?" Amanda asked.

"Surviving."

Her eyes went wide, and then she slapped his arm—hard. "Don't even talk like that! Of course, it's worth it. Don't pretend you're the type to give up. I'm not, and I'm not going to let you give up."

He shrugged. "Are we supposed to live up here forever? What kind of life is that? I have a teenage daughter. Is this our future? I have to be honest, Amanda; I'm not looking forward to living in that house with all those people for the rest of my days. I love my brother, but I don't think I can live with him."

She studied his expression, and he didn't look away. "Did you walk across the country only to turn around and walk back home, wherever that is?"

"Maybe. I do have a house."

"You have no way of knowing if that house is still standing or if the area where you lived is safe. Look what happened at my place," she reminded him. "The world we knew is gone. The sooner you accept that, the sooner you can start thinking about the future. You can't go back. None of us can."

He closed his eyes. She was right. Going home wasn't an option. He looked through the trees, listening to the sounds beyond his little piece of quiet on the rock. He had to rethink things and decide what to do. He felt as if there was a clock on things, knowing winter would make it difficult to travel.

"Doesn't it feel like we're giving up in a way anyway?" he asked.

She shrugged. "I don't think we're giving up. We're making sure we can survive until something changes."

"What if it doesn't change?" he asked, meeting her eyes again.

"Austin, you are getting way ahead of yourself. It's only been a few weeks—"

"Months, Amanda, it's been almost two months since everything went to hell in a handbasket," he retorted.

"Okay, fine, months, but that doesn't mean *this* is the forever future. We cannot be the only ones out here who are sane and ready to survive. I know all about the prepping movement. I know guys who had HAM radios, and some of them belonged to their own militia-type groups. We are not the only ones ready to rage against the machine. Let's focus on today and tomorrow. We have that information to comb through. Maybe there is some secret code word that will change everything. Crazier things have happened," she pointed out, and he couldn't argue with her.

"We'll figure this out," she added seriously, her tone full of hope.

"One way or another, I'm not going to have my little girl living forever in a house with men I don't know, and one young man who I know she has a serious crush on—and vice versa," he snarled.

Amanda chuckled. "Savannah is a smart girl. We talked about building cabins. Savannah will have her space, and the men from the revivalist group don't seem to be a threat. They're nice enough, and most are older," she said.

Austin shook his head. "It feels like a commune."

"Communes don't have to be a bad thing."

Austin stared back at her, frowning. How could a commune be a good thing, after the world they'd known before? How could they settle for something like this little corner of a forest being their whole world? He shook his head, looking away from her. Maybe he was being unrealistic.

"I don't like the idea of her living with a boyfriend, even if I am right here," he complained.

Amanda laughed outright. "You're being a protective daddy.

Fight that battle another day. The living situation is more like living in the same apartment building. We'll all keep an eye on her."

"That's what I'm afraid of," he said dryly.

She laughed again. "You're freaking out over something that hasn't happened. You took on a crazed gunman without thinking twice and this is what keeps you up at night?"

He shrugged. "I can't help it. She's my little girl."

"I love how protective you are, but you are stressing yourself out over nothing. Don't make a problem that isn't there," she advised him.

He let out a long breath, knowing she was right once again. He had to let go a little. Savannah was a smart girl and knew how to protect herself. "I tend to be overprotective," he admitted. "It's something Savannah and I have been butting heads over for too long. I'll back off, but that doesn't mean I'm totally sold on the idea of staying here indefinitely."

Amanda smiled. "Good enough. Now, come with me, okay? I want to do a little exploring and see if we can find a natural spring. With this hillside, there has to be a winter run-off. We'll look for the greenest, lushest part of the forest. We can do a little digging and I bet we'll find water. We can follow it up the hillside and find the source," she said, and with more enthusiasm than he felt for anything at the moment.

Still, he nodded, sliding off the rock and wiping off his butt before he knelt to help her re-collect the moss she'd gathered and press it into pockets within her cargo pants. His leg twinged when he stood back up, but he managed to keep from showing it; the limb had healed, but tended to be a little sore now and again. This was one of those times. He wasn't looking forward to climbing the steep, rocky terrain, but Amanda was right about one thing. He needed to get his mind off things and stop dwelling on problems he couldn't solve, or else he was going to drive himself crazy.

2

Savannah walked upstairs to the room she shared with Amanda, Bonnie, and Gretchen. They'd all agreed to give the single bed in the room to Bonnie. She was still grieving the loss of her husband, Bill, and she was the oldest of the four of them. It seemed right for her to have the bed.

"Hi," she said when she saw Gretchen reading in one of the chairs in the corner of the room. Although the woman was in her thirties, Savannah felt closer to her than any of the other women in the home—her calmness was comfortable, and friendly.

"Savannah," she greeted her with a friendly smile, setting her book down in her lap.

"What are you reading?" she asked.

Gretchen held up the book to show her the cover, which displayed a picture of a woman eating a handful of berries.

"This is a book on the wild edibles in the Rocky Mountains. I'm brushing up on the plants that are new to me, different than what we had in the Appalachians."

"My uncle had that book?" Savannah asked.

Gretchen smiled bigger, her freckled cheeks dimpling. "He did. He has an entire library filled with books on surviving off the grid and in the wild. Your uncle is a smart man. I had a bunch of these books on my Kindle. Fat lot of good that does me now," she joked.

"I'd like to go with you if you go out foraging," Savannah volunteered.

"I'd like that. I'm hoping to get Tonya to go, too. She needs to get some fresh air and sunlight."

Savannah glanced back out the door, down the hall, but saw no sign of the other woman. "Have you spoken to her today?"

Gretchen shook her head, her face creasing with the worry that Savannah herself felt. "No, I tried to take her some breakfast, but she's been holed up in that room unwilling to come out. Malachi said she was sleeping. I worry she's sleeping too much. I saw her yesterday and she looked extremely pale; the weight loss is really showing."

Savannah nodded, having sought Gretchen out just for this purpose—to talk about Tonya. She'd gotten an idea and wasn't sure if it was a good one, but she was confident Gretchen would know. "Listen, I was thinking… What if we had a service outside, like you guys used to do with the tents and stuff?" Savannah offered. She'd hesitated to bring it up, but couldn't imagine what else might do Tonya more good, and Malachi was so worried about her. So was she, truth be told.

Gretchen's eyes drifted back to the door, thoughtful, but her voice sounded hopeful when she spoke. "That's a great idea. We can put down some blankets under the trees and Malachi can give a sermon."

Savannah smiled, relieved that Gretchen liked the idea. "I think he'd like that."

"Maybe some of the others would like to join us?" Gretchen suggested. "Make it more like old times with a good group of us."

"I wouldn't count on my dad attending. He's not the religious type," Savannah admitted.

Gretchen shrugged, smiling again now. "It isn't about religion; it's about celebrating the fact that we're alive and worshipping our Maker."

She didn't think she could sell that to her dad, but that was okay. This wasn't about him. "Do you think we could do it tomorrow?"

"I think that would be perfect," Gretchen replied. "How about we plan for that, and tell Tonya at dinner once we've got it more settled?"

Savannah grinned, excited to have a good reason to talk to Malachi. "I'm going to go find Malachi and tell him. That will give him plenty of time to put together a sermon." If anything would get him to talk to her openly, it would be the subject of finding a way to help his mom out. She felt thrilled that they were under the same roof, but he was still convinced she was no good for him. This was the perfect way to show him she wasn't so bad.

Sure, Savannah knew he'd been reluctant to spend a lot of time hanging out with her, but this would be something else. With that in mind, she took a quick look in the mirror, brushing her hair to a shine before tucking her tank top into her shorts. The shorts were approved by her father, which meant they practically went to her knees, but at least they were fairly clean. She longed for the days when she had a wardrobe to actually choose from. Now, she had a pair of pants or the shorts—and that was it.

"Have fun!" Gretchen called out as Savannah practically bounced from the room.

She headed downstairs where she found Wendell sitting on the leather couch beside her uncle. They were in a heated conversation about the Denver Broncos. It seemed silly to be talking about football, but she guessed maybe it made them feel normal. Whatever got them by.

"Have you seen Malachi?" she asked.

Wendell looked up at her. "He went outside with a couple of the other ones."

She stared at him, and when he didn't back down, she responded. "Other ones?" she asked, not appreciating the way he referred to the others.

She'd gotten the feeling Wendell didn't like the group of

revivalists she had traveled with, yeah, but he didn't have to talk about them like that. Her dad assured her Ennis didn't mind them sticking around. After all, they had kept her alive, and they all owed them for that. Wendell's opinion didn't matter. It wasn't his house, according to her dad, but this was ridiculous.

"Those Bible thumpers you hang out with," Wendell replied with a look of utter distaste. "You know, the God squad," he joked, looking to Ennis for congratulations on what he clearly thought was a funny joke.

She shot him a dirty look, appreciating the fact that her uncle looked slightly embarrassed on his behalf, rather than appreciative. "We're going to be holding a service, Wendell. You should come. You might learn something about human kindness," she snapped before spinning on her heel and heading for the front door.

She would have loved to make a grand departure and slam the door, but that was far too risky and she knew it. The steel plate that had slid over the door was up, supported by some heavy cable Nash had rigged, but there was no guarantee the thing wouldn't loosen, and the door could slam down. Ennis and Nash assured her it was safe, but she preferred not to risk getting squished by a heavy door just to prove a point.

"Malachi?" she called out, looking around and beyond her uncle's dead SUV in the driveway, her eyes scanning the flat area and the surrounding woods.

She listened, waiting to hear him reply.

"Over here!" his voice called out from the right.

She followed the sound, finding him on the other side of the line of trees along the steep driveway to the house. He was standing near a pile of large red fir wood rounds that Ennis had explained he'd had delivered last year for the oncoming winter. He stood with two other men and there was an ax in his hand. The smell of the wood reminded her of home. She inhaled deeply, thinking about the last winter with her mom, sitting in front of their woodstove at home and drinking hot cocoa. She quickly brushed away the nostalgia, though, not wanting to get melancholy. This was about Malachi and his mom, and not her own heartbreak.

"What are you doing?" she asked, immediately feeling like an idiot for asking such an obvious question.

He had taken his shirt off and had a fine sheen of sweat over his naked torso. His long black hair was pulled back in a ponytail that hung down his back. Seeing him like this had left her stumbling over her words a few days before, though she thought she'd managed not to gawk at him today, at least. Even if she'd sounded like an idiot, asking what he was doing.

"Splitting wood," he replied in a dry tone, looking irritated.

The two men he was with smirked. "I'll take over," Jordan said, stepping forward to take the ax from Malachi.

Malachi yanked his t-shirt from the tree limb it had been hanging on and used it to wipe his face before turning to Savannah and pulling it on.

"What's up?" he asked as he stepped toward her, the scowl on his face revealing his irritation.

"Can we talk for a minute?" she asked. Then, not wanting to have an audience, she started to move away—Malachi didn't follow.

"Fine, but I need to get back to work soon."

She stopped in her tracks, realizing he wasn't planning on following. With a sigh, she turned back to face him and stepped nearer, hoping the men wouldn't overhear her as they continued chopping at the wood. If he was about to shoot down her idea, she wanted it to be in private.

"Gretchen and I were thinking we could hold a service under the trees tomorrow evening. There's that spot over there, which could be nice." She pointed to a flat, wooded area where there was a decorative park bench tucked under the trees.

"A service?" he asked.

"You guys used to have some kind of worship every day. We were thinking you could give a short sermon and then maybe sing a few songs. I want to help your mom. Getting out in the fresh air and doing what your father always did might help."

He looked thoughtful, and then shook his head. "I don't want to speak."

That, she hadn't expected, and it took her a moment to find words to respond. He looked ready to turn away by the time she found the words. "Malachi, your father would have wanted you to keep going. You told me he expected you to take over as the head of the group one day. That day is now," she said in a soft voice.

The men, standing a few feet away, were watching Malachi. The ax hung at Jordan's side while they waited for him to decide, signaling they'd heard everything. Malachi looked over his shoulder, staring at them before turning to face Savannah again.

"Okay. I'll do it."

Savannah grinned, just refraining from clapping her hands together. "This is going to be awesome! What do you need me to do? We could do it right before dinner tomorrow, after things cool down a bit."

"There will be a lot of mosquitoes," Jordan chimed in.

"We have all those citronella candles and bug spray," she said, already thinking about how she could organize the space and help get everything together to make it more comfortable.

"I'll talk to my mom, but I'd prefer to wait until I can put something together to say," Malachi said, a frown on his face.

"Is tomorrow long enough?"

He didn't look happy, but nodded anyway. "I suppose. I'll stay up tonight and work on something."

"Great! I'll talk to Gretchen and Bonnie. We can make a big meal for after the service, just like you guys used to have before all this happened!"

Finally, Malachi smiled. "Thank you, Savannah. It's a really good idea, and you're right, it's time for us to start rebuilding our lives. We can't forsake God. We have to worship in times of sadness and joy."

Savannah nodded, satisfied just knowing that Malachi liked her idea. Slowly but surely, she was going to prove to him she was worth having by his side. She was convinced she loved him, but he was certain she wasn't worthy. She only had to prove to him she was.

"I can't wait!" she told him honestly.

Malachi looked back at her, his eyes still holding that sadness she'd become familiar with. "Savannah, I have to get back to work. I promised your father and uncle we'd split and stack this wood before it rains."

She glanced beyond him to the men who were already back at the wood, and then caught his arm to stop him. "Mal, can't we go for a walk or something? You've been working for the last couple of days and we haven't had a chance to talk. There's not a cloud in the sky," she protested.

He grimaced. "Talk about what? If you're talking about what I think you are, I told you yesterday, I have to focus on taking care of my mom."

She let out a dramatic sigh. "I can help you."

"I've got work to do."

"Mal," she said, trying her best not to whine.

"Enough, Savannah, this isn't the time for this. I have responsibilities now. None of that other stuff matters," he said, turning back towards the men splitting wood.

She watched him walk away, pushing down the rejection she felt. In her mind, nothing had really changed. She had a serious crush on him, and was sure he liked her. She wasn't going to give up on him yet. He might be the last boy around that was worth crushing on, and she wasn't going to let him get away.

3

Ennis Merryman carried his plate of food outside, more than ready to enjoy the meal prepared by several of the ladies from the revivalist group. They were relying on the freeze-dried stuff for now, but after dinner, it had already been decided there'd be a discussion about long-term survival. They needed more food. They needed *fresh* food. His brother and what he had decided was his girlfriend, Amanda, had come to him earlier, letting him know they were going to broach the subject at the evening meal. It worked for him.

"Can I sit with you?" he asked his niece, who sat cross-legged on the blanket she occupied alongside her father and Amanda.

"Of course," Savannah replied, barely looking at him—she was already digging into the food, which hadn't yet grown old for her like it had for him. Being hungry was near enough in her memory that she seemed to think it was delicious.

He wished he agreed.

Still, the ladies seemed to know what they were doing with the stuff in his pantry. He ate as he looked around the clearing, where other blankets had been spread out for the large group to use; everyone was choosing to eat outside and appreciate the fresh air. It was a comfortable night, in the mid-seventies, while the house was hovering in the eighties. He didn't mind eating outdoors, but wished he would have had the foresight to have set up an outdoor eating and cooking area. He had a small patio table and chairs, but they weren't enough. Truth be told, he'd never anticipated needing to eat outside.

He looked around the area, listening to the quiet murmur of voices from the many conversations going on. Everyone was talking about what they'd done during the day and how nice it was to sit down and eat. It was like being at a camp of sorts. He didn't mind all the extra bodies, and appreciated the community feel. He had done this—or at least made it possible. He'd built a fortress that was now host to a new community they were creating. He kind of felt like the honorary mayor.

"Ennis, we need to know if you have any objections to everyone sticking around indefinitely," Austin said, his voice low.

"What? Why?" he asked.

"Because there's no point in talking to them about long-term goals for stocking up food and water here if they do plan on leaving. But we don't want to roll out the welcome mat if you prefer they go," Amanda whispered. "This is your place."

Ennis nodded, a little surprised at the idea of anyone leaving.

He had just assumed they were all staying. He hadn't really thought about six months down the road. Part of him still believed everything would be fixed, the government would rise again, and things would eventually go back to normal.

"I don't know. I thought some of them were talking about moving on, but nobody has actually said when," he murmured.

Austin looked to Amanda, who gave a very slight nod. "It could be beneficial to have sixteen people defending this place and working together to stay alive," he said, still whispering.

Amanda looked back at his brother and smiled. Austin shrugged in return. Ennis had no idea what they had just said in their own, private, unspoken language, but he had to fight down a twinge of jealousy. Austin and Amanda were so close, it was hard not to feel left out.

Ennis looked around at the revivalists, considering what had just been said. They weren't exactly Army material. They were actually soft, in his opinion. The strongest members of their group had been killed on the journey across the country from what he had been told. It was nothing short of a miracle they had made it at all. In fact, that's exactly what they were chalking their survival up to—a miracle created at the hands of the God they worshipped. He didn't know how much defending they could do... but they could cook, clean, and he did like the company. Sometimes, a few of the ladies would break into song, singing a hymn while they worked. It was nice to know he wasn't alone. Those days he'd spent alone in the house, thinking he would die, had given him a new appreciation for company.

"Those two, Jordan and Mike, they would be good assets. I think one of them could end up being a leader within that small group," Ennis said quietly.

"Those two would definitely be good help, but do you want them here? Do you want me here?" Amanda asked Ennis directly.

He nodded, not having to think about it. "I do."

"We need to talk to each of them and get a feel for what their plans are," Austin said.

"I think we can take some time," Ennis replied, not wanting to make any rash decisions. Couldn't they just relax for a few more days?

"The NWO is pushing folks out of the cities, Ennis," Amanda pointed out. "Those displaced people are going to be here as soon as they flee, looking for somewhere safe to live. We need to be ready for that. If they're going to stay here, they have to be ready to defend the house and all of us in it."

Ennis scoffed. "I'm not exactly in the suburbs."

"No, but they're running out of places to hide. People are going to be flooding the mountains to get away from those men we saw," Austin said, defending Amanda—as usual.

"So, what's your plan? What if they all decide to pick up and go? I heard Harlen talking to a few of the others. They want to try and get to Seattle. They still believe there's a retreat over there," he said, shaking his head at the silly notion.

"They don't like to fight. They really hate guns," Savannah added, chiming in for the first time. "I don't know if they'll want to stay here if you're going to try and make them fight back."

Austin glanced at her, but shook his head. "Too bad. If they're going to be here, they need to know how to defend the place. Four or five of us isn't going to be enough. If they're here, they're a part of it."

"Do you want to teach all of them? What about Wendell and Nash?" Ennis questioned.

"I think Nash is pretty capable. He proved he has what it takes already," Austin said, looking at his daughter and flashing back to Nash's role in rescuing her.

Ennis agreed with him, but was glad to hear it said. "When do you want to have this little come to Jesus conversation?"

"I want to broach the subject after dinner," Austin said, keeping his voice barely above a whisper. "Amanda can train them. She's ex-military and can teach them some basic self-defense, as well as how to shoot."

"I can help, as well," Ennis offered.

"Good. We need to start thinking more offensively," Austin said, finally digging into his meal.

"I agree. We can't take anything for granted. There are roads that can lead here. Someone is bound to find the house," Amanda said.

Austin looked up, chewing his food thoughtfully before he

spoke again. "I think we need to keep the number of guns we have in the stockpile to those of us sitting here."

Ennis raised an eyebrow. "Not Wendy?"

Austin shook his head. "No. Not yet. He knows about the ARs and he saw the full-automatics we brought back. That's all he needs to know about. That's all anyone else needs to know about. We don't know them all that well, and I don't think we can trust them implicitly, not yet. The guns and ammunition are too valuable to risk."

"Fine. It's locked down anyway," Ennis replied.

Amanda cleared her throat. "About that—I think it would be smart to hide some weapons around the property in case we're attacked and unable to get to the weapons cache."

Ennis felt his mouth gaping at her. How far were they going to take this army mentality? "What? Why?"

"What if we're hunting or out walking and there's an attack? Either we carry weapons all the time, which is dangerous for those who aren't familiar with using guns or tend to be jumpy, or we keep a stash for easy access. We also have to prepare for the house to be overtaken. We don't want to put all of our eggs in one basket, so to speak," Amanda explained.

Savannah was nodding. "I think that's a good idea."

Ennis knew he was outnumbered. He didn't like the idea of having his guns outside, exposed to the elements and up for grabs, but he did see the need to be prepared.

"Along with the guns, we should add some basic survival

stuff, like matches, some of those water purification tablets, and food," Savannah said.

Ennis looked sideways at her, pride over his niece suddenly overshadowing any other worries. "That's an excellent idea. I read about using PVC pipe to make caches, but I don't have any. We could use trash bags. We'll double-bag everything and add some of the silica gel packs I've stored."

"Will that be enough to absorb the moisture and condensation that will happen inside the trash bags?" Amanda asked.

Ennis thought about it. "There was something else I read that we can try. I have ice melt on hand, calcium chloride. We could make little sachets and put them inside the bags to keep the guns and ammo dry."

"Ice melt?" Savannah asked around a bite of food.

Ennis nodded. "It's a desiccant. You know how you were told to put your cell phone in a bag of rice if it got wet? It's the same thing. The calcium chloride will absorb moisture just like salt, rice, or even powdered coffee creamer."

Ennis looked to Austin, who seemed impressed. That made him feel good. All the years of studying survival were finally paying off.

"We'll do it," Austin said.

"Do we tell them about the emergency caches?" Amanda asked.

"I think we tell them about a couple, not all of them," Austin replied. "Especially not all of the weapons."

Ennis looked at him for a moment, raising an eyebrow. His brother kept coming back to the weapons, like they were an army encampment and not a group of strangers trying to survive. "Fine. Let's finish eating, and then we'll ask them all to participate in combat training. I'm sure that will go over great," Ennis said, a little sarcastically.

Austin shot him a look, but didn't say a word. Instead, they all got back to eating. They were halfway through their meal of roasted chicken and rice that had been pulled from the pantry, and Ennis wanted to enjoy what was left of it rather than worry about logistics of weapons training and long-term plans.

"This is really good," Savannah commented.

"I agree," Wendell said, coming to sit on the edge of the blanket.

Ennis noticed his brother stiffen. He knew Austin didn't like Wendell but wasn't sure why. Wendy was a little annoying, but he was nice. But then he leaned forward, convinced he'd caught a whiff of whiskey coming off the guy. He couldn't be sure, though, and chose not to say anything. There was enough tension without adding any more to the mix. He'd talk to Wendell about it later.

"We have to get fresh meat," Austin replied.

"Why? Ennis has plenty of food in the pantry," Wendell replied, stuffing his face with a healthy bite.

"Because this stuff is fine for the short-term, but it doesn't have all the nutrition of fresh meat. We need to supplement our diets or we're all going to end up sick and weak," Amanda replied as if it were obvious.

Ennis cleared his throat. "The packaging states it has all the nutrition we need."

"Not if it's the only thing you're eating," she retorted.

Ennis shrugged, wondering for a moment whether to believe this woman veterinarian or all of the packaging and prepping materials he'd studied. "I have a supply of multi-vitamins that would rival any Walgreens."

"Good, because you'll need it if this is all you eat for the rest of your days," she replied.

"Ennis isn't stupid. He's been preparing for this for a long time," Wendell said, defending him.

"I can see that. He's done an amazing job. I'm only saying fresh food is healthier. We need to take advantage of the summer to stockpile more food and water in case this thing we're living in lasts a long time. No matter what, his stores won't last forever."

Ennis nodded, acknowledging the point. He certainly hadn't planned on this many people being around for any length of time. Even as she'd spoken, though, Wendell had been getting ready to dig himself another hole.

"We don't need any more water. Ennis has plenty," Wendell replied in a haughty tone.

Ennis grimaced. He already knew what his brother would say, and he would be right.

"Enough water?" Austin scoffed.

"We're going to need more water. We can always use more water," Ennis replied gently, not wanting to insult or offend his friend.

Wendell looked as if he'd been slapped. "Of course. I only meant it doesn't need to be a priority."

Austin made a sound that said otherwise. Fortunately, he didn't say anything more. Austin could be a little stuck up at times, but at least he seemed to sense that this was a time to keep his mouth shut before the tension grew worse. Ennis shut out the exchange and focused on food, chalking it up to his brother being his brother. He had always had an air about him that made him seem untouchable, and it sometimes rubbed people wrong, just like it sometimes made Austin forget he was a mortal like the rest of them. His big brother was better looking, more charming, and they both knew he had always had an easy life—at least until his wife had died. That had been rough on him.

"I'm going to put my dish away and then I'll try and talk to everyone while we're all together," Amanda said, rising from the blanket.

"I'll go with you," Austin said, rising and following her back into the house.

"Talk to everyone?" Wendell asked.

Ennis needed to choose his words carefully, and he knew it. Savannah was loyal to her dad and would tell him anything that was said.

"We need to talk about defending this place," Ennis said lightly.

"My dad and Amanda want to teach people how to shoot and defend themselves," Savannah added.

"I know how to shoot," Wendell spat. "Do they honestly think they're the only two people who know how to use a gun?"

"Can you hit a moving target?" Savannah snapped back.

Ennis grinned, nudging his niece with his shoulder. "I taught her how to shoot, and she's good. I can work with you if you'd like," he told Wendell.

Wendell seemed to relax a little. "I'd like that. I'll admit I might not be great at moving targets, but I know how to use a gun. These other people, I don't see them picking up a gun. They're all peace, love, and joy," he said with a sneer.

"Uh, those people had to walk over a thousand miles to get here, and we all had to fight for our lives against bad guys," Savannah said, always quick to defend the revivalists.

"You saved them, Savannah," Ennis said quietly. "You did."

She looked at him, her brown eyes holding a hint of sadness. "I had to. I want them to know how to protect themselves in case they ever find themselves in that same situation and no one is around to do the saving."

"We'll teach them." And he would. He'd do anything for his niece.

Malachi had told him about Savannah shooting a man at point-blank range to save him. That was a huge burden to put on anyone's shoulders, especially a young girl. He hated that she'd had to do it, but was glad she known how. Austin hadn't been thrilled when Ennis had taken his little girl target shooting last year when they'd come for a visit, but it had saved her life and those she was with. He was proud of her.

Austin and Amanda came back out of the house with Gretchen and Tonya behind them, carrying their plates of food after feeding the rest of the group. He appreciated the way the newcomers were willing to help out, dividing responsibilities between themselves without complaining a bit. It made him hope they stayed around.

Gretchen and Tonya settled nearby on one of the blankets under the trees. Ennis swatted away a mosquito, hoping the coming lecture was short. The mosquitoes would be coming out in force with the cooling temps. While they didn't have to worry about Malaria, West Nile was a concern, even in the Rocky Mountains. He'd stocked bug spray, but not enough to last sixteen people all summer. Gretchen had said she knew a plant that would act as a bug repellent, and he hoped she was right. Getting eaten alive by mosquitoes was not his idea of a good time.

Ennis put his plate on the rocky ground beside him and gave his brother and Amanda his full attention. He was used to Austin taking charge, and at the moment, he didn't mind all that much. Why would things be any different in the apocalypse?

4

Amanda took a deep breath and scanned the crowd of people who were scattered around sitting on tree stumps, fallen logs, and blankets. She felt like she was walking into church and asking the congregation to pick up weapons. She looked up at Austin, standing beside her and silently supporting her in front of this group.

"Hi everyone," Austin said from beside her. "I know we've all been living together the past few days, but I don't think we've all had a chance to get to know one another. Amanda is ex-military. Please, give her your attention." Austin's voice had rung out loud, clear, and with an authoritative tone that had quieted the small crowd.

Amanda looked over at him and smiled, silently thanking him for the support. Somehow, somewhere over the past few days, Austin had emerged as their leader. She didn't know how it had happened but was used to the phenomena. In the service, there was always one person who had that *it* factor that led people to trust them and look to them for advice. Austin was that person in their group, and she was happy to support him in the role. It wasn't a role she wanted for herself, though she'd agreed to try to break the ice tonight and pull their group together.

Amanda took a deep breath. "I know it sounds really cheesy, but can we please go around the area so that everyone can introduce themselves? And maybe tell us something about yourself as we go?"

She felt a little goofy for using such an old-school method of breaking the ice, which she'd been exposed to even in grammar school, but it was all she had. If she was supposed to live with the people in the group and count on them to keep her alive, knowing more than their first names didn't seem like too much to ask.

The man she knew to be Jordan, and probably in his mid-twenties, raised his hand from where he sat on a blanket next to Malachi.

"My name is Jordan. I worked in the coal mines in West Virginia. I was in Kentucky visiting family when I met Jim Loveridge. I was at the meeting the night everything went black," he finished.

"Thank you," Amanda said, grateful that she hadn't had to pick on someone to get them going. Jordan's voice had done the job, too.

Malachi raised his hand and introduced himself next, although everyone knew who he was. Next came the man on his left.

"Name's Ezra. I'm nobody special. I lived in Kentucky, worked as a farmhand, and was at the tent thing when it happened," he said simply.

Amanda studied him, guessing him to be in his twenties, as well, and also in good shape. He and Jordan had paired up with Malachi almost naturally, and all three of them had been more than willing to work, and seemed like good people—she hoped they'd stay around.

The next man to speak stood up awkwardly and looked around, nodding at everyone in turn. "Mike, thirty-one, recently divorced and was looking for something to keep my interest when I came upon the Loveridge family... kind of became a hanger-on, I guess you could say," he said with a friendly smile.

"We're happy to have you," Tonya said, looking to him from her blanket across from him.

"What did you do, before all this?" Austin asked.

Mike shrugged. "Construction mostly."

Amanda and Austin exchanged a look as the man sat back down. That would certainly be a useful skill. Mike was over-weight and didn't look to be in the best shape, but that would change soon enough, the way things were going. And he'd come this far, which was no small thing.

"I'm Gretchen, I think I've met you all. I've been with the

Loveridges for some time. I'm a hippie," she said with a giggle. "I love to live off the land. I'm very much about living for God and taking care of the earth while I'm here."

Amanda hid her grimace. Her eyes ventured over to where Ennis and Wendell were sitting. She had confirmed their suspicions. Gretchen, at least, was going to be a hard one to convince to hurt someone, even if she had to.

"I'm Bonnie, and my husband Bill and I were traveling when it happened. Jim and Tonya were kind enough to take us in," the woman added quietly as Gretchen reached over and took her hand. "My husband was killed, but I'm here."

Amanda nodded when it seemed clear that was all that Bonnie would say. She was another one who would be very unwilling to shoot someone. She was middle-aged, and had been in something of a daze since Amanda had met her—grief, probably, and shock.

Tonya raised her hand. "I'm Tonya, and you all know me," she said.

They did know her, and Amanda guessed that most of them recognized she was the weakest link in the group, given her current condition. She was pale, barely eating, and just a shell of a woman. The woman looked nothing short of fragile, and the idea of her defending anything was laughable. Savannah had told Amanda that the widowed revivalist hadn't always been so withdrawn, and had proved to be more of a quiet force, supporting her husband, but that had clearly changed. When he'd been killed, Tonya's world had been turned upside down. Amanda hoped she could find her way back to being that strong woman Savannah claimed she'd been.

Amanda's eyes moved to the two men sitting back from the others. They were probably the oldest in the group, and seemed to have bonded over that fact. She nodded at them, hoping they'd take the cue without being pushed.

"I'm Drew, and this is Harlen. I guess we're the old-timers of the group. I was a pastor before I got tired of the church politics. I met Jim at a gas station of all places when he was filling up down in Florida. I've been with them for six months," he explained.

Drew was an average-looking guy, with nothing outwardly noticeable about him. He was of average height, maybe five-ten, and had a slim build. He wore slacks and a button-up shirt, which seemed out of place in their current situation, but made sense for him. She smiled at him, noticing he had the kind eyes of a pastor, too.

Amanda looked to Harlen, the tall black man with a bald head and bushy gray eyebrows. She could practically see the wisdom in his eyes. He reminded her a bit of a bald Morgan Freeman with his gentle way and calm demeanor.

"Like Drew said, I'm Harlen. I'm a retired drug and alcohol counselor. I just happened to be in the right place at the right time when all this happened," he said.

Amanda nodded, unsurprised. That would explain why it was rumored he was one who was considering moving on to Seattle. He had no ties to the group. He was only with them because he didn't have another clear option. She pegged him as one to watch. He'd potentially want to divide the group, taking some away and leaving some behind. It was something she made a mental note to share with Austin when they were in private. He could be a strong asset or a strong dissenter. She needed to talk to him, as well. If Harlen wanted to go and others wanted to join him, that was great, but that needed to happen sooner rather than later. The people who chose to stay had to be all-in. If they weren't, she had a feeling they'd walk away at the first sign of trouble. She didn't want to depend on anyone who wasn't committed to the idea of surviving together.

An older woman, probably in her late fifties or early sixties, raised her hand, drawing Amanda's attention. She was petite in stature. Amanda had almost not seen her at all. In fact, she barely remembered seeing her over the past week—she'd simply blended into the background of the others.

"I'm Audrey. I'm no one special. I was bored and thought I'd see what the tent revival was all about. I'm a widowed, retired school teacher. The most exciting thing that ever happened to me before all of this craziness was an unplanned fire drill," she said with dismissive laugh.

Everyone laughed in return as Audrey motioned to the figure next to her to take his turn.

"All right, Nash, let's move on to you," Amanda said.

Nash, Ennis, Savannah, and Wendell all got the chance to say their piece as they continued, and Amanda felt the change in the group dynamics almost immediately. Everyone seemed more at ease, which was exactly what she'd hoped would happen.

Amanda took a breath when the introductions finished, and then she got started. "This is great. I'm glad we've taken a minute to breathe and get to know each other. I wanted to talk to all of you about our future here, together. I think we need to be prepared for there to be others who want to try and take what we have here," she began, hoping to approach the situation with kid gloves.

"You think we're going to be attacked?" Gretchen asked.

"What if it's people like us who need somewhere safe to stay?" Bonnie asked.

Austin stood up again, waving down the voices who'd begun murmuring. "We need to be careful, cautious about who we open the door to. That's all. What Amanda is trying to say is that we need to be prepared for those who don't want to join us, but wish to take from us, and possibly even try to hurt or kill us," Austin clarified.

Jordan nodded. "We saw it first-hand. We know what it's like out there."

"Exactly," Amanda breathed out with relief, glad that someone besides her and Austin had chimed in to offer support, "and I know you suffered some tragic losses. I want to show you all how to defend yourselves in case there's an attack, whether you're here or out taking a walk in the woods, or if you do choose to move on," Amanda explained.

Tonya looked down at the mostly full plate of food in her

49

hands before looking up at Amanda, her eyes full of sorrow. "What happened was tragic, but I cannot hurt another person. I can't take a life."

Malachi moved over to her blanket before Amanda could think how to reply. "Mom, I don't want to lose you. You have to learn to fight. Dad would want you to. He was prepared to do whatever it took to keep you and me safe," Malachi insisted.

Tonya only shook her head, her eyes remaining on her uneaten food.

"I understand that most of you have strong beliefs," Amanda said gently, "but this is truly a life or death situation. Sadly, there are going to be fewer good people and a lot more bad guys."

"I won't hesitate. I'm willing to learn," Ezra announced.

"Good, we need people to step up," Austin said. "None of us *want* to hurt someone. However, if it comes down to my life or my daughter's life, or any one of yours, I will do whatever it takes," he finished, his voice leaving no room for argument.

"I think we can learn self-defense without raising a weapon," Gretchen offered. "Right?"

Amanda shrugged. "Do you think you can outrun a bullet? Self-defense is designed to disable an attacker and give you time to escape. If your attacker has a gun, the stakes are high. You have to be able to disarm your attacker and disable them. You don't want them coming after you a second or third time.

Self-defense is worth spending time on, but it's not everything."

"I can't shoot one of God's children," Tonya insisted, sounding more alive than Amanda had heard her since she'd first met the woman.

"Tonya, I understand your convictions, I do, but what if that person was going to hurt your child?" Audrey asked.

Tonya looked at the older woman, who appeared to be very meek. Audrey was the last person Amanda had been counting on for support, and the shocked faces surrounding them suggested she hadn't been the only one surprised to hear her speak up.

"I'd pray," Tonya replied in a soft voice.

Wendell made a loud scoffing sound, earning glares from everyone.

"Look, this isn't something any of us wants to do," Amanda said loudly, "but I want to live. I know you all do, as well. You wouldn't have walked over a thousand miles and dealt with all that you did if that weren't true. You are not ready to lie down and give up," Amanda added, her voice rising as she spoke.

A moment passed in quiet, but there were nods all around.

"When do we start?" Jordan asked.

Amanda looked at Austin. "Tomorrow?" he suggested.

"Sounds good to me," she breathed out, looking around. "We'll start with some basic self-defense. Ennis will teach you all how to use a gun. Ammunition is too valuable to do a lot of target practice, but it's important you know how to use one, how to load it and how to be safe," she said, watching the hackles on a few of the revivalists go up.

Ennis got to his feet. "I know you guys don't like guns. That's okay, but something I taught my niece and something we learned from our father," he said, looking at Austin, "is you need to know a gun. You need to be comfortable with it. You need to know how to use it and how to be safe around one. That's all we're asking. Trust me, I think those of you who were in that cornfield and either saw or heard about what Savannah did have to agree that things would have been much different had she not had the knowledge."

Everyone remained quiet as his words sank in. It was the hard, cold truth. They could hate guns all they wanted, but they were a necessary evil.

"He's right. We have guns here. I don't want someone to pick up one of the guns and not know what to do with the thing. That is far more dangerous," Austin added, and Amanda was thankful that even Tonya nodded in response to that comment.

Ennis cleared his throat. "I understand some of you aren't sure what your plans are for the future. I get it. I'm not pressuring you—we're not pressuring you, either way—but you will need to decide if you want to stay here or move on. If you want to stay, you are welcome to, but everyone has to work together to keep this place safe."

"Move on?" Audrey asked, looking a little confused.

Ennis nodded, looking at his brother. "Yes. I believe some of you had intentions of going to Salt Lake City or further west to Seattle. We aren't forcing you to stay here. If you want to move on, I'll give you a supply of food to take with you on your journey."

"He's right," Austin chimed in. "You only have a few months before the weather changes. If you are all planning to stay here, we need to think long-term housing, food, water, and so on. Winter in the mountains is going to be tough."

"Are you asking us to leave?" Tonya asked quietly.

"Absolutely not!" Amanda answered quickly. "We're just saying that we all need to plan for the future, wherever that future will be, and that's going to be hard to do until we know how many people plan to stay here around the house."

"Mom, we'll talk about it later," Malachi said, his voice low and soothing.

Amanda looked around at the faces of the others, waiting to see if there was an immediate answer. It looked like they were all on the fence. She understood the feeling. Since talking with Austin earlier, she knew he was hesitant, as well. It was to be expected, she supposed. They were running scared, and they'd been on the move for long enough, planning to move on until they got here, that it had become a sort of autopilot setting. Coming here hadn't been like buying a house in a neighborhood you had scouted ahead of time and then settling in. Everyone there knew everything could change in the blink of an eye. Nothing was certain.

What was playing out now was the fight or flight instinct, but in slow motion. Stay or go—that was the decision all of them were facing. What if the grass was greener on the other side? What if there was a refugee camp in Seattle that would provide protection from the faction trying to take over the world? Or, what if this really was the best option?

"So, just a lot to think about, everyone, but we'll start working on weapons tomorrow. And self-defense," Amanda added with a nod to Gretchen, who smiled back at her. After all, that couldn't hurt. "Everyone have a great night, okay?" she offered, and there were nods all around as people began to speak to those who were close by. She heard murmurs about guns and travel, and 'this world,' and tried to take comfort in the fact that at least they'd gotten the conversation started.

"You okay?" Austin asked quietly.

"Yes, I just suddenly had a very clear understanding of your apprehension to stay."

He grimaced. "I'm sorry."

"Don't be."

The briefly relaxed mood they'd experienced after the introductions had evaporated, though. The group broke apart, a few going inside to take care of the dinner dishes and the rest going for walks or retiring for the night.

"Well, that went over like a lead balloon," Amanda said on a sigh.

He shrugged. "It had to be said. I don't want to live with a bunch of people relying on me to do all the dirty work while they sit back and pray."

She laughed. "I don't think that's exactly what they were expecting, but I'm not sure anyone was thinking about it one way or another."

Austin shook his head, his eyes narrowing as he stared at the house bathed in oranges from the setting sun. "Well, it's not gonna happen, and everyone needs to start thinking and being a part of the group if they're gonna stay. I'll protect my daughter, you, my brother, but I'm not going to put my life on the line if they aren't ready to fight for themselves. If they want to stay, they'll learn to fight."

5

The stove was coming together off to the side of the clearing, where they'd made a habit of eating their nightly meal together. It had become a sort of courtyard for the inhabitants of the house. Austin piled another one of the semi-flat rocks he had collected onto the box he'd made from rocks of mostly equal sizes. He'd dug a hole in the ground first, which would serve as the heating element where the fire would burn. He'd been lucky enough to find a nice, stone slab that was about two inches thick and two feet wide. The stone's surface only went about a foot deep, but he was hoping to use the rack from the oven in the house to extend the heated surface.

He'd already made walls, as well, stacking rocks on top of one another to run about a foot high around the rectangular hole, and he planned to use another oven rack across the top as a roof, with more rocks to anchor it. There would be enough air gaps for smoke from the fire below to escape while trapping in most of the heat. The oven was something he'd seen in his mind, and Nash had agreed it made sense, but he honestly had no real idea if it would be effective. He hoped so, though—it certainly looked like it would be a useful tool, and seemed more impressive than he'd expected it to, now that he was pretty much done.

Taking a breather and drinking down some water, he took a seat on a log over on the side of the house, where he could watch Amanda working with the women from the revivalist group, showing them some basic self-defense moves. He looked on proudly as Savannah helped demonstrate. After their meeting last night, he hadn't been sure any of them would actually participate. It was a pleasant surprise to see them all listening and watching Amanda intently.

It was a mild day, sporadic clouds blocking the heat of the sun and making it far more comfortable to be outside in the middle of the day, so he stayed where he was. He'd at least wait till Amanda took a break, he decided, wanting to talk with her about something she'd mentioned earlier.

"Why don't we demonstrate on Dad?" Savannah asked.

Austin blinked. "What?"

Amanda grinned. "I think that sounds like a great idea!"

He scowled at her, but reluctantly stepped into the impromptu ring, eyeing the women who were about to unleash their new moves on him. It wasn't exactly how he had anticipated his day going.

"Okay, the first scenario we're going to practice is an attack that you can see coming. Austin is going to approach you and try to grab you. I want you to think back to *The Karate Kid* and the moves you saw there. If you don't know the movie, think of your hands as clocks," Amanda explained, demonstrating a half-circle motion with each her arms. "An attacker who's trying to grab you is going to go for your hand, wrist, or forearm. The windmill is going to keep him from getting a grip on you. This is also an effective way of defending your face from being hit."

He and Amanda demonstrated such an exchange, using different approaches before each of the women took their turn fending off his attempts to grab them.

Amanda applauded everyone as they congratulated each other, and then went on. "The next option is one we all know—a kick to the groin area. I don't care if your attacker is male or female; a solid foot to that area is going to send them to their knees. Once that happens, you either run or you get in a few more good blows to the face, using your knee," Amanda said.

Austin winced at the idea of even gentle demonstrations, and then let out a purposely exaggerated sigh of relief when Amanda motioned him back to his log to observe. Released, he added, "Don't stop with one kick, ladies. If you see an opening, take it. This is a good way to get an attacker to drop a weapon if they have one."

Amanda nodded, and then faced the women again after she'd had them practice some hard kicks into saplings. "Next, we're going to talk about the heel of your palm. Punching someone hurts, and you can injure your hand if you don't do it right.

Instead of making a fist, use the heel of your hand and shove it at your attacker's face. Eyes, nose, mouth, jaw, wherever you can hit, do it," Amanda ordered them.

"Don't forget, you have built-in weapons on your body," Austin told the ladies.

"Weapons?" Audrey asked.

"Your elbows, knees, and your head are your built-in weapons. Use them to your advantage. An attack from behind can be fended off by a few sharp elbow thrusts to the rib cage," he said, rising again to demonstrate how one might jerk their elbow sideways. "A knee to the face, shin, or groin is brutally painful. If you're pulled against an attacker from front or behind, slam your head against their face. It might sting you, but your head is going to do some damage," Austin told them.

Savannah was smiling. "Yep. I've used that move to get free from people a couple of times now," she said proudly.

Austin swallowed down emotion—some sort of mix of pride and horror over the fact that his daughter could say such a thing now, and so casually—and sat back down as Amanda took center stage again and eyes went to her.

"Exactly. It doesn't matter how big or small you are; it's about using your weight to launch an attack and hitting soft targets," Amanda confirmed.

Moving on from there, everyone got in more practice as Amanda educated and guided each of the attacks and more demos, taking it slow and easy on the ladies as they got familiar with the moves. When everyone had broken a real sweat and Amanda declared they were done for a day, it was Audrey who stepped forward to thank both her and Austin.

"You're welcome. I hope it has helped give you confidence," Amanda said. "Hopefully, you'll never have to use any of these techniques, but if you do, you'll be ready."

"I always said I was going to take one of those classes they offered at the senior center. I never did. I'm glad to learn now," she said with a smile.

"Amanda is an excellent teacher," Austin commented. "You're lucky you had her."

Audrey winked. "She is that and so much more, huh?"

Austin chuckled as Amanda blushed, not giving the woman the response she was clearly angling for. When everyone had left, he turned to face her.

She was looking at him expectantly. "What's up? I know you didn't come over here to watch me show them how to escape a chokehold."

He shook his head with a small smile. "No, not quite. Ennis told me you guys want to hide the horses. That's a good idea, and I'm done with the outdoor stove—for now, at least. I'll go with you to scout a location."

She sighed out loud. "Thank you. I don't worry about them wandering off—they're too lazy and attached to people for that—but I worry about them not having any shelter from rain, and I'd like to make sure we have a place to hide them when strangers are around."

"Are you talking about a barn or something permanent?" he asked.

"I don't know about building a barn today," she said sarcastically.

"But you are talking about a permanent structure?" he clarified.

She shrugged. "They need shelter. As you said, winter will be here before you know it."

"I get it, but I think we can get by with doing something temporary for now."

"Temporary?" she questioned.

"There's other stuff that needs our attention more than a full barn, Amanda. We need to scout the area, see if there are people close, get an idea of local resources, and know our options for escape, should something happen," he said. "We need to prioritize. I know the horses need shelter, but we also need to make sure there isn't an impending attack. Soldiers could be out there right now. Putting our time and energy into building a barn could cost us everything."

She stepped closer to him, one hand reaching out to take his. "Austin, I know you're feeling anxious about staying here— we all are—but on the other hand, this place is too good to pass up. We can take steps to make it more secure."

He stared into her eyes. "But what if they come for us anyway?"

"Then we fight," she said simply. "We can't focus all our time and energy on what's on that USB drive. We have to live. The only way we live is by taking care of things like hunting for food, and building and planning for the future."

Austin stepped away from her, trying to decide whether what he felt was more paranoia or realism. "We're cut off up here, which is good and bad. We need to see if things are still in a bad way. If we cut off the head of the snake, things might not be as bad as we think. That drive could be the weapon we need," he insisted.

She looked thoughtful when he turned back to her, and then replied, "Okay."

"What?"

"Okay, you and I and maybe Nash can try and go into the city, do a little scouting, and see what we can find out," she said.

"Really?" he asked. He'd been expecting convincing her to his way of thinking to be more of a challenge. He knew it was that internal need to stay on the move that he felt, to run from the thing that was making him uncomfortable. He wanted to be active if they stayed here, and prepare as much as they could for the unknown—even though that might mean going out into areas that might be dangerous, he thought the risk was neces-sary. He just hadn't quite expected her to agree so readily.

She grinned. "I think we can look for supplies, medicine, and whatever else we can carry while we're out scouting. Killing two or three birds with one stone," she teased.

"For the horses?" he asked.

"I don't see why not. We need to scout a location for them, and you want to look around for supplies or danger. We'll just do at the same time."

"Great, then," he answered after a beat. "We'll go tomorrow at first light. I'm going to find Nash and see if he's up for it."

"What about Ennis?" she asked.

He shrugged. "We need someone here to hold down the fort, and I guess since it is technically his fort, he's the right man for the job."

"Okay, I'm going to find Ennis now then. He was going to be teaching the guys how to use a gun, and I can only imagine how that's going. Half of them were way too eager and the other half acted as if we were asking them to train venomous snakes," she grumbled.

Austin chuckled. "Oh, but he has good old Wendell with him, and Wendell knows everything there is to know about guns."

She slapped his shoulder. "Stop. He's trying to be helpful. He can be a little obnoxious, but I'm sure he doesn't think we're real peaches."

Austin narrowed his eyes. "He's dangerous."

"What? How so?"

"He thinks he knows a lot, and he doesn't. That's a dangerous combination."

After a few seconds, she nodded her agreement. "In that way, I guess he is dangerous. But I'm sure it will be fine. He's trying to fit in, and I think he has a bit of a man crush on you."

Austin rolled his eyes. "Great."

Crack!

Austin jumped, instinctively reaching for the Glock at his waist.

"They're using bullets?" Amanda gasped.

"I don't know. Ennis said he was only going over gun safety, not actual shooting!" Austin exclaimed, already making his way around the house and heading in the direction of the shot.

And then Raven broke through the trees, running scared.

"Whoa, whoa, girl," Amanda said, racing after the dragging lead of her cherished Raven. In minutes, she'd caught up to the horse, the trees having helped to slow her down.

Ennis burst through the trees just as Amanda got Raven turned around and back to a walk.

"What the hell happened?" Austin demanded, laying a hand on Raven's neck as Amanda brought her back around.

Amanda turned, glaring at Ennis and looking too angry for words. Austin knew she was about to give him a lecture he wouldn't soon forget when suddenly Wendell walked out of the trees. And upon seeing him, Austin didn't need to ask. He knew. Wendell had screwed up.

Ennis had been running at full-speed, and needed a moment to catch his breath, but when he did, his eyes were on Amanda and the horse. "I'm so sorry! I didn't know she was grazing nearby," he gasped.

"You were shooting? I thought you said you were teaching them gun safety!" Amanda growled. "If we'd known you were going to be shooting, the horses wouldn't have been anywhere near you."

Ennis nodded, still catching his breath. "I was, but—" He stopped mid-sentence and looked back at Wendell.

Austin rolled his eyes. "That's why he shouldn't be around the guns," he hissed, low enough so Wendell couldn't hear.

"I'm going to agree with Austin on that one. This could have ended a lot differently," Amanda said, her anger palpable.

"Sorry, guys, I didn't realize it was loaded," Wendell said, finally deciding it was safe to approach.

Austin shot the man a glare. "Why were you handling a gun if you didn't know it was loaded? You always handle a gun like it's loaded!"

"I'm not an idiot, Austin. I know how to shoot and load. I was only in the little gun class to help Ennis," Wendell shot back.

"Help? You could have killed someone," Austin retorted. "Or scared Raven into breaking her neck!"

"It was an accident," Ennis said, defending him.

Austin shook his head, holding up one finger. "You don't get to have accidents when guns are involved. I don't want you anywhere near my kid if you have a gun," he added, staring at Wendell.

"I'm going to get her some water and check on Charlie," Amanda said, leading her horse away.

"Sorry, really, it was an accident," Wendell said to her back, finally showing a little remorse.

"Why don't you go tell the rest of the guys we'll pick up where we left off tomorrow?" Ennis suggested.

With that, Wendell walked away, his shoulders slumped as he headed back down the driveway before cutting across and disappearing into the trees.

"Why is he here?" Austin asked.

Ennis glanced back to him, raising an eyebrow. "This is my house, Austin—I think you need to remember that. Wendy is my friend. He made a mistake, so just relax."

Austin swallowed down the curses in his throat, and then looked back to the trees where Wendell had disappeared. "Ennis, you have to see that guy isn't fitting in. He's constantly butting his nose in or saying things that are rude and inappropriate. He dropped an entire can of dehydrated potato slices on the ground yesterday. I'm pretty sure he was drunk when he did it, which is an entirely different problem. That's a lot of food to waste, and now he nearly kills someone with a wild shot?"

"Nobody was nearly killed—the shot went high. Could have killed a bird, if anything. And he isn't fitting in only because you won't give him a chance. You and your little girlfriend are running around this place like you're the bosses on a work farm," Ennis accused him.

"I'm not trying to be a boss. I'm trying to keep us alive. Amanda is trying to help people stay alive by teaching them how to defend themselves. You're supposed to be teaching them how to use a gun without blowing their own head off so that she can teach them some defensive maneuvers," he replied, fighting to keep his voice even.

Ennis stepped back. "It was the first day. It was one accident. I'm sure, with the way you handled things, he'll never screw up again."

"Good! That's the point. If he's going to be here, we need him helping, not hurting."

"Who is we?" Ennis asked, his lips pulled back in a sneer. "You and your girlfriend? Are you the *we* that's trying to be our saviors?"

Austin closed his eyes, taking a deep breath. His little brother was always questioning him, wanting to go against him. Circumstances didn't matter. It had been one thing when they'd been kids, but they were adults now, and in a fight for their lives.

"Put it aside, Ennis," he said in a low voice, exhausted from the constant bickering.

"Put what aside? The fact that you and Amanda have teamed up and left the rest of us in the dark is irritating. This is my house. I'm the one who built it. I'm the one who stocked it, so I would expect a little more respect!" Ennis snapped.

Austin put up both hands. "I'm not trying to step on your toes. I'm trying to help. You won't survive up here alone. You almost died before Nash saved you. I want this to work, but it isn't going to work if we can't get along and come up with a plan."

"Then let's *talk* about a plan. Don't *tell* me about the plan," Ennis replied.

"I am. I have been," he argued, though a voice in his head told him that he knew that wasn't the case. He'd been planning with Amanda, not Ennis.

Ennis shook his head. "No, you and Amanda have talked about a plan and then told me it was going to happen. Not the same thing, Austin," he pointed out, more quietly now.

Austin studied his brother, noticing the wrinkles around his eyes and his soft body. He sounded hurt, like they were kids again and fighting for someone's attention or over the same toy, and Austin had won. There had always been a bit of jealousy between them, but it seemed amplified now. Then, as Austin looked at him, the light came on.

"You're jealous of Amanda," he chuckled.

"What? That's ridiculous. Why would I be jealous?" Ennis spat out.

Austin smirked. "You don't have to be jealous of her. You're still my little brother."

"I'm not your little brother," he retorted, crossing his arms over his chest.

"You are. There's no getting around that. Amanda is my friend. We've been through a lot and I've come to trust her and depend on her opinion. That's it," he said, hoping to diffuse what he could see was a growing problem.

"I'm not jealous of her. You act like everything she says and does is perfect, and my friend is the one who's a total screw-up. Wendell made a mistake, but he's my friend and I don't want him to leave," Ennis said, all but sticking out his lower lip and pouting.

"Fine, but you need to have a talk with him. He's insulting and driving everyone crazy."

"Again—my friend, my house. He stays," Ennis said before stomping back down the driveway.

Austin watched him go, shaking his head. There was little he could do to heal forty years of sibling rivalry. It had always been this way. They loved each other, but loved each other more when they weren't in the same state. Austin turned around, looking at the big house and feeling even more convinced that living in the house with his brother and a bunch of other people was a ticking timebomb.

It wouldn't be long before Wendell did something that pushed the last button for someone, but Ennis seemed to have hitched his wagon to the guy. Austin had a feeling that had been Wendell's plan all along, too. He had enmeshed himself in deep with Ennis, the true owner of their little fortress. No one could kick him out.

"That's what you think, buddy," Austin muttered, heading into the house in search of Nash.

The kid was young, but he had a good head on his shoulders. Austin wanted to put this little fiasco behind them and talk to him about their plan to go into town.

But when he looked around the house, he came up empty. Nash wasn't anywhere to be seen. Everyone he talked to said that the last time they'd seen him had been early that morning.

Austin walked back outside, going in search of Amanda with the thought that maybe she'd know where the kid had gotten off to. Austin really hoped he hadn't decided to ditch them. He needed him to decipher all the technical jargon on that drive. Amanda might not think it was all that important, but he did.

Knowledge was power. He needed to know what they were up against and what they could expect in the coming weeks and months.

He was not going to be blindsided—not again.

6

Amanda crept downstairs quietly, doing her best not to disturb the two figures sleeping on the couch. She was craving coffee, and wanted to watch the sunrise in peace. Finding a peaceful moment with so many people around was next to impossible, but doing so in the early morning made it slightly easier. Moving slowly made her feel like she caused less of a disturbance as she filled the pot with a little over a cup of water and placed it on the stove. She left all the lights off, not wanting to wake anyone. A little niggle of guilt ate at her over using the stove instead of going out and starting a fire in the oven Austin had built for them to use, but she assured herself it was only a little propane.

"Caught you," Austin's deep voice cut through the dim light in the kitchen.

She nearly jumped and spilled the pot of water. "You scared me! Why are you up?" she asked.

"Wendell snores like a train," he grumbled, moving to pour himself some water. "I've been up for a while."

She raised an eyebrow. "You slept down here last night again?"

He nodded. "I feel better when I'm near that door."

"Why?" she asked, still whispering as she lit the burner, its blue flame casting a soft glow in the room.

"I want to know if someone is coming or going. I guess that's the benefit to only having one working door," he quipped.

She turned to him and smiled. "Do you want coffee?"

"No, thanks. I need to wean myself off. That supply isn't going to last forever, and there are certain people in this house who need it more than I," he teased her.

"Hey, you better not be talking about me!"

He shrugged. "If the shoe fits."

He re-filled his glass with water and headed out the front door. In the kitchen, she waited for the water to boil before quickly stirring in the spoonful of instant coffee. It was weaker than she liked, but Austin was right that their supply wasn't infinite. It made sense to wean herself off before she had to quit cold-turkey.

She found him sitting on the single park bench outside and sat down beside him. It was a cool morning, the sun barely coming over the horizon. She had on one of Ennis's old plaids, something she'd taken from him a few days before and not bothered to return. They'd all been pilfering his clothing, but he didn't seem to mind.

"It's nice out here," she murmured.

"It is. Can you imagine what this place will look like in the winter?" he asked.

She laughed. "Yes, white and pretty as a postcard."

Austin nodded beside her, but then frowned. "Pretty, but dangerous. We really have to get some meat in that freezer. Otherwise, there's no way we'll survive the winter with all of us here. That food supply is going to be gone within a few months," he said, expressing the same thought she had.

"Do you think it's smart to load up a freezer?" she questioned.

He shrugged. "With the turbine and the panels, I think it will keep the freezer going during the day. Even if it's a really cloudy, snowy day, the freezer will hold temp for at least three days if we don't open it. If it looks like the power isn't going to be enough to run it, we'll put it outside. I'm sure we can count on it being below freezing. Maybe we should build an outdoor freezer anyway, planning on using the cold to our advantage."

"Good point. And we can stock up for winter with anything we can find. We'll go into town and scout for anything to add to our stockpile. I'd like to find a bow, and maybe even some arrows. I know Ennis has a healthy supply of ammo, but if we start shooting a bunch, hunting or not, it's going to draw attention."

His eyes scanned the area, his gun holstered at his waist. He was the only one wearing his gun constantly. She did if she ventured into the trees, but avoided it at other times; she didn't care for the weight of the weapon on her leg or waist.

"That's true. I saw a book in his library about trapping. That's a good option, as well. I don't think we have to worry about Fish and Game coming after us for hunting in the off-season," he quipped.

She giggled. "No, I don't think you do. I think we should hit a Goodwill or one of those other secondhand stores also," she commented.

He turned to look at her. "Got a hankering to do some thrifting?" he asked dryly.

She rolled her eyes. "No, but I have a hankering to change my clothes. We could all use some clothes and, like you keep saying, winter is coming, and we need to have the right clothing for it. I'm sure the malls and department stores have been raided, but maybe we can find some stuff at a thrift store," she explained.

He smiled at her, his blue eyes dancing with laughter. "Good thinking. I never would have thought about looting a Goodwill."

"I have a good idea now and then," she said with a laugh.

"I'm going to see if Harlen, Mal, and Mike are ready to move. They said they were up for a scouting mission. Let's see if they were serious," he said, getting to his feet.

"What about Audrey? She mentioned she wanted to go," Amanda said.

Austin turned to look at her. "I don't know if that's a good idea. We don't know what we're walking into. We need those who are quick on their feet and able to move. She's not exactly nimble."

Amanda understood his point, but also knew that they all needed clothing, and any extra set of hands could make a difference if they found supplies worth carrying back. "I'll tell her, but I don't think she's going to be happy about it."

"We're not always going to make everyone happy, but I think she'd be less happy if she got shot and killed."

Amanda nodded. "Good point. Eventually, we'll have to get all of them used to the idea of scouting and hunting, though. And we all need supplies like clothing. One person can only carry so much."

"Yes, but let's cross that bridge when we get to it."

"Fair enough."

Austin headed inside the house, and Amanda watched him move and found herself wondering what her life would be like without him. She wasn't sure she wanted to find out. They had come together in the strangest of circumstances, and those first few weeks he had tested her patience, but now she didn't want to do this without him. If he decided to leave the house, she'd be going with him, no matter how much she yearned to make this place a long-term home.

The realization opened up a new door in her mind, but it was one she wasn't ready to explore. Starting a relationship was about the last thing she needed.

She pushed the thought aside, demanding her mind focus and keep those feelings tucked away where they belonged. She had no business thinking romantically. Plus, she wouldn't make a hypocrite of herself. At least not this soon. She'd talked with Savannah about her and Malachi, and letting things cool down while they figured out this new world. She wasn't about to show that she couldn't take her own good advice.

Savoring the last drops of her coffee, she spent a few more minutes on her own enjoying the peace before heading into the house to get ready for what she'd internally been referring to as their mission. Going into town would be dangerous, but it had to be done. They needed to know what might be headed their way, and she really wanted to find a change of clothes.

When she walked inside, Malachi, Austin, and Harlen were in the kitchen. Austin waved her in. She glanced over and saw Wendell sprawled out on one couch, a blanket pulled up to his eyes. Drew was draped on the other couch, still sound asleep.

"What's up?" she asked in a quiet voice.

"It's going to be us, and apparently Gretchen is coming along," Austin said.

Amanda raised her eyebrows with surprise. "Gretchen? Really? No Mike?"

Harlen nodded. "She wants to look for some plants on the way and Mike offered to stay behind."

"Works for me," Amanda replied.

"They've all agreed to carry guns," Austin said, looking at her before the others.

"Good. I think it's a very good idea."

"I'm going to wake Ennis and let him know we'll be leaving. I'll retrieve the weapons, as well," he said.

Amanda nodded. The weapons were being kept out of plain sight for the time being. It was dangerous to have them all easily accessible. She didn't like the idea of not trusting the people in the house, but she didn't know them all that well. They couldn't risk one of the revivalists deciding to up and leave, and helping him or herself to their weapons supply before they left. They claimed to be peaceful people, but it could be an act, and even the most peaceful among them understood that there were people out there who'd take advantage of anyone they could. Weapons meant self-defense as much as anything. With that in mind, she wasn't ready to trust any of them wholeheartedly just yet.

"Do you have packs loaded?" she asked Malachi and Harlen.

Both men nodded. "We took care of it last night. They're the go-bags Ennis had here. We took out a few things to make room for any supplies we might find."

"Good."

"Maybe we can find extra backpacks while we're scouting," Malachi added.

"I hope so. We should have enough for every person here," Amanda agreed.

Gretchen walked into the kitchen then, her red hair pulled back in a ponytail and a smile on her face. Amanda thought she looked chipper and ready, though she always had a look of innocent serenity about her. Amanda assumed it had something to do with her firm belief in God and those freckles that gave her such a youthful look. Amanda envied her mindset in some ways, but preferred reality to spirituality.

There were only four backpacks in the house, which she'd thought had meant someone would be going light, but Gretchen held something else in her hand.

"What's that?" Amanda asked the redhead, pointing to the cloth in her hand.

Gretchen smiled and held it up. "It's one of those reusable grocery bags. I'm borrowing it to carry any plants I find."

Amanda grinned. "Good plan. If there are more of those," she added, "we could put them in the pack in case we find small supplies that they'd work for." When Gretchen agreed to find some more and distribute them, Amanda turned back to the men. "I'll be right back," she told them, heading off to find Austin.

Ennis's bedroom door was slightly ajar. She knocked.

"Who is it?" Ennis asked, his voice sleepy.

"Amanda."

"Come in," Austin called out.

She walked in at the prompt, feeling a little out of place in the room with Ennis still in bed. "Hi," she said with a friendly smile. She knew he didn't care for her all that much.

"Your leg holster is there," Austin pointed to the dresser.

Amanda quickly donned it, sliding the Glock into place.

"Do we have holsters for the others?" she asked.

Ennis nodded. "I do," he mumbled, throwing the blankets off and getting out of bed. "Austin will be carrying one of the ARs, as well."

Amanda looked at him. "You don't think that's too obvious?"

He shrugged. "Obvious might be a good thing. If we encounter anyone, I want them to know we aren't in the mood to be messed with."

She smirked. "Got it."

They gathered the three remaining holsters with another Glock, a Beretta, and the smaller thirty-eight semi-automatic for Gretchen. Austin slung the semi-auto rifle over his shoulder before they walked outside to join the rest of the group.

Amanda watched for Gretchen's reaction to the rifle on Austin's shoulder. There was a brief look of shock, but the woman quickly wiped it away. That seemed like a good sign.

"Here, put these on," Austin instructed, handing the holsters out.

Amanda helped Gretchen before giving her a very quick tutorial on how to use the gun. It was smaller than what she'd practiced with, and would be easier for a beginner to handle.

"I hope I never have to shoot the thing," Gretchen muttered.

Austin chuckled. "You and me both. Are we ready?" he asked.

There was a round of head-nodding before they set off, walking out of the house and straight down the driveway. Amanda took a last look back at the house as they did, hoping it wouldn't be the last time she laid eyes on it.

7

Austin froze, goosebumps popping up over his flesh as his ears strained to identify the exact direction of the noise he'd heard. They'd been walking an hour or so when he'd sensed something or someone.

"Stop," he whispered.

Amanda was the first to do exactly as he'd instructed. "What's wrong?"

"Stop!" he hissed again when he saw the other three were still moving.

Malachi halted, reaching out to touch Harlen's arm. Gretchen had been staring at the ground, oblivious to anything around her as they walked through the thick forest.

"Go, that way." Austin pointed into the trees in the opposite direction of the noise he'd heard.

Everyone did exactly as ordered, but the sound of their footsteps was equivalent to a stampede of elephants. When they'd gone about a hundred feet into the trees, they all stopped, turning to stare at him.

"What'd you hear?" Amanda asked.

"Voices. Men's voices," he said.

"It could have been someone out hunting or looking for refuge," Gretchen spoke out softly.

Austin nodded. "It could have been, but I would prefer we saw them first."

"I hear them!" Malachi exclaimed.

"Shh," Austin scolded.

"Get down and hide behind the trees. It sounds like there are several of them," Amanda said, moving to pull the gun from its holster on her thigh.

Gretchen stared at the gun in Amanda's hand. "Do I have to?"

Austin shook his head. "Not yet. If we tell you to shoot, though, do exactly as Amanda told you."

Gretchen dropped to her knees behind a thick tree trunk. "I have a confession," she whispered then.

Austin's blood froze, anticipating something horrible. "What?"

"I know how to shoot," she admitted.

Harlen chuckled while the rest of them looked at her in complete shock.

"What?" Amanda asked.

"My dad was a cop. He taught me how to shoot. He was killed in the line of duty. I *hate* guns. I loathe them, and I swore I would never, ever use one," she said with regret, "but I know how."

Amanda offered her a fast smile. "I'm glad you know how to shoot. Hopefully, you won't have to."

"I see one," Harlen said from where he was crouched about ten feet away, behind the trunk of a massive pine.

"Where?" Austin asked.

Harlen pointed. "About two hundred feet to the east. It looks like he's wearing a jumpsuit," he said, confusion in his voice. "You know, the kind race car drivers wear?"

Amanda's mouth fell open. "No!" she breathed out.

Austin felt the world tilt briefly and then suddenly right itself. He'd known it was too easy. There was no way a group like the NWO would get taken out so easily, in just one swoop. They were still around, and they were searching for them.

"No one say a word," Austin ordered.

He pulled the rifle from his shoulder, checking to make sure the magazine was locked in tight. None of them moved a muscle as a group of six men fanned out through the forest. They were all carrying the same automatic rifles seen at the tower. Austin glanced at Harlen and Malachi, seeing that both men had the barrels of their semi-automatic handguns trained in the general direction of the men.

They were no match for the ARs, though. They'd be mowed down before any of them could ever get a shot off. All they could do was hope they'd go unseen.

As if there was some twisted hand of fate hovering above them, a bird directly over their heads called out before fluttering away. The sound spooked the soldiers, who all turned their weapons in the group's direction. Austin hoped none of them were the nervous sort to shoot at anything.

"Who's there? Show yourselves!" one of the men shouted.

Austin shook his head when his fellow housemates looked to him for guidance.

"Shoot into the trees; see what runs out," another one of the men called out.

He knew it was a ploy. They were trying to scare them into moving.

"We haven't done much target practice this week. I bet you we could shoot a moving target," a man said with a laugh.

Gretchen whimpered. The sound was barely audible, but in the forest, it was as loud as a ringing bell.

"There!" a man shouted.

There was a cacophony of ear-splitting gunfire. Fortunately, Gretchen's whimper had been slightly misleading. The men were shooting about twenty feet south of where Austin and the others were now lying flat on the forest floor.

The gunfire stopped as suddenly as it had started. Austin's heart pounded in his chest as he waited for what would come next.

"Nothing!" a male voice shouted.

A thump against the ground drew his attention. He looked to where Amanda was lying prone in a pile of pine needles intermingled with pine cones. She had hit the ground with her palm to get his attention. She pointed behind her, indicating that she wanted to move. He shook his head.

The men started talking again. Austin dared to lift his head, finding himself not thirty feet from one of the soldiers wearing the signature all-black jumpsuit. The man's back was to him, but he was too close for comfort. When Austin turned to look back at Amanda, her eyes were wide with fear.

He used a finger to point away, telling her to take the others and go. She nodded, moving a hand to get Malachi's attention. Austin kept watch as they silently slid across the forest floor on their bellies. When they were nearly out of sight, hidden by forest foliage and trees, he made his move.

And he did his best to go undetected, but he was too close to the men.

"Stop!" one of the soldiers shouted.

Austin froze, hoping they hadn't actually seen him. When he

looked up, though, there was an ugly black barrel about twelve inches from his forehead.

"I'm just out here hunting for food," he said.

"Get up on your feet!" the man with the gun on him shouted.

Austin stood slowly, his hands in the air; the AR remained on the ground beside where he stood.

"Hunting, huh?" another man asked, kicking the gun away from him and removing the handgun from the holster on his thigh.

"Check out that holster," an older man grumbled, pointing to Austin's thigh.

"Looks a lot like ours, don't you think?"

"I've been out here, living off the land. I fled the city and have been holed up here for a few weeks, just like you guys said to do," Austin said, willing them to believe him.

"Alone?" the older man asked.

"Yes."

He fought the urge to look into the trees to see if Amanda had made it away safely. If he looked, they'd know he was lying and likely open fire. He leveled his gaze at the man with graying hair, much shorter than himself.

"Why don't I believe you?"

Austin shrugged, his hands still raised. "I couldn't tell you."

"You always hunt game with a Glock and an AR?" the man asked, eyeing him up and down.

"It's all I have. Does the trick," he replied easily.

"Why don't you take us back to your camp. We'd like to see it," another man said.

"Why? You told us to flee the city and we did," Austin shot back.

The man with the gray hair grinned. "I guess you could say our boss has changed his mind. He's a little irritated about a recent uprising. We're out here to find anyone who might try and come after us again."

"Again, huh?" Austin replied with a smirk, before he could stop himself.

"You know, this guy, doesn't he fit the description of the Merryman dude?" a middle-aged soldier asked, standing watch a few feet away.

Austin's heart skipped a beat. They *were* actively looking for him.

"Nah, they said that guy was at least two-fifty, much taller, and traveling with a ragtag gang," the older man said.

"I'm alone," Austin repeated, his voice even.

The six men exchanged looks before the man standing directly in front of Austin nodded.

"We're going to take you back to headquarters, just to be sure," he announced.

"What? Why?" Austin grumbled.

"Because I like to be sure," he replied, raising his rifle and aiming it directly at Austin's chest. "Move, toward us. We're heading back that way," he added, gesturing into the trees, directly toward where Austin and his group had originally been heading.

Austin stepped out of the thick trees, following the man ahead of him. He knew he wouldn't be coming back. There'd been too many men and women at the tower who had seen him when he'd been brought in. They hadn't all been killed. It wouldn't take long before he was identified and killed for taking out their leader—or, rather, one of their leaders.

He tried not to let himself think about Savannah and what she would go through. He was confident Ennis and Amanda would take care of her, though that was small comfort on the way to one's own death.

The men talked amongst themselves as they kept a steady eye on their surroundings. Austin scanned the area, hoping Amanda didn't try to stage a rescue. They were outgunned, and didn't stand a chance with the four handguns between them. He stumbled over a root, quickly catching himself.

"Don't try anything stupid, or I will shoot you," the man behind him grumbled, shoving the barrel of the gun into his spine.

"I tripped," Austin retorted.

There was a sharp whistle. Austin assumed it was more of the NWO members filtered throughout the forest. It was only when all of them held their weapons up, forming a semi-circle with Austin in the middle, that he realized they weren't expecting company.

"We'll shoot!" one of the men called out.

The whistle came again, directly in front of them. A second later, gunfire erupted as all six men opened up, aiming their rifles straight ahead at the unseen whistler. The sound of the gunfire was deafening, disrupting his senses. He struggled to orientate himself as movement attracted him from his periphery.

It was Amanda. She gestured for him to run, now, while the semi-circle had broken and the men were all focused forward. The gunfire in front of him was the perfect distraction. Without hesitation, he turned and sprinted as fast as he could away from the soldiers.

"Stop!" one of the men shouted, the gunfire suddenly coming to an abrupt halt.

Another shot rang out, followed by several more. Two of the soldiers dropped where they stood as Austin was pulled into some brush, yanked in by Amanda. He held his breath and looked back, still beside her.

"We're under fire!" one of the men shouted, aiming his weapon to fire into the trees where the shots had come from.

He never managed to get his finger on the trigger. There was a flash of red hair followed by two rapid shots that dropped him where he stood. Bullets came from elsewhere and caught the soldiers' attention as Austin used the distraction to bolt for the clearly visible shock of red hair; he tackled Gretchen to the ground at the same time bullets began flying over them.

Several more shots rang out from all around them, and then there was nothing but silence. Austin was afraid to move. He didn't think he'd been shot, but the eerie silence had him wondering if he'd died or was on the verge of death.

"You can get off me now," Gretchen muttered from below him.

"Sorry," he mumbled, rolling to the side.

"Clear!" Amanda's voice rang out.

Austin jumped to his feet and raced back towards where the men had been. They lay scattered around the forest floor in various poses. All of them dead. Amanda was already kicking guns away from the bodies in case anyone was playing possum.

He quickly jumped in, picking up the fallen weapons along with all spare magazines and checking for pulses. He looked up to see Malachi and Harlen standing next to each other, staring down at the bodies, stricken looks on their faces.

"Are they all dead?" Gretchen whispered.

Austin turned to look at the woman who'd gone pale as a ghost, making her freckles look even more pronounced. "They are."

She was shaking her head. "I hated doing that."

"I know you did," he said, and then he reached out and

gripped her shoulder, holding his hand there for support until she finally looked up from the bodies and met his eyes. "Thank you. You helped save my life." He looked around at the group. "Thank you to all of you for saving my life," he said.

They nodded, and then Amanda met his eyes pointedly. "Let's get out of here. We don't know if there are any more out here."

Harlen went to Gretchen, wrapping the woman in a bear hug. He looked at Austin before silently passing him, Gretchen on one side of him and Malachi on the other. Austin knew it had been too much for the trio. They needed to recuperate.

"Wait!" Austin called out.

Harlen turned back. "We're going back to the house."

"I know, but take these. We need the weapons," he said, picking up two of the automatics, handing one to Malachi and one to Harlen.

He'd had no intention of giving one to Gretchen, but she held out her hand. "I'll carry one," she whispered.

Austin silently gave her the weapon. He knew she was going to be struggling with what she'd done for a long time. He hated that she'd had to kill a man, too, but was grateful she'd found the strength to do it. The three of them walked ahead, leaving him and Amanda behind with their promise that they'd catch up.

"Thank you," he said, though the words felt incredibly inadequate.

"Of course," she replied, shrugging—as if killing six men wasn't a big deal.

"Are you okay?" He stopped her when she moved to follow the others.

"I'm fine."

"Amanda, are you sure you're okay?" he asked again.

She let out a long sigh. "I'm fine, really I am. I've been trained for this. I'm somewhat desensitized to what happened here. It's them I'm worried about."

He realized that she must have gone back into soldier mode, and that was the new vibe he was getting off of her. She really was fine, even if they couldn't say the same for the others. "I think we'll know very soon if they're going to stay or go."

"I think so, too. They all agreed to help me rescue you. I gave them the option of walking away, Austin. They all wanted to do what we had to," she added.

Austin wrapped her in a hug, the guns clanking between them. "You're an amazing woman. Thank you for saving me."

She laughed, pushing him away. "You saved me. I was returning the favor."

"We should probably head back. I think it's safe to say it isn't safe out here. They're actually looking for me personally," he muttered.

She grimaced. "I guess it was a little too much to hope they would just forget all about us."

With that, they followed the others, erasing their tracks as they went and then veering off as they got closer to the house, circling back and laying out a false trail away from the bodies, keeping a watchful eye around them as they tracked in a different direction and then took a long detour back to the house. They couldn't risk leaving a trail right to the front door. The soldiers were looking for them. And when those bodies were found, it would become clear there were people in these woods who were willing to fight back. Burying them wouldn't do any good, either—disappearing in this area would be just as suspicious.

This fight they'd engaged in would certainly increase patrols and hunting parties. Unless, by some chance, it would be taken as a warning to stay away. Austin could only hope.

8

Nash sat on the couch in the living room, the house virtually empty. Everyone was outside doing chores while others stood guard. The events yesterday had shaken them all. The soldiers were looking for people in the mountains, and Austin specifically; that didn't bode well for them. Nash was only irritated it had taken them this long to get with the program. He'd tried to tell them there was a good chance soldiers would be roaming the mountains, but not looking for survivors. They were there for another reason entirely. If anyone would stop moving long enough to listen to him, he could explain it.

He'd spent all of yesterday going through the files on the drive. The more he read, the more he realized they weren't dealing with normal, sane people. It was a collective group of crazy people, but they were crazy people who were crazy smart and had a crazy amount of resources at their disposal.

"Hey," Austin said, coming through the door.

"Hey," Nash replied.

"What's up?" he asked, sitting on the other couch.

Nash stared at him. "What's up? I've been trying to tell you what's up. You ignored me and nearly got yourself killed yesterday."

Austin frowned. "I'm sorry. What is it you wanted to tell me? Is it something you found on that drive?"

Nash took a deep breath. "Yes and no. I found a file filled with information about bunkers and secret hideouts. And remember that cave, where we got the laptop from? There was a door on the far wall."

Austin nodded. "I remember."

"I think there's more to that bunker," Nash said.

Austin shrugged. "Possibly, but we can't go back there, especially if you think they've been there since we stole the laptop."

"What if that's their real headquarters?" Nash demanded.

"What? We've been to their real headquarters—Zander admitted that much," Austin pointed out. "And what if it is? You want another shoot-out?"

Nash shook his head. "No, of course not, but we need information, and there weren't people there before or they would have stopped us taking the laptop itself. That drive is loaded with files, too many files for me to go through on my own. A lot of them have information in them that doesn't make any sense. I feel like there's something I need to see, but there's so much crap to filter through that I'm getting distracted; it's hard to know what's important and what's not. I think we should go directly to the source."

"The source? The source of that information is dead. I can't ask him what's on there," Austin said, frustration evident in his voice.

"I know that, but I think that door could be something worth investigating. Your friend, he gave you this information because it could be used for something," Nash argued.

"You heard what happened yesterday. It's dangerous out there," Austin reminded him.

"What if the soldiers are out there because they're going to that cave? What if they're protecting the real headquarters?"

Austin scowled. "They're out there looking for survivors."

"It doesn't feel right. Something bigger is happening. I think we have the answers right here, and I just haven't found it yet."

Austin stared back at him, as if measuring his words, and then shook his head, looking away. "Nash, you're working day in and day out on that thing. Take a break before you make yourself crazy."

Nash sighed, feeling like he was talking to a brick wall. "You don't understand. I think that cave is important. I think it's the key to shutting this whole thing down, Austin. We just have to figure out how to use it."

"I get it. I do. We saw there were a lot of electronics and other equipment in there. That's a big deal, and it's probably what you're seeing on that drive. They hid the electronics in there to keep them safe from the EMP. We need to focus on what to do next here. That laptop isn't going to help us right now. Right now, we need to think about defenses," Austin said, getting to his feet. "I want to solve the mystery of it, too, but we've got bigger things to worry about right now."

There was no point in arguing. Austin had initially thought the drive was a priority, but things had shifted. No one was paying attention to Nash or his opinions.

Austin walked out of the living room, leaving Nash alone in the house once again. He reached for the laptop once more, opening it up and staring at the screen. Maybe he was too wrapped up in the stupid thing. The idea that there was a magic button to shut everything bad down and return the world to normal was nothing more than a fantasy. Even the idea that a single button could dismantle that organization and make things safe again was likely a pipe dream.

"Hey there," Wendell's voice came from the kitchen.

Nash looked up, surprised to see him. He'd thought he'd been in the house alone. Wendell stumbled as he watched him, smiling as he righted himself before walking into the living room and flopping onto the other couch.

"What are you doing? Are you drunk?" Nash asked.

Wendell shrugged. "I'm not drunk. I had a drink."

"You're in here drinking while everyone else is working?" he asked with disgust.

Wendell rolled his eyes. "I wasn't drinking. I had a drink while I did inventory."

"Inventory?" Nash echoed.

"Yes, Ennis wants me to do a full inventory and then budget out what we have to make it last as long as possible. When it was just me and him, we would have had food for at least a year."

Nash smirked. "It was never just you and him. I was here before you, and Austin and Savannah are family. They were on their way before you were."

Wendell waved a dismissive hand. "Well, fine, but the rest of them, they're more mouths to feed."

"The rest of them are out there hunting and doing things that will make life easier," Nash reminded him.

"I'm doing my part in here," he replied easily.

Nash shook his head, dismissing Wendell and returning his focus to the screen in front of him.

"I think you're right, you know," Wendell said after a time.

"What?" Nash asked, looking up at him.

"I overheard you and Austin talking. I think you're right, or at least I think you think you're right, which is about all that matters since we all know you're some kind of genius. My opinion is they should listen to you," he replied.

"About?" Nash asked, one eyebrow raised.

"About that cave you're talking about. Why don't you go check it out yourself if you think it's important?"

"Because I'm not an idiot, and I don't go running off on my own," Nash shot back.

Wendell grinned. "You mean you listen and do as you're told."

Nash closed the laptop and got to his feet. "I'm going outside for some fresh air."

Wendell smiled, still slouching on the couch. "Suit yourself."

Nash took the laptop with him. He didn't trust Wendell not to purposely break it or mess with the files. The guy was strange. He honestly got the feeling Wendell wanted them all to leave the house to him and Ennis, or maybe even just to him, and would stop at nothing to get what he wanted.

9

Wendell watched Nash walk away. The guy hated him. He could feel it every time the kid looked his way. Nash was one of the valued members of this little group of survivors, too, and Wendell knew Austin tended to believe whatever the kid said. Nash was likeable, if someone liked that kind of thing, which was not good for him.

It wouldn't be long before the entire house was against him.

Right now, Ennis was his only ally. If Austin and Nash had their way, he'd be sent packing. Wendell wasn't interested in trying to survive out there all by himself. It was nothing short of a miracle he'd made it as long as he had. Somehow, though, he had to secure his place in this group, and the only way he knew to do that was to get on Nash's good side.

He'd make a point of talking to Ennis about checking out the stupid cave. That would prove to Nash he wasn't a bad guy.

Then, he'd align himself with the genius and slowly win over Austin and his girlfriend.

With nothing better to do at the moment, and that plan in his thoughts, Wendell headed back to the pantry. He didn't mind hanging out in the dark space. After all, it's where the alcohol was stashed.

He sat on the floor, cross-legged with the notebook in his lap, a pen in one hand and a bottle of Southern Comfort in the other. It wasn't necessarily his drink of choice, but it certainly got the job done. He stared at the notebook, trying to remember what he'd been counting when he'd heard Nash and Austin talking.

"Corn, canned corn," he mumbled to himself, taking a swig directly from the bottle.

He held it up to the light as he swallowed and told himself not to forget to add some water to the bottle once he was finished. The others would be pissed if they found out he was helping himself to the stash of liquor. It was one of the luxuries that was supposed to be regulated to make sure everyone got some —not that the Bible thumpers were big drinkers. He hoped it stayed that way, too—more for him.

"Wendell?" Ennis called out.

Wendell squeezed his eyes closed as if that would make him invisible. "Yes?" he asked, trying to appear innocent and sober.

"What are you doing?"

"Inventory," he replied.

"Are you drunk?" Ennis asked, anger in his voice.

"No."

Ennis stared down at him, his lips pursed. "Wendell, get up."

With some serious effort, Wendell managed to get to his feet, using one of the shelves to pull himself up.

"What?" he snapped.

"Nash said he thought you were drunk, and now I'm asking, are you?" Ennis asked, his tone softening a bit.

Damn kid. "I'm not drunk. I had a few drinks," he said, hoping that would be enough to get his friend to back off.

Ennis reached for the bottle, taking it from his hand and walking out of the pantry. He put it on the kitchen bar before turning back to him with a look of disgust. Wendell had followed him, but standing wasn't working well for him, so he slid onto a barstool, waiting for the lecture he felt sure was coming.

"Wendell, what's going on? I've smelled alcohol on you the past few days. How much are you drinking?" Ennis asked.

Wendell shrugged, realizing he was caught. One excuse after another went through his mind, but he knew none of them would work. "I have," he admitted. "I mean, I am. I'm sorry," he muttered.

Ennis stared at him for several long seconds. "Is this a problem for you?"

Wendell looked down at the counter, a rush of shame rising up in his gut and making it difficult to look Ennis in the eyes. "Yes. I mean, no. It used to be."

Ennis sat down on the stool next to him. "Wendell, I don't know a lot about this, but I don't think there is such a thing as 'used to be.'"

Wendell nodded. "You're right. There isn't. I got treatment for it a few years back. I've managed to stay sober until recently. The stress has been too much."

He opened his eyes wide as he looked down, trying to bring on some tears. When he finally looked at Ennis, he knew his eyes were glassy, but not only from the alcohol. He *hoped* he looked like he was on the verge of tears, at least. Maybe something good could come of this.

Ennis reached out and put a hand on his shoulder. "I didn't know. I wouldn't have put you in charge of inventory if I had known. I put the bottle right in your hand."

Wendell shook his head. "No, no. That's not the problem. I'm the problem. I let my demons get ahead of me. I knew better. I knew one little drink was too much."

"We'll figure something out," Ennis assured him.

"No!"

"What?" Ennis asked, shock sounding in his voice.

"I mean, please don't tell anyone. I don't want anyone else to know about this. Can we keep it between us?" he pleaded.

Ennis hesitated before nodding. "Yes, I won't say anything, but I want you to promise you'll come to me if you feel like you need a drink."

"I will, I swear I will. I'll quit cold-turkey right now!" Wendell promised.

Ennis looked at him, his eyes saying it all—he didn't believe him. "Okay. For now, let's give inventory duty to someone else. We'll remove the temptation."

Wendell hid his reaction to the news well. He wasn't looking forward to one of the other many jobs around the house. His drinking wasn't really a problem, either. He just liked drinking, and it helped dull the stress of living through an apocalypse. What was the harm in enjoying the liquor while they had it? He'd have to find another way to get his fix, though. For now, he'd be on his best behavior.

"Thank you. I really appreciate everything you've done for me. You're a good friend."

Ennis clapped him on the shoulder. "You're welcome. Now, come on. You need to get cleaned up and brush your teeth. I'll take care of this."

"Thanks, Ennis, I owe you big for this," Wendell said, sliding off the chair and doing his best to walk a straight line out of the kitchen.

But he cursed himself as he left. He'd screwed up. It'd been stupid of him to get caught. He knew his limit, but he'd let himself get carried away. Now he was off inventory duty.

And then, once he reached the living room, he stopped in his tracks and smiled. In some ways, getting caught had been a good thing. He and Ennis shared a secret—one that could bite Ennis if he were to tell. Austin would be mad that he'd kept something from him.

Wendell took the stairs slowly as he gripped the handrail. The whole thing might actually work out very well for him. And besides that, Ennis would never kick out a friend in need.

10

Austin walked out into the dark night, illuminated only by the moon surrounded by a million stars. The view was phenomenal. Without any light pollution, the stars looked so much brighter and closer to earth. They reflected colors, looking more like prisms hanging high in the sky than plain, white stars. It was such a beautiful sight, it was hard to think of the ugliness happening beyond the forest.

He followed the hushed sound of voices, finding Amanda and Ennis sitting on the park bench under the trees, enjoying a nightcap. Crickets were chirping all around them, trying to outdo the sound of the owls high in the trees. The forest could be very loud at night if you actually stopped and listened.

"Hi," Amanda greeted him, scooting over on the bench and making room for him.

He took a seat, his thigh pressed against hers on the small bench. "God, it's so beautiful out here," he commented.

Amanda laughed softly. "It really is. It's hard to imagine anything horrible happening in the world when you can see this night sky and hear the forest remaining so alive." She inhaled deeply. "Everything smells so fresh, so clean... so new and full of promise. Can't we pretend everything is normal?" she asked wistfully.

"That's moss and wet pine needles you're smelling," Ennis joked.

"Ha ha ha. You know what I mean. This is the kind of place people dream of retiring to, and we're living it," she replied.

"If only there weren't crazy people not more than a dozen miles away, ready to take over the world and all the people in it," Austin quipped.

"Seriously, though. What if we could hide this place? Make it our own private retreat that the rest of the world will never find? Think about those people who live in the Amazon. They've lived away from the world in general, maintaining their own little corner with no one bugging them," Amanda said.

"It's a nice idea, but it isn't realistic," Austin said, unwilling to dwell on a fantasy.

"It could be," Ennis replied.

Austin leaned forward to look at him, peering around Amanda's wistful expression. "How? There are too many people, and this place is too close to the city."

Ennis shrugged. "Not really. There are a lot less people living in the city than there were two months ago. I would guess a large chunk of the population fled to their own secret hidey holes, and another large chunk's been killed or perished for one reason or another," he reasoned.

"That is so sad," Amanda murmured, half to herself. "What do you think the population is right now? And it's been what, a matter of a few months?"

Austin shook his head, sighing at the gravity of the situation. "I don't know. By the end of winter, I think it's safe to assume the population of the United States alone will drop in half. With no food supply, few people with electricity to heat homes, and sickness in general, it's going to be devastating," he said. "And the South is probably losing people to heat stroke as we speak."

There was a silence among them as they all digested the information. Austin hadn't let himself think too much about the devastating effects that the EMP would have had on people all around the country. He'd been caught up in his own world, trying to save his daughter, and now just trying to survive. He'd seen some of the death first-hand, but knew that was only a small glimpse into what would have been happening in the larger cities. He pushed it out of his mind, preferring to stay in a place where he didn't have to think about children dying or their parents dying and leaving them alone in the world to fend for themselves.

"Want a drink?" Ennis asked, holding up a bottle of whiskey and cutting through the gloomy silence that had wrapped a heavy cloak of dread around them.

"Sure," Austin said, grabbing it and taking a swig directly from the bottle.

"Austin, we need to make a plan," Amanda said.

"A plan for what?" he asked.

"For staying here."

He looked at her, then his brother. "Even after we saw those men in the forest?"

"They were a good five miles away. Maybe more, considering how fast we were walking. We don't know they would ever have found this place," Amanda pointed out.

"And if they had?" he asked.

"We can take steps to hide this place a little better. We talked about it before, and I think it's more important than ever to do it now," she explained.

"What do you have in mind?" he asked, resigned to the idea at least for the immediate future.

"We block the road leading to the driveway first," Ennis answered.

"With?" Austin asked.

"There's enough manpower here, we can put some large boulders into place, maybe a couple large logs," he said.

Austin chuckled. "The guys we saw were on foot; they'll go around."

"If the road is blocked, we eliminate the threat of people

coming in by car. You said those soldiers you encountered on the way here were in Humvees?" he asked.

"True—Amanda and I saw them when we were traipsing around to cover our tracks. I guess that will slow them in that respect," he agreed, though unconvinced it would help prevent people in general from finding the house.

"The dirt road leading up here is already fading with lack of use. We'll help it along. People might assume it's an old logging road," Amanda said, reasonably enough. "We can cut some tree branches and toss them over the roadway off the main road. We'll make it look as natural as possible. So far, everyone has been smart, not using the same paths around the area when they go out looking for plants or for walks. We talked about that early, and everyone listened."

Austin nodded. "Okay, I like that. What about creating some kind of alarm system to give us warning when someone is close?"

Amanda nudged him with her shoulder. "That's the spirit. We have all those cans from the canned food we've been eating. We can attach them to some fishing line strung low to the ground. They'll clank together when someone trips the wire."

"How are we going to hear that?" Ennis asked.

Austin looked at him and shrugged. "We might need to talk about having security running around the clock. And at night, when there's no one talking, sound carries pretty far."

"What? Really? You want someone to stay on watch all night?" Amanda exclaimed.

"Yes, really. Wouldn't you rather be safe than sorry?"

She looked thoughtful before nodding in agreement. "You're right. I have to keep reminding myself we're not in Kansas anymore, so to speak. Even in the barracks with hundreds of airmen sleeping in their bunks, there was always a night shift keeping watch over things. There are enough of us to take turns, too. Do you think the revivalists will participate?"

"They have to. This isn't only for our safety. They're here too," Ennis replied. "And it's not like we're talking about shooting anyone. We're talking about keeping watch. They see anything, they'll be raising an alarm, not going on attack."

Austin took another drink from the bottle before handing it back to Ennis. "I agree. Plus, we saw what they're capable of. I know they all have their own beliefs about taking a life, but human instinct is to survive. If they're threatened, they're going to fight back. Really, worse comes to worse, all we need them to do is fire a shot in the air and alert the rest of us that we have a problem."

"Good point. When we present it to them, that's exactly what we need to tell them. I think that will help it go over a little easier," Amanda said.

"What about setting traps?" Ennis offered.

"Like, human traps?" Amanda asked, her voice full of disgust.

Austin chuckled. "I don't think he meant for eating. I think that's a good idea, but we're going to have to make sure we're all careful not to trigger them ourselves."

Amanda playfully slapped his leg. "I knew that, Austin. But, okay… We can rig something in the trees. When a person triggers the trap, a bucket of something will dump over their heads."

"That works. What are we going to put in the bucket?" Austin asked.

She shrugged a shoulder. "I don't know; poop, rocks, thistle heads, pee," she said.

"I like that—well, not the poop, but the other things are great," Austin agreed.

Ennis chuckled. "I think poop is a great idea!"

Amanda giggled, taking her turn with the bottle. "I know if a bucket of poop dumped on my head, I'd be turning around and going the other way."

The three of them laughed, enjoying the peaceful night together as they kept brainstorming for another hour before deciding to turn in for the night. It was nights like these that made it easy to forget about the destruction happening all around them.

Austin couldn't shake the feeling that the worst was yet to come, though. Maybe it was his journalist's intuition in overdrive, but something felt off. There was no way they could all live up here happily ever after, not with soldiers actively hunting them and others. It wasn't a matter of *if*, but *when* the house would be found. He wanted to be prepared as much as possible.

11

Malachi sat down next to the tiny creek flowing downhill from what appeared to be a natural spring. Amanda and Austin had come across it on one of their scouting adventures, telling everyone they had found a source of running water. With no real destination in mind, he'd set off on his own to explore the mountainside, eager to see the creek. He knew he wasn't supposed to, and knew it was risky, but he needed time alone.

It had been three days since the encounter with the soldiers in the woods. Austin and Amanda were already planning their next scavenging mission into the city, claiming the risk was a necessary one. Malachi had volunteered to go. He needed to see what it was like out there. Plus, he wanted to get away from the constant barrage of opinions from the other revivalists who were looking to him as their new leader amongst the group. They all wanted him to hold regular sermons. He wasn't up to that—not yet.

He needed time to think and get his head straight. Everyone had an opinion and wanted him to hear it. He was only fifteen, though! He didn't know what to do. He wanted Austin or Ennis to make the decisions. Unfortunately, there was an obvious divide between the two groups. There was his group and there was Savannah's family. And he, even though he was the youngest, had somehow become the person the revivalists were turning to. It was like they needed him to give them the okay to stay or go. It was too much.

It felt like he'd been in a nightmare that wouldn't cease. Everything was wrong. His life had been so easy, so boring, even if it hadn't been the life of a typical fifteen-year-old. Traveling the country, preaching and spreading the word of God while being homeschooled was all he knew. His mom, dad, and grandpa had been his whole world. He'd never had close friends his own age, or even a cell phone to surf the internet with before the EMP had happened, but he'd had his family. He had known what he was supposed to do with his life, too, and now all of that was in question.

His father had always assumed he would carry on the family torch, but he was supposed to have learned more from his father before the torch was passed to him. He hadn't learned enough yet, no matter what the others thought. Worse, he no longer felt that draw to be a part of the family business. In fact, he wasn't entirely sure he had ever felt the calling. He'd always assumed it would come later, when he got older. Now, he felt like he was at a crossroads in his life and he had to make a decision, but there were no clues or knowledge for him to base that decision on.

Malachi picked up a stick, stirring the crystal-clear water and wondering what to do next. They had traveled west with the intention of going home. Staying at the house hadn't been part of the plan. Things had just kind of happened that way. But at least his mom was perking up. The sermon he'd given last night seemed to have helped her. She'd smiled for the first time in a long time and fallen into some of her old ways, leading the very small group in song before sitting and chatting with everyone.

He took a deep breath, inhaling the clean air before slowly making his way back to the house. He didn't want anyone to notice he'd been gone. Savannah would probably be looking for him already. She was trying to be his friend, but he'd been pushing her away. He didn't want the distraction of a pretty girl. He was having a hard enough time trying to keep his mind right.

When he returned to the house, he found his mom sitting alone under the shade of some tall pines about fifty feet from the house. He sat beside her on the hard ground.

"Why are you out here all alone?" he asked.

She offered him a small smile. "I like to come out here alone and think. It makes me feel closer to your father. I swear I can hear him beside me sometimes."

Malachi nodded in understanding. "I believe he is watching over us."

"How was your walk? Did you find the answers you were looking for?" she asked softly.

He grimaced, realizing he'd been caught going off on his own. "Sorry," he muttered.

"Don't be. I know you needed some time away. I would have sent out a search party if you were gone too long," she teased.

"It was good to be alone… really, truly alone for a little while. It feels like everything is so much louder now. Do you know what I mean?" he asked her.

She smiled, and he noticed that the dark circles that had been under her eyes for so long seemed to be fading. "I do know. We have to remember to give ourselves time to hear the voice of the Holy Spirit. He can bring us peace if we allow Him to."

"I know. It's like all the bad stuff has pushed Him away."

"Which is why it's time to find Him again. We need His presence to guide us," she advised.

"I do feel lost," he said on a sigh.

She paused, and then answered, "You've made me very proud these past couple of weeks, my son. You've really taken on such responsibility, filling his role. Your father would be proud, too. It's okay to feel a little lost; we all do. We're finding our way," she assured him.

"Thank you. I just needed some time to think. Some of the others came to me last night," he added.

She stopped the weaving of the tall grass she had piled up beside her. "Oh? What did they have to say?"

"Some of them think we should be going into town to help

others," he said, knowing this was what had been weighing most heavy on his mind since they'd first told him the night before.

His mom put a hand on his arm. "Malachi, you are a natural born leader. They are looking to you because they see you as a leader."

"But what about Harlen or Drew, or you?" he protested.

She smiled and shook her head. "You are the next in line. You were born into this life. You already demonstrate leadership qualities. With time, you will feel comfortable."

"What do I do now?" he asked.

She shrugged, staring off into the trees. "I think you know. What would your father do?"

"You think we should go into the city and offer help?" he asked, a ball of nerves in his gut. He'd known she would say that, and that that was what his father would have said. What he felt was something else.

She smiled. "I think we are in a position to help others. We have a doctor of sorts who could offer medical attention to those in need. Gretchen is studying the medicinal plants in the area. The vast library Ennis keeps has given us a huge advantage. Think about the volunteer work we used to do. Think about the meals we provided for those who had nothing to eat, and the shelter we offered to those who had nothing."

Malachi sighed. "These things are not ours to offer," he pointed out.

"No, but we can pray with those who need hope. We can offer them help in many ways, even if it isn't giving them a home. We have so much here, how can we not share? What do you think God would do, were He here?" she asked, posing the question he had heard so many times throughout his life.

The question was meant to provide him with a Due North reading on his moral compass. And, deep down, he knew what to do, but he also knew he didn't have the support of Austin and the others. They weren't big on charity. They were more concerned about keeping the house protected, and protected those who resided within. He could understand that, too.

"It isn't ours to give," he reminded her.

"We don't always give material things. We give love, support, and understanding. If we have a single loaf of bread and there are others starving, what should we do?" she asked, her voice soft.

He sighed. "We share. God always provides if we do the right thing."

She smiled, her eyes lighting up. "You're a good boy, Malachi. I know you're struggling. You can always talk to me, and God is there for you, as well, don't forget."

"Mom, do you want to stay here?" he asked bluntly.

She let out a long sigh. "I don't know. I don't know that we have a home to go to. I thought that's what we were meant to do, but I don't know if that's our destiny."

"Harlen keeps talking about that refugee camp," he said.

She shook her head. "I don't think it's wise to travel that far. Not again. Salt Lake City, perhaps, but Seattle? Here, we have safety, community, and we can live freely. I don't want to put your life at risk again. We don't know if that camp is real or a rumor started by the people who've put out that disgusting literature. It could be a ploy, a way to get us all in one place to make their jobs easier," she said vehemently, shocking Malachi.

"So, you want to stay?" he asked, finding he was almost hoping she would say yes.

"Yes, I think that is the right decision. If things change, we'll reevaluate."

He slowly nodded. He was happy to know his mother was okay with hanging out a little longer. He'd feared that, as she'd begun feeling better, she'd have become more anxious to move on.

"Do you think the tension will ease?" he asked, knowing she'd understand his meaning.

"I think we all have to learn what it means to live together. I talked with Amanda yesterday. She talked about building some cabins to provide us more living space. There is tension because none of us really know each other. It will take time. If it's meant to be, it will be," she said, her voice firm.

Malachi smiled. "It's nice to have you back, Mom."

She chuckled as she picked up her weaving. "I'm sorry I wasn't there for you the past couple of weeks. I was over-whelmed by grief. I feel like I can breathe again. You can always talk to me. Never feel like you have to carry your burdens alone. You have me, you have God, and your father is always present."

"Thank you. I needed to hear that." He watched her work for a few moments, and then stood. "I should go find Jordan and Ezra. We're going to be stacking that wood we chopped," he said, dusting off his pants.

"I'll see you at dinner," she promised.

He started to walk away, then turned to look back at her. "Austin is planning a trip into town tomorrow, and I'm going to go with him. I want to see for myself what things are like."

She nodded, still focused on her own work. "I think that's a good idea. We'll pray for your safety as well as that of the others tonight."

"What's tonight?" he asked.

"A few of us are getting together for a Bible lesson. You're welcome to join," she offered.

"We'll see. I love you, Mom," he told her, and when she echoed the sentiment, he headed towards the house to begin the grueling work of carrying the split logs the hundred-some feet to the lean-to they were going to be building to shelter the wood.

He felt a little lighter as he headed downhill through the trees, but raised voices drew his attention. He followed the sound, recognizing one of the voices as Ennis, and the other sounded like Ezra, but he couldn't be sure.

"It has to be closer to the house," Ennis nearly shouted.

"What's going on?" Malachi asked, finding Ennis, Wendell, Ezra, and Jordan in a face-off.

"The wood pile has to be closer to the house. These two are building it over there." Wendell pointed to the place where a lean-to built with branches was already taking form.

"I thought that was the agreed upon location," Malachi said, not sure what he'd missed.

Ennis shook his head. "I didn't agree to that."

"These two aren't the ones doing all the work," Ezra snapped, looking to Malachi.

Malachi fought down a grimace, understanding where Ezra was coming from. Wendell and Ennis seemed to have jobs that kept them inside out of the heat, and neither of them did any manual labor. That had fallen on Malachi and the other men.

"Why isn't the spot going to work?" Malachi asked Ennis.

"Because it doesn't!" Wendell snapped.

Malachi ignored him, his gaze on Ennis.

"In the winter, the snow is going to be deep. That location works for a back-up pile, but it would be better if we didn't have to walk so far from the house to get wood for the fire. The farther away it is, the more shoveling we'll have to do. That takes time, energy, and could be dangerous," Ennis explained.

Malachi looked around the area, realizing everything he'd said was true. This whole area would be buried in snow. "Where do you want the wood?" he asked, resigned to the idea that it was going to have to be closer.

Ennis pointed to an area next to the side of the house. There was little shelter, which meant they were going to have to build another lean-to.

"You gonna help build the cover?" Ezra asked sarcastically, looking at Wendell.

"Well, I, uh, I, there's inventory to be done, and organizing," Wendell stammered.

"I think it would be helpful if we had more people working out here on these chores that can't be done at night and have to be done soon," Malachi said, crossing his arms over his chest and looking at Ennis, then Wendell.

Ennis nodded immediately. "You're right. We'll need to switch around some jobs. We'll get the new shelter built right away."

It was the best they were going to get.

Malachi used his eyes to tell Ezra and Jordan to follow him. They were quiet as they walked away, leaving Wendell and Ennis in a heated discussion.

"Why are we the ones out here doing all the heavy lifting?" Jordan snapped.

"I don't know. We have to appreciate them letting us stay here and eat their food, though. A little hard work never killed anyone," Malachi said, repeating the same advice his father had told him so many times.

"It seems like they want us to stay so they can treat us like we're their slaves," Ezra grumbled.

"The new shelter isn't that far, and like Ennis said, it will be necessary for winter. Do you want to be the guy shoveling several feet of snow to get to the wood pile?" Malachi asked.

Ezra shook his head. "No, but there needs to be a better division of labor. How long does it take to count the supplies? How much is there? You notice they never let any of us in that pantry?" he growled.

"We're guests," Malachi reminded him.

The tension in the house was mounting. Malachi hated feeling it and knew they were going to have to find a way to diffuse the mounting frustration. Everyone was feeling it. Pushing it all to the side, the three of them got busy, hauling the split wood up the hill to the first shelter as a back-up. Within two trips, they decided to break from carrying logs and build a sled they could use for hauling them. Maybe even a cart if they could find wheels for one that would be sturdy enough to support the weight of the wood. He was going to sleep very well that night, he decided on his fifth trip.

12

Austin's skin felt electrified, as if there were a million needles pricking him as they moved through the forest on their way to the wealthy suburb perched high above the city. It was a place filled with huge houses with panoramic views of the mountains and Denver. He looked to his left, seeing that Nash and Malachi were walking purposely, their eyes wide and scanning the area, each of them carrying one of the ARs from Ennis's stash. Malachi looked bigger, older than Austin remembered. It was the times, he realized, and the life they were being forced to live. He'd noticed the same growth in Savannah.

These teens were being forced to grow up practically overnight, as he guessed was happening to children all over the country.

A crack of a branch from his right had his eyes darting towards Amanda. She grimaced and mouthed the word *sorry*.

He nodded, assuring her it was okay. Drew was on her other side, looking completely out of place and terrified. He had insisted on coming along. Austin had a feeling he was doing his own scouting. Several members of the revivalist group had spoken up at dinner last night, expressing their desire to venture out and offer aid to any survivors. The idea had been shut down quickly, by Austin and several others. And although Malachi had supported the idea verbally, Austin guessed from the expression he'd had while doing it that the boy also had more sense—he was simply being torn between roles, and Austin didn't envy him the position.

So, among them, Drew was on his humanitarian mission. Malachi was trying to prove his worth as man of the house or leader of the revivalists. And poor Nash, he was seeking a break from going stir-crazy from staring at the laptop all day and night. Only Austin and Amanda were simply on the mission to scavenge and scout.

They walked along in silence, each of them armed—even the good pastor, although he was carrying a Glock and Austin seriously doubted the man would actually use it. Austin had chosen to carry one of the automatics they had lifted off the NWO soldiers. These guns would do a lot of damage in a little time, giving him and the others plenty of time to escape if they needed it.

The trees started to thin out the more they went uphill. His pulse raced when the back of one sprawling house came into view.

"Wait," he whispered to the others.

He crept forward, staying in the trees and scanning the back-yard for any signs of life. It looked deserted. The backyard pool water was green and covered with algae. Some patio furniture lay overturned, and one of the large picture windows overlooking the backyard had been shattered.

"Empty?" Amanda asked.

He shrugged. "I guess we're going to find out."

They spread out, walking down the rocky hill that opened into the neighborhood of expensive homes and what had probably been perfectly landscaped yards. Amanda led the charge as they entered the first house through the sliding glass doors at its back.

"What's that smell?" Malachi groaned.

"Sewage," Amanda replied, pulling her shirt up to cover her nose.

The boy grimaced. "What?"

"Someone was living here. I'm guessing the toilets are backed up," Amanda answered.

"Why?" Malachi shot back.

"The main city sanitation pumps require electricity. People probably flushed as usual in the days following the shutdown, but with nowhere for the crap to go, literally, and no pumps to push it and sanitation systems, it would have nowhere to go but back up," she explained.

Austin stared back at her, also horrified. "You mean it's going to be like this in all the houses? Is that safe? I mean, should we bother scavenging? Isn't that like walking in disease?" he asked.

She shrugged. "Don't step in any liquid you see on the floor. If it is raw sewage, we don't want to be carrying that back to the house. Otherwise, we should be okay."

They all nodded back at her, their initial excitement at the idea of shopping for goods deflating a little with the strong smell of human waste.

"I'm going to check the master bedroom for clothes. Drew, you check for a junk drawer in the kitchen. Grab any batteries, string, duct tape, shoestrings, paperclips—anything that we can use at the house," Amanda ordered.

"I'll check the garage—look for hunting or fishing supplies," Malachi said. "Could be a junk drawer in there, too."

Austin waved for everyone's attention, meeting everyone's eyes in turn. "And pay attention, too. There could be people roaming about," Austin told them. "If not inside, outside to see us through the windows."

Malachi nodded. "Got it."

"I'm going to search down here," Austin said.

The five of them split up, scavenging what they could from the house that had already been gone over. They met back in the huge kitchen area, spreading their loot on the counter.

"We need these clothes, but they're going to be heavy,"

Amanda said, looking at the armload of men's and women's clothes she'd found.

"Wait, I have an idea," Malachi said, rushing out of the kitchen and back towards the garage.

He returned a few minutes later with a large steel garden cart, with large wheels that would make it fairly easy to pull through rough terrain.

"That works," Austin said with a grin.

"And, this is going to make my life much easier moving the split wood up to the lean-to where it's being stacked," Malachi said, clearly very pleased with himself. "We built that little sled, yeah, but compared to this, it's nothing."

"It'll come in handy when the snow comes," Austin said—not wanting him to think the sled would go to waste, and knowing that this cart wouldn't be worth much in the snow.

"Right," Malachi answered, nodding with what looked like relief.

"How are we going to get that through the trees?" Drew asked.

"We'll carry it if we have to," Austin replied easily. "In fact, we'll check the other houses, too; if we find another one, we take it. It looks sturdy, too; I think it'll be fine if it gets bumped around some."

"What about a mountain bike?" Nash asked.

"Is there one in the garage?" Austin asked with surprise.

Nash nodded. "Yep. It was behind a bunch of boxes and stuff."

Austin looked at Amanda, who shrugged. "I haven't ridden a bike in about a million years."

"I'll ride it back," Nash said quickly. "I've done mountain biking on some pretty crazy trails. We could really use a bike," he said, clearly eager.

"Why do we need a bike?" Amanda asked.

"There are the roads to the house still. The bike will make it quick and easy for us to get around. We can use it to go hunting and foraging. It'll keep up with the horses, too, if three people want to go out at more than walking speed."

Austin couldn't see a real need for the bike, but having wheels couldn't hurt. "If you're up for trying to get it back, I'm game. Who knows? It might come in handy one day."

"We have the horses," Amanda replied.

"And now we have a bike," Nash added.

"Okay, let's leave this stuff here and check out some of the other houses. If there's medicine, first aid supplies, matches, whatever you find, grab it. If we can't get everything on this trip, we'll come back tomorrow," Austin said.

"We need to look for building supplies," Drew said almost offhandedly.

Austin stopped walking and looked at him, smiling. "Good thinking. I didn't even think about that. Nails, screws, hammer, all of that. Ennis has a good toolbox, but the more we have, the better. We'll need to consider weight, but grab as much as you can."

"There's a shed in the back of that house," Nash said as they exited the first place.

"Malachi, go with him. And watch for wasps, guys," Austin warned.

"Is anyone allergic?" Amanda asked.

Everyone shook their head before Nash and Malachi headed towards the shed, the rest of them moving across the yard to go to the next house.

"Is it strange this area is completely deserted?" Drew asked.

"I think the NWO has probably been doing sweeps through the neighborhoods. They've cleared it out," Austin replied. "Probably taken a lot of supplies themselves, too."

"Stay vigilant," Amanda warned.

Austin reached out then, jerking her backwards just as she was about to open the back door of the luxury home they'd approached. He pointed to a large wasp nest under the eaves of the home, and they slowly backed away.

"Dang, there are wasps everywhere," Drew complained.

"With no one spraying them, they're getting free rein. We'll find another way in. We'll make another trip here in a couple days and get to any houses we don't get into today. I think we need to try and get down the hill and into the city, too," Austin said.

"That's going to be dangerous," Nash warned, joining them

and shaking his head when Austin gestured to the shed to ask if they'd found anything.

"We haven't seen anyone. Shouldn't we be seeing people even if they did sweep this area?" Drew asked.

"I think they're hiding, scared," Austin answered as they made their way in a broken window.

"Maybe the NWO has prisons or camps set up," Amanda suggested.

"That's horrible!" Drew gasped.

They all fell silent as they thought about the possibility, stopping briefly now that they were inside the dim luxury home which had long been abandoned, and smelled just as bad as the first they'd entered.

"It makes sense," Austin finally said.

Nash nodded in agreement. "That tower. They could be holding prisoners or recruiting the people who stayed in the city to be their own little foot soldiers. They could easily house hundreds, maybe more, in that building."

"I think we need to scavenge in places people wouldn't normally think to look for supplies," Amanda said.

"Like?" Austin asked.

"Like business offices. Not medical clinics, but lawyers' offices, company headquarters and things like that. Every business is required to have a first aid kit, and plus, you know people stash stuff in their desks. Snacks, painkillers…"

"What about storage units?" Austin suggested.

Amanda grinned. "Exactly. We'll find tools, camping gear, fishing and hunting equipment, and I bet a lot of clothes and shoes!"

"Manufacturing places, warehouses, and even the marinas might have valuable materials," Nash suggested.

"Don't you think the soldiers would have already scoured the city for every available resource?" Malachi asked quietly.

They all turned to look at him. It was definitely a possibility they needed to consider.

"We have to try," Austin said.

"I agree. We need to come at night when we can use the darkness to our advantage," Amanda said.

"Walking through the forest at night would be dangerous," Drew pointed out.

"We'll walk in during the day and hang out until it's dark," Nash proposed.

Austin nodded. "That's a great idea. Let's hurry up and go through at least this house and one more, and then get out of here before we press our luck."

As they had in the first house, they spread out again, searching first the house they'd found entry to and then two more, gathering what they could. By the time they'd gotten that far, their packs and hands were full, and it was getting late enough in the day that Austin figured it was time to call it quits.

They walked back to the first house, paying close attention to their surroundings as they moved. It was remarkably quiet. He kept expecting to hear people talking or ordering them to stop. It never happened.

After piling the garden cart with as much as it could hold, and using a blanket tucked over the sides to hold it all in, they set out for home. Nash walked the bike until they were deep into the woods, just in case they were ambushed and he needed quick access to the gun.

But, as they traveled, the group remained even quieter than before, and Austin guessed they were processing the same emotions as him.

Austin couldn't shake the feeling of loss he had felt while they'd pilfered through the belongings of other people. It seemed so pointless. The pictures of happy families on the walls of the homes had reminded him of all that had truly been lost. He wondered if there would ever be those trips to Disneyland or ski resorts again. He also realized just how lucky he was to have Savannah still by his side. He would never take that for granted.

13

S avannah felt so mad she could scream. The men in her life were making her crazy. Malachi was avoiding her like the plague, sticking to his conviction that the apocalypse was no time for teenage romance. As if! And as for her father —well, the lack of power seemed to have transported his attitude back into the dark ages. If he could, he'd lock her in a tower and keep her from talking to anyone, but most especially Malachi. He was treating her like a little girl, and she wasn't.

She had proven she was capable of defending herself and surviving against some pretty tough odds. But it wasn't enough for him. He was acting as if she should be treated like a porcelain doll, with no one allowed to look at her, let alone touch—or kiss.

She kicked a small pebble, sending it skittering across the gravel road.

"Alright, what's going on?" her uncle asked her.

She looked at him and shrugged, glowering. "Nothing."

"Savannah, I know you better than that. Plus, you've sighed a good twenty times and assaulted I don't know how many rocks with your shoe. Something's on your mind," he said, walking alongside her.

She shifted her fishing pole to her other arm, being careful not to get the hook snagged in her shirt as she glanced toward her uncle and saw him observing her.

"It's my dad," she muttered.

"What's wrong with him?" Ennis asked.

She heaved another dramatic sigh. "He's treating me like I'm a little kid."

"How so?"

"Well, for example, he doesn't want me leaving the house. He thinks I need to sit inside or close by, as he says, and do stupid stuff with the other women," she complained.

Ennis chuckled. "You mean make fish baskets, bake, do laundry and things like that? Things that keep the house running smoothly and food in our bellies?" he teased her.

She barely held back from stomping her foot. "I know it's important work, but I want to learn more. I mean, like this. You're taking me fishing. I need to learn how to fish if I plan on living on my own one day."

He laughed. "Are you planning on moving out soon?"

"You know what I mean. If this thing lasts forever, I don't want to live with my dad the rest of my life. I want to have a husband one day. I'm going to have to know how to live on my own," she said.

Her uncle nodded, though he didn't look amused. "I understand, but I think he just wants to protect you. I can't imagine how scared he was those weeks the two of you were apart. It's going to take some time for him to loosen the hold."

She scoffed. "Yeah, right. He was like this before everything happened. He didn't like me seeing Malachi even before—or any boy, for that matter."

"Seeing Malachi? Were you two dating?" he asked.

She smiled, appreciating that he didn't sound horrified so much as curious. Her dad had made it very clear he didn't want to hear about Malachi. It was nice to have someone to talk to who treated her like she was her own person. It wasn't like she had many friends in the group. The one close friend she'd thought she had was currently not talking to her at all.

"We had talked a little, yeah, and the night the EMP happened... don't tell Dad?" she said, and when her uncle raised his eyebrows and nodded, she confessed, "We shared our first kiss." She felt herself blush before her uncle could react, and looked back at the trees ahead of them.

Ennis was quiet for a few seconds. "That's a big deal."

"It is! I thought Malachi liked me, but now he doesn't want to talk to me. It started before we ever left the ranch. His dad didn't like me," she added. "And that's what got us off-track."

Her uncle stopped walking, reaching out and turning her to face him. "What do you mean he didn't like you?" he asked, his eyes on hers.

She shook her head, realizing she'd given him the wrong impression. "Not, like, in a mean way, but he didn't think I was right for Malachi. They want Malachi to be with a girl like them, all into the Bible and stuff," she explained, not wanting Ennis to dislike Malachi. "More religious, I mean."

She needed an ally, and her uncle seemed to be the only person she could think of as being on her side in the whole situation. She still liked Malachi, though, and didn't want her uncle to be like her dad and hate him.

Now, her uncle chuckled, apparently put at ease, and started walking again. "Sounds to me Malachi's parents are just as protective of him as your dad is of you."

"I'm not exactly a sinner of grand proportions," she said, feeling herself pouting. "I could be good for him."

"Savannah, I say this with total honesty: you're too good for him," her uncle replied.

Her mouth dropped open. "Uncle Ennis! Don't say that!"

He grinned, winking at her. "You're my niece. My only niece. I don't know if there will ever be a boy who is good enough for you in my eyes. However, with that said, I think Malachi is a good kid. I think he's got a lot on his shoulders right now and needs to work through it. I've spoken to a couple of those revivalists, Savannah. They're turning to Malachi like he's their messiah, born to lead them to salvation of some sort.

That's a lot of pressure to put on anyone, especially a fifteen-year-old kid. Give him a break and let him come to you," her uncle said.

They were putting a lot of pressure on him, she knew—she could see it in the way he was working so hard, and the way they looked to him when he passed by. Truly, she didn't want to add to that pressure, but was it too much to ask for him to be her friend? "I guess, but he doesn't have to shut me out. He could talk to me."

"He could, but you're going to learn boys aren't big talkers," her uncle said, clearly just holding back a laugh.

"No kidding," she muttered, unamused.

Patting her on the shoulder, Ennis moved ahead to lead as the trees got closer together, making it harder for two people to walk beside each other like they'd been. They made their way down to the edge of the river that was some three miles south of the house. Ennis and several of the others had been going fishing, and deemed it to be relatively safe. They hadn't run into anyone yet, and there were no signs that anyone had been in the area.

"Alright, have a seat and let's catch some dinner," her uncle said with a smile.

Savannah watched him bait the hook with some corn from one of the cans they had opened specifically for fishing.

"The fish like corn?" Savannah asked.

"We're after trout, and trout love corn. I used corn even when

I had easy access to worms and other bait. It's effective, cheap, and plentiful. Relatively speaking," he said after a moment, apparently remembering that even corn wasn't plentiful now that the world had gone crazy.

He showed her the basics of casting with the spinning reel next, and then stepped back and let her do it on her own. It felt good to feel capable, and doing something to really help. Her dad had been making her feel like such a baby over the past few weeks since they'd been reunited, and it was making her miserable.

"Do you think you could show me how to hunt?" Savannah asked her uncle as they settled down on the bank to wait for fish to bite.

"Yes, absolutely. We'll start small—maybe some pheasant or grouse."

"What kind of gun will we need for that?" she asked.

He shrugged. "Just the twelve-gauge shotgun. Anything bigger and we'll destroy the meat."

She nodded, vaguely remembering shooting the gun before. "Can we go tomorrow?" she asked.

He chuckled, shaking his head. "We'll see. After the hike down here today, you might want to rest tomorrow. Grouse hunting is physically taxing. We might end up walking a good ten miles."

She groaned. "Why?"

"That's hunting for you. Hunting is a lot of walking. Nash got that bike, which will be great for when we go out hunting for deer or elk, but it will scare off the birds hiding in the brush if we try to use it for smaller prey."

"That's why you said you wanted to try trapping," she said, suddenly understanding the conversation she'd overheard earlier that morning.

"Yes. Hunting is a lot of work. We could spend a week hunting for game and never get anything. Let's say four of us go out hunting every day—that's four of us burning a lot of calories, which means we need more food to keep our strength up. We'll also need more water to stay hydrated if we're hunting during the warm months," he explained.

"Wouldn't you eat the same amount of food as you normally would?" she questioned.

"No. We'd probably want and need double the amount. Plus, if four of us are gone all day, think of the stuff around the house that isn't getting done," he pointed out. "It wouldn't be just the four of us needing more calories, either."

"But there's so many of us, we'd still be able to keep the house clean, and get the wood chopped, and I could go fishing to keep fresh meat coming in," she reasoned.

He shrugged. "True. One of the benefits to having so many people at the house is for that reason exactly. We can divide and conquer. If it was just us, we would seriously struggle."

She nodded with her eyes still on the water, understanding exactly what he meant. Having the large group was both a blessing and a curse—at least, that's what she'd heard Amanda tell her dad.

"Do you think they'll leave?" she asked Ennis.

"Who? Malachi's family?"

"Yes, do you think they'll leave?"

"I don't know. All we can do is wait and see," he replied.

"Do you want them to leave?"

He smiled. "I don't know. I like having the extra manpower, but it is also a burden. I think it's too soon to say for sure."

She agreed, though she'd hoped he might have more insight. As much as she wanted to get close to Malachi again, it was scary to think of that happening, only for him and the others to move on. Still, she appreciated her uncle actually talking to her about the situation in the house. She could feel the tension between some of the adults, and especially between Wendell and her dad. No one was acknowledging it, though—at least not to her. Her uncle was at least admitting there was an issue, however indirectly. She appreciated him treating her like one of the adults in the house and not like a little kid who was always underfoot, which seemed to be her dad's default attitude.

14

Nash walked into the kitchen to find Austin sitting at the center island, the laptop opened and a notebook off to the side where he was taking notes. Austin hadn't been at the group dinner outside, and Nash had had a feeling he'd find him inside with the laptop.

They'd been tag-teaming reading the information on the USB for the past few days. When they'd gotten back from their scavenging mission yesterday, Nash had gone straight back to work, feeling it was his duty to decipher all the files. He'd created new files and put shortcuts to them on the home screen in an effort to organize the information on the USB based on main topics. It was a huge undertaking.

Austin looked up at him. "Hey," he offered.

"How's it going?" Nash asked, taking a seat on one of the stools.

Austin rubbed his eyes. "Grueling. Where is everybody?"

"Outside, having one of their sermons or revivals or whatever they call it," he answered.

"Is Savannah out there?" Austin asked.

"Yep. You're going to hurt your eyes, you keep staring at that screen like that," Nash warned. "Looks like you've about stopped blinking."

Austin sighed, shaking his head as he pushed the laptop away. "This stuff is crazy, like sociological warfare. They've combined tactics used by some of the worst dictators in history."

"I know. It's insane, seriously. I think this group has been at this a lot longer than anyone recognized. Did you see the screenshots of the newspaper clippings about that militia group down south?" he asked.

Austin nodded. "I did. I think that was their trial run. They spread hate about the group of migrants and the militia group ate it up. They killed all those people. After reading the literature on this drive, I fully believe that militia group was manipulated into killing those people. They were guinea pigs and didn't even know it."

"These people, the ones behind this, purposely created stories that would appeal to the lowest common denominators of society. They planted stories, made up crazy lies, all with the goal of inciting hatred and violence."

Austin rubbed at his beard, frowning. "Amanda and I came

across some of the flyers they were handing out. They were disgusting, calling for open attacks on anyone who believed in God. Then, on the flip side, it was the religious people attacking those who didn't believe and blaming them for what they'd determined was some act of revenge from God. People are playing right into their hands."

"That's the goal. The world's population has turned on itself," he muttered.

Austin remained quiet for a moment before he looked at Nash. "How long do you think it will be before it lands at our front door?"

Nash shook his head. "I have no idea. I think it's closer than anyone knows. That bunker in the cave? I still think we need to check it out. It could lead to some big underground head-quarters, like the Cheyenne Mountain Complex. If these guys have the money and means like it appears they do, they could have a huge underground facility."

"Are you suggesting we try to find one of these bunkers and attack? We don't have the manpower to do that," Austin said, his eyes narrowing.

"No, but don't you think we should know what's around us?" Nash shot back.

Austin didn't answer. His attention was focused on something behind Nash now. Nash turned to see what it was that Austin was watching, and saw Ennis and Savannah sitting on one of the couches. They looked to be in deep conversation. When

Nash turned back to Austin, he got the sense the overprotective father was not pleased.

"What's that about?" Austin grumbled.

"What's what about?" Nash asked, still irritated that no one was taking him seriously about what could very well be a bunker housing the NWO leaders.

"That, my daughter and brother. They've been awful chummy lately."

Nash shrugged. "It's your brother—your daughter's uncle. They went fishing earlier; maybe they're talking about their catch."

Austin watched them a little longer before turning back to the laptop. "I found a file I can't open. Have you been able to?" he asked, returning the conversation to the USB.

"What file?" Nash asked.

Austin made a couple of keystrokes and pulled up a file. "This one."

Nash pulled the laptop towards him, recognizing the one Austin had pulled up; he hadn't yet had any luck with it. "It's encrypted."

"What does that mean?"

"It means, someone didn't want anyone to read what's in this file."

"Can you get into it?" Austin asked.

"No. I mean, I'm okay with computers, but this is next-level hacking. I don't know if it's one-twenty-eight or two-fifty-six, but I'm going to go with the latter. There's no way I can crack the encryption code—at least not in this lifetime," he muttered.

"Why would this one file be encrypted and not the others?" Austin asked.

"I would say there's something big hidden in this file," Nash replied, feeling unease settle in his belly. "But that doesn't help us get into it."

"Maybe plans?" Austin suggested.

Nash nodded. "Plans, schematics for whatever they used to trigger the EMP, or maybe locations of where they're hiding. You know they're somewhere, watching and appreciating their handiwork as the rest of the population kills itself off. The ones who survive the initial cleansing are going to die of starvation, exposure, or illness, and they'll be watching."

When Nash looked up, he noticed Austin was ignoring him again, and staring into the living room where Wendell had just joined Savannah and Ennis.

"I don't like that guy, and I definitely don't like him buddying up to my daughter," Austin said quietly.

Nash shrugged, though he agreed. "He's not my favorite person in the world, but I don't think he's a pervert. Your brother'll watch out for Savannah."

"He doesn't have to be a pervert. I don't want him filling her head with garbage. I've seen the way he kisses up to my brother. Ennis eats it up," Austin grumbled.

"I'll take over here," Nash said simply.

"Alright. Let me know if you find anything that's particularly alarming. I think we're going to have to make some big decisions about our future here in this house."

Nash stared at him, wondering if there were plans he wasn't hearing about. "How so?"

Austin only shrugged. "We're too close to the heart of the NWO. I don't like it. We can't expect to hide here forever."

Nash smirked. "Good luck convincing your brother of that. He's positive this place is invincible."

"I don't have to do anything my brother says. I make my own decisions for me and my daughter. If you'll excuse me, I need to go find out what's going on in there," he said, sliding off the stool and heading for the living room.

Nash watched him walk away. There had been tension brewing between Ennis and Austin for the past few days. Nash had avoided most of the conversations about staying or going, or how to prepare for winter. He'd been keeping his head down, focusing on the USB and trying to figure out what it all meant. He'd never been one to play into drama. In school, he'd always been younger than everyone else because of his smarts and skipping grades, making him the odd man out. Because of that experience, he'd gained an uncanny knack for blending in and staying out of the line of fire when things got ugly—and they always did.

15

Austin examined his daughter, who stared back at him defiantly from her seat on the couch. Ennis was on the opposite end, with Wendell making a move to sit on the other couch. They were acting as if he'd intruded on a private conversation.

"What's up?" Ennis asked easily.

"I thought you guys were listening to the sermon?" he asked, staring at his brother and then Savannah.

Savannah rolled her eyes. "It's boring. Malachi is a much better speaker than Drew."

Austin was about sick of hearing about Malachi. His little girl was infatuated with the kid. He'd been working hard to keep them apart, but he could only do so much.

"You need to go upstairs and take your shower before everyone else gets back inside," he ordered his daughter.

She made a face of disgust. "Dad, I know when to shower. Will you stop treating me like I'm a little kid?"

"I'm not treating you like a little kid. I'm telling you to shower now. There's a system in place for a reason, so everyone can shower at least once a week. It's your day, and I know you like to shower at night. That means now. If you're not out there listening to the sermon, then you can get upstairs and shower."

"We were talking about some of the traps I'm going to show her how to set," Ennis said.

"What traps?" Austin asked, his eyes on his brother now.

"For deer and rabbit, and whatever else might be out there," Savannah replied.

"I'm going to help," Wendell chimed in.

Austin shot him a look, wondering why the guy was even involved in this conversation at all. The idea of Wendell hanging out with his daughter did not sit well with him, for traps or any other reason. Wendell was a creep as far as he was concerned.

"Don't you think that's a job best left to one of the men?" Austin asked.

"Dad!" Savannah protested.

Ennis shook his head. "Savannah pointed out the fact that if this new world we're living in persists, she's going to need the skills to survive on her own, and maybe even one day keep her own family alive."

Austin felt as if he'd been slapped. "Her family? What are you talking about? She's fourteen!" he said, his voice rising.

"I'm saying that she needs to learn these skills," Ennis argued as Savannah let out an exaggerated grown. "It will only help her and us. What if one of us is sick or injured and we have to rely on her to take care of us while we heal? I'm going to be with her. I'm not going to let anything happen to her," Ennis promised, his voice going gentler.

"I can teach her later, when it's more appropriate," Austin replied after a moment. He could see in his brother's face that he was overreacting, but this was his daughter. His little girl. She didn't need to be out setting traps and worrying over their survival. That was his job.

"Dad, is there ever a more appropriate time than right now? I want to learn. I don't want to sit around here like a pet," she complained.

Austin closed his eyes, searching for patience. He was used to dealing with her typical teenage attitude, but he wasn't in the mood for it right now. He also didn't appreciate his brother taking her side. He felt like the odd man out here, when it was about *his* daughter.

"Savannah, please, just go take a shower," he said, hoping she'd realize he was at his wit's end and just needed a break from the bickering.

She grumbled, making a big show about getting up and walking out of the living room. He watched her disappear up the stairs before he turned to look at his brother again.

"Why are you glaring at me?" Ennis asked.

"Where were the two of you all day?" he asked.

"Fishing, Austin," he replied nonchalantly. "We were fishing. Nothing dangerous about it."

"Alone?" he shot back.

Ennis shook his head. "Yes, alone. I had my gun. It wasn't like I dragged her into the city. We went to the same place we've been going. You need to take a step back. She's not a two-year-old."

Austin leaned in, wishing they were alone for this and didn't have Wendell watching them like they were a television program. Still, he couldn't let Ennis's remark slide. "Don't tell me how to raise my kid."

Ennis shrugged. "Someone should."

Austin felt rage boiling to the surface. "Ennis, when you're a parent to a teenage girl, you can give me parenting advice."

"I think he's only trying to help," Wendell chimed in.

Austin shot him a look that warned him to shut his mouth before he did it for him.

"I wasn't trying to parent her," Ennis told him, getting to his feet. "She asked to go fishing. You never had a problem with me teaching her how to shoot before. What's the problem now?"

"The problem is, we're not living in a world where you can

call nine-one-one if something goes wrong. You can't traipse around the forest with her," he said.

Ennis shook his head at him, as if he was the one being sane here. "You're being ridiculous. You think you're the big boss around here. Need I remind you that this is my house? My beds? My food," he said, stepping closer to Austin.

"I don't see you stepping up and taking the leadership role," Austin snapped.

"Not every leader has to rule with an iron fist," Ennis argued.

"I'm not ruling anything. I'm trying to help people live through this. We need some direction," Austin told him, not for the first time.

Ennis shrugged. "Whatever you say, Austin. We're not all your kids. You can't boss us around."

Austin took a deep breath and was just getting ready to rip into his little brother when Amanda stepped in, apparently having heard the last of the argument. "Austin, let's go for a walk. I need to check on the horses."

Austin glared at Ennis and Wendell before stomping out of the living room, not bothering to say another word. He walked outside ahead of her, taking in big gulps of the humid night air. Somewhere in the back of his mind, as he breathed in and told himself to calm down, he realized there was a thunderstorm brewing. He could feel it in the air, and immediately started to think about what needed to be done to prepare for an early summer storm. This, at least, he could do.

"Hey," Amanda said, coming up to stand beside him.

"What?"

"Don't bite my head off. Come on, we need to walk," she said, heading away from the house.

After a moment, he followed her, suddenly recognizing that she'd stopped an argument from getting out of hand, and then he'd bitten her head off in return. "I'm sorry. I shouldn't snap at you. That guy, though, he's on my last nerve," he muttered.

"Your brother?"

"Yes."

"Why? I came in at the end. What were you two arguing about?" she asked.

He felt a little ridiculous admitting to the reason, but couldn't lie to her about it. "Savannah."

"What about her?"

He shrugged. "I feel like she's dumped me and chosen Ennis to be her new dad."

Amanda chuckled, knocking her elbow against his. "I don't think it works like that."

"You know what I mean. I've been so busy with planning the missions into town and taking care of the defenses and that stupid USB drive, I hadn't even noticed the two of them have been spending the last week together. He took her fishing today! I used to always ask her to go fishing and she never wanted to. Now, he's going to show her how to set traps and take her hunting," he complained.

"That's a good thing, though, isn't it?" Amanda asked.

"Yes, but why can't I be the one to show her that stuff?"

"I'm sure you can. Maybe you need to set aside some time with her," Amanda suggested.

Easier said than done, Austin thought to himself. Could he do that? Yeah, absolutely… if he could bring himself to take a step back from worrying about the house and their safety, which was something else entirely.

They made their way to where the horses' makeshift shelter was underway. It was nothing more than a tarp stretched between two trees, which they were in the process of covering over with branches in order to muffle the sound of rain on plastic and also camouflage the shelter a bit, but Amanda had grand plans to make something much bigger and sturdier. Now, Amanda reached out, stroking Raven's nose.

"I don't think she wants to spend time with me. She's always mad at me," Austin confessed, feeling hurt by the realization.

"She's a teenage girl who's been through hell and is trying to figure out life, just like the rest of us. Unlike the rest of us, she doesn't have maturity and wisdom on her side. I think she's also a little upset about the Malachi situation."

"What? What Malachi situation? What did he do?" Austin asked, ready to rip the kid limb from limb.

Amanda smiled, her face illuminated by the muted moonlight filtering through the trees.

"He hasn't done anything but ignore her. You yourself said she had a crush on him. Malachi is pushing her away, and she's hurt by it," Amanda explained.

Austin wrinkled his nose. That was new information. "Good."

Amanda swatted his arm. "No, not good. She's got a bit of a broken heart."

"So, she's hanging out with Ennis?" he asked incredulously.

"Austin, I'm going to say something, and I'm sure it's going to make you mad and you're going to want to deny it, but just think about it, okay?"

He shrugged. "What?"

"You're a good father. You have done a great job with Savannah. You've done everything you can to protect her and shield her from the harsh world. You've been on the road with her traveling, keeping her all to yourself, controlling her environment in order to keep her safe from everything and everybody in the world," Amanda said, her hand still on his upper arm.

"I wasn't trying to control her world," he defended himself.

She cocked her head to the side. "Are you sure about that?"

He inhaled a deep breath. "She'd just lost her mom. Things were bad. I wanted to get her away from it all."

"*And you did.* You did what you thought was best for her, and maybe it was. Scratch that," she corrected herself when she

160

saw he was about to argue, "I bet it was. Maybe she's the well-adjusted, happy girl she is today only because you did that for her. You gave her the safety and security she needed at a time when her life had been turned upside down, Austin. But that was then, and this is now. She's changed. She's grown up, and she's had some huge life experiences that have given her strength and courage," she went on.

Austin looked into Amanda's eyes. "What are you saying?"

"I'm saying, that little girl that you swooped in and wrapped up with love and protection has grown up some. She's growing into an independent woman. You have to take a step back, and help her grow and guide her when she needs it. You've raised a smart girl, so don't try and hold her back now," Amanda said.

Austin shook his head, wanting to reject the idea that his little girl was growing up. "She's only fourteen."

"She's fourteen, yeah, but she's seen more and lived through more than most adults," Amanda reminded him.

Austin groaned. "I hate that I'm losing my baby girl."

"You're not losing her, but you will if you don't let her stretch her wings. Be the one that supports her growth, okay? Just like Ennis is doing. Your relationship has to evolve. She's moving into a new stage in her life. You have to get on board or she's going to throw you from the moving train."

He nodded, letting Amanda's words sink in as he stroked Charlie's muzzle. "You're right. I'll try, but it's hard to see her changing right before my eyes."

Amanda giggled. "My dad used to say the same thing about me. When I went on my first date, he actually followed us. I spotted him at the movie theater. Let me tell you, I was so mad! I didn't talk to him for two full weeks—not until my mom sat us down and made us hash it out. He agreed to give me some room, and I agreed to check in with him."

Austin felt himself grinning at the idea of following Savannah on a first date, and then checked himself when he saw Amanda glaring at him. "Thank you. I will talk to her. I just hope it isn't too late," he muttered.

16

Zander rolled to the side of the bed he'd been laid up in for too long. Merryman was going to pay for what he'd done. He'd not only cost Zander several good soldiers, but had nearly killed him in the bargain. The shot to his arm had barely missed his brachial artery—he'd bled like a stuck pig and had nearly died from the injury. It was only his anger and need for revenge that had kept him going, and still recovery had been too slow for his liking.

Merryman was going to know what it was like to lose everything. Zander's mission had been deemed a failure by his bosses and that was unacceptable. The powers that be were not happy with him, and he needed to fix that. He couldn't stand to be a failure. He had devoted too much time and energy to making this transition a success.

There was a quiet knock on the door, distracting him from the pain shooting down his arm.

"Come in!" he barked.

"Sir, I've got that list of names you wanted," one of his captains said, stepping forward and into the office space he had claimed as his own living quarters.

"Did you secure the horses we'll need?" Zander asked, skipping any niceties.

Captain Davis nodded. "I have five right now. How many guys do you want on the hunting team?" he asked. "This is a list of the best options—those who will obey orders and not hesitate," he said, handing over a piece of paper.

Zander took the list of names handpicked by the captain and glanced over it. "I want at least six. Five men and myself. We have to find these people."

"I'll get on it. Do you know who you want?"

Zander didn't recognize the names on the list, though that was no real surprise. They had been recruiting soldiers for the past two months. It was easy to get people to sign up to be a part of the new controlling force when you took everything away from them. They'd secured quite a few former American military personnel, as well, and were actively hunting for more. The ones who were already trained for war were the most valuable, especially now.

"I don't know these men. I'm trusting you to select the right team." He looked up at his captain and passed the list back to him. "I need at least one person familiar with tracking. I have a feeling these guys are smart enough to try and cover their tracks," Zander hissed.

"I'll do that, sir. How long of a journey should I prepare them for?" Captain Davis asked.

Zander shrugged his good shoulder. "As long as it takes. They've got our weapons and they still have that stupid USB. We have to get it back. You know the leaders will kill all of us if we fail to find and destroy that drive."

Captain Davis looked like he might leave, but then hesitated, and instead asked, "How will they access the information on it?"

Zander glared at him until the man nearly cowered, and did take a step back. He didn't need his men questioning him about the mission. That wasn't their place—particularly when they obviously weren't thinking. "They don't have to access it. All they have to do is get it into the hands of the wrong people. You can't think we're the only ones who were prepared to function after an EMP. If that information is leaked, our entire mission fails. We'll have done all of this for nothing. We'll be sought out and get a needle in our arms for our role in taking down the country. I'm not interested in dying, are you?" Zander seethed.

"No, sir. I'm sorry I questioned your mission. When should I tell them we'll be leaving?"

"Two days. In the meantime, I want scouts out asking questions. I want to know if Merryman and his crew were dumb enough to stay in my city. If they are here, I want them brought to me—all of them," he ordered.

David nodded, already backing away. "Dead or alive?"

"Dead, except Merryman. I want him alive. I want to be the one who kills him."

"Yes, sir. I'll report in later."

"Good. Send in the nurse on your way out," he added.

"Yes, sir," Captain Davis replied as he quickly exited the room.

17

Austin swatted away an annoying mosquito buzzing near his ear as he tried to sleep for at least an hour. The trunk of the tree he was leaned up against was digging into his back, and the hard ground he sat on was extremely uncomfortable. After a couple of weeks of having a couch or even a carpeted floor to sleep on, he'd forgotten how miserable it could be to sleep outside with nothing but the ground to lay on.

He, Amanda, Malachi, and Nash had left that evening, hiking through the forest and hunkering down at the edge of town. Now, he guessed it was well past midnight. They wanted to get a look in town, take the temperature of the situation, and maybe scout out more locations to scavenge. This initial trip was all about getting the lay of the land and determining just how dangerous it was.

"Are you asleep?" Amanda whispered.

He guffawed. "No. These dang mosquitoes are relentless."

"We should have brought bug spray," she replied.

"We'll know better for next time."

"Maybe we should just go now," Malachi mumbled from a few feet away.

Austin stared into the darkness. He had no idea what time it was for sure.

"We probably have an hour or so of walking into town," Nash reasoned. "I think we can move now and keep a close watch on activity. If it's too busy, we'll find somewhere to wait it out until the early morning hours when everyone will hopefully be asleep. None of us are sleeping now, after all."

Austin looked to Amanda for her opinion. In the muted light of the stars, he caught the outline of her head moving up and down. "Sounds good to me," she confirmed. "I don't think any of us are going to get any sleep, no matter what we planned."

With their new plan decided, the foursome headed down the hillside. The smell of fire filled the night air as they hit the paved road leading into the outskirts of the city. It looked and sounded completely deserted. They stuck to the shadows cast by the small buildings lined up along the road.

"What do you think is burning?" Malachi asked after they'd been walking a bit.

Nash scoffed. "It's hard to say. It could be soldiers burning people out or survivors trying to cook food or boil water. It's best to stay away from the fires."

"We'll go north, up towards the tower," Austin said quietly.

"Is that a good idea?" Amanda asked.

"I'm not saying we go directly to the tower, but there's a good four miles between where we are and the headquarters. It's the financial district. You're the one who said we could scavenge the businesses—"

"Get down!" Nash shouted when a flaming ball came flying through the air directly at them.

Austin and the rest dropped to the pavement and rolled in opposite directions. Austin rolled to a stop in the ditch and peered above the road line. The flaming ball smacked into the road a few feet from where they'd been walking. It was followed by another flame in the sky and a group of men coming behind it, carrying a variety of pitchforks, shovels, and what looked like hammers. A couple of men in the group were carrying torches to highlight their progress.

"Come out now! This is our block!" one of the men shouted.

There really was nowhere to run or hide without making targets of themselves, and so Austin got to his feet, his hands raised, his rifle still slung over one shoulder.

"We don't want any trouble. We're just passing through," he said as the men got closer.

Amanda and Malachi stood up from where they'd been hunkering down on the other side of the road.

"Where's the other one?" the man snapped.

Nash rose from the shadows and stood with his hands up, as well. Austin looked from side to side then, and realized the guns they were each carrying didn't make them look remotely peaceful. Malachi had the Glock in a holster at his side while he, Amanda, and Nash had each opted to carry both a rifle and a back-up handgun. They looked outfitted for war.

"Passing through, huh? You look like you're out for trouble," the man in front of the group said, stepping forward until he was within ten feet of them.

Austin studied the middle-aged man, who had a scraggly, unkempt dark beard shadowing his face. His hair was shoulder-length, and looked dirty and greasy. His clothes matched the facial hair. He had the look of a man who was weary, with nothing to lose.

"We're travelers, trying to get through, nothing more," Austin said quietly, trying to keep his words even and calm.

The man studied him for another few seconds before looking to Amanda, then Malachi. His upper lip curled in disgust.

"You're traveling with them, huh?" he snapped. "All of you mixed together. What a disgrace."

Austin looked at Amanda, then Malachi, wondering what it was the man was referring to. Then it dawned on him. Their skin color. He looked back at the white faces filled with hatred in front of him, and had a flashback to the literature he'd read on the USB.

"We'll be on our way," Austin said, hoping the fear he felt wasn't showing.

"Not with them, you won't," one of the men in the crowd growled.

Austin stepped sideways, putting himself between the men and Amanda. "Look, I understand you have your beliefs, but we have our own. They're as American as you and I. They're not a threat," Austin warned, noticing that not one of these men looked to be armed with guns, giving them the advantage. They'd thrown some flaming balls, and he saw more rubber in a bag, ready to set aflame, but even those wouldn't do the damage of a bullet. These men were carrying what weapons they had, but they wouldn't stand up to ARs.

He cast a glance at Nash and made a point of looking at the barrel of the rifle sticking up high above his head. Nash nodded in understanding. The pitchforks and shovels and torches were no match for their guns.

"We don't want their kind around here," the man in front continued. "This is our block and we keep it the way we want it," he added, his bluster deflating somewhat. He must have realized he was seriously outgunned.

Austin shrugged, meeting his eyes again. "We're not asking to move in. We're passing through."

"You think the others are going to welcome you with open arms?" he snapped.

Austin shook his head, sensing that the conversation had moved more toward conversation than confrontation—and being glad for it. He didn't want to shoot anyone who was just trying to survive, no matter how skewed their world view might be. "We're not asking anyone to welcome us."

The man looked Austin up and down, and then his eyes lingered on the rifle hung over his shoulder. And Austin saw the very moment when the man recognized the black strap with gold thread.

"You're one of them!"

Austin shook his head again, trying to keep his voice even. "No, we're not. We relieved some of them of their guns after they attacked us."

The leader stared, unsure, and then another man came up to whisper in his ear. Whatever the exchange was, it worked in their favor. He turned to look at his small gang before facing Austin again. "We'll let you pass. I don't know what you think you're going to find in the city, but it's ugly. You'll be killed."

"Ugly, how?" Nash asked.

The man shifted, scowling. "Ugly, as in there's no food and there's a riot unfolding about half a mile from here. Some of those soldiers tried to take over a building that's already been claimed by some preachers. The preachers and their people been real nice, trying to help the survivors by offering food and blankets. A couple of them are doctors and were helping all of us. The soldiers caught wind of what was happening and went in there, guns blazing, throwing grenades and trying to kill as many as they could. A bunch of the other groups living around here fought back. They'll all be killed, which is why we're staying over here."

"Why are you out here, on the road?" Amanda asked.

The man looked at her and sneered before turning to look at Austin. "We're out here protecting our block."

Austin was growing tired of the man's open hostility towards Malachi and Amanda—many of the men in his group were glaring at them and whispering to each other at their expense, and doing nothing to hide it. Clearly enough, these men weren't worth their time. "We'll be going," he said.

"Then you'll be going down that road. You're not coming through here with them," the man snarled. "They want to turn back, you and the young guy are welcome to pass through, but that's it. Otherwise, you want to travel with them, you go around our blocks."

Austin looked down the dark road behind the group, which led into what looked to be older apartments. This side of town had been the poorer one, with low-income apartments and convenience stores on every corner.

They could have it.

"We'll go left," Nash said.

There was some laughter from the men. "They'll be killed before they make it to the next block," one of them joked.

Austin took a few steps back, signaling the end of the exchange, and Nash led them down a road to the left as Austin kept his own focus half-tuned to the men behind them. Before they'd gone thirty feet, the men had melted back into the darkness of their claimed space. Austin turned back around, satisfied that that particular danger had been navigated and content to let Nash lead them. He knew the city, which was why he had come along in the first place. Amanda still walked backwards, keeping an eye on the road leading to the group that had confronted them.

"What was that about?" Malachi asked.

"From the way they talked and the looks on their faces? I'm guessing your and Amanda's dark skin wasn't their cup of tea," Austin muttered.

"It's exactly what the NWO wants to happen. It's what they've been encouraging. They want to divide the survivors, make them turn on each other. They've created gangs," Nash explained. "Anything to separate people and pit them against each other—religion, blame for the EMP, skin color, whatever. They want us fighting each other instead of them."

"You mean they're actively inciting racism?" Amanda asked.

"Yes. Absolutely. But like I said, I'm sure it isn't just different races that are turning on each other. It's going to be a class war along with that underlying religious war we've all seen already," Nash pointed out.

Reading about the hatred had been one thing, but seeing it in person was entirely different. The moon provided little light, but as they went further, Austin could see graffiti sprayed on the streets, sidewalks, and the buildings they passed. The messages were hateful and racist, and clearly territorial, as if every citizen who remained in the city had claimed territory and joined a gang of like-minded, hateful fellows. Moving down the street, he read words he hadn't heard used in a long time, and words that he imagined Malachi wouldn't even know the meaning of. He had no desire to enlighten him, either. The decades of progress in striking down racism seemed to have been lost along with the electricity.

"Over there." Malachi pointed around the corner.

Austin jogged the distance to catch up with him and Nash, and see what had caught his eye. It was a huge bonfire burning in the middle of a four-lane street through the heart of the city. They had made it to the commercial part of the city, which was lined with three- and four-story buildings lining the road —realtor offices, insurance companies, nondescript businesses, and a handful of medical buildings. Shouts and screams echoed down the otherwise quiet streets, and along with the fire burning in the distance, Austin felt the scene wouldn't have been out of place in a high-budget horror movie.

"Are they fighting?" Amanda gasped.

Austin watched shadowy figures outlined by the glowing fire strike out to a nearby building, gunshot suddenly echoing. It looked to be at least ten people, maybe more, fighting right in the street. This was the riot they had been told about. Or at least a part of it.

"Get off the street," Austin ordered as one group struck out toward a building in their direction, not wanting their presence to be seen.

"Oh my god! He's gonna—" Amanda was cut off with the

reverberating sound of a gunshot coming from a nearby building.

One of the shadows that had been fighting dropped to the ground. Another shot rang out and another shadow dropped to the street, and suddenly a new crowd of people was flooding from between two nearby buildings that were no more than forty feet from where their small group had been hiding. They were preoccupied with the fight heading towards them, but Austin didn't want to trust that that would last. Pointing in the direction they'd come from, Austin gestured with a sweeping hand, and they began to run. Amanda covered her mouth with her hand as they fled, and when they fell to the ground behind a building, Malachi began whispering a prayer.

Austin shook his head. There was no amount of prayer that would help those people. The crowd had erupted into violence as some people fled and others had stayed to fight, only to be shot or beaten with what Austin guessed were shovels and pipes, judging by their shapes.

"Let's go," he whispered.

"Are we going to check any of the buildings?" Nash asked.

"No, it's too dangerous. This place is going to self-implode, and I don't want to be anywhere nearby when it does. The NWO has succeeded. They've created total chaos—at least they have in Denver. We're witnessing what amounts to the fall of civilization, and it isn't pretty," Austin said, sliding along the wall and heading back the way they'd come. They walked in silence along the sides of streets until they could no longer hear any sounds of the fight, and Austin was sure he heard the others breathe a sigh of relief that echoed his as they created more distance between themselves and the city behind them.

"What will you tell your people?" Nash asked, without specifying who he was talking to. Austin knew well enough, though, and was sure Malachi did, as well.

"My people?" Malachi asked, his voice gruff.

"You know what he means," Austin interjected, heading off any chance of discord. "He didn't mean offense, Malachi. There's no denying we're in two groups, living together."

"They wanted you to come out here and see what it was like," Nash said. "If they could help. Now that you've seen it with your own eyes, what do you think?"

Malachi took a deep breath. "I think it is much worse than they can imagine. I think it is too dangerous to come back here. I also think it would be pointless to try."

Amanda sighed, and Austin saw her put a hand out to grip Malachi's shoulder in quick support. "I agree. I know we all have that instinct to help others, especially those who are suffering, but this is out of our control. We can't save them all. I fear it would be a suicide mission for you or anyone else who tried."

"Guys, I think we need to pick up the pace and get back to the forest before the sun comes up," Nash said when a sudden explosion of gunfire echoed up over the road.

"I agree. Now we know. I don't even think it's safe to attempt more scavenging missions," Austin confessed, hating to admit that their one way of bolstering their own supplies was cut off. But, tellingly, nobody disagreed with him.

From there on, the group traveled home in silence. The realization that civilization was truly crumbling, leaving nothing but rioting and death in its wake, was devastating. Austin had assumed it could never get so bad. He'd assumed people would see through the tactics being shoved down their throats. He'd been wrong.

18

Malachi had crashed on the floor when they'd made it back early in the morning. Nash had taken the bed in the room only at Malachi's prompting.

By the time they'd made it back to the house, everyone else had been up for the day. Malachi had simply promised his mother he'd fill her in on the details once he slept for a couple of hours. In truth, he needed some time to process everything and didn't expect to sleep at all. His heart hurt at the thought of the death and destruction they'd witnessed, along with the pain and suffering of the survivors.

When he woke up, he noticed the bed where Nash had crashed was empty. He rubbed his eyes, staring up at the ceiling and wondering how to tell his mother and the rest of the revivalists about what he had seen.

He got up and, with a heavy heart, headed downstairs to find his mother first. She would know how to tell the others. He found her in the kitchen with Gretchen, making what looked to be flatbread. Her hair was pulled back in a ponytail, flour dotting her shirt and pants. It was something they had been eating often. The flatbread they made was filling, and helped stretch the various stews and casseroles they'd been making.

"Hey, Mom," he said, watching her work.

"Hi there. Did you get enough sleep?" she asked.

"Where is everyone else?" he asked by way of answer.

She shrugged. "The usual. Splitting wood, building that shelter for the horses, and laundry, never-ending laundry," she said with a quick smile.

He nodded absently.

"What's on your mind? You said you wanted to talk after you slept," she said.

He looked at Gretchen, elbow-deep in flour, and quickly decided he could talk to his mom in front of her. She was going to find out anyway. They all were.

He took a deep breath and met her eyes. "We can't help them," he said simply.

Gretchen and his mother both froze. "What do you mean, son?" his mother asked.

He swallowed the lump in his throat and looked into her eyes, willing her to believe him. "We can't help the survivors in the city. It isn't safe. They were rioting and shooting people in the street. We ran into a small group of men who looked at me as if I were garbage, Mother. Austin said they were racist, and though I didn't realize it at first, I believe he was right. It's just not safe. If we try to go into the city and help people, we'll regret it. The way those men looked at me, and Amanda… there's no chance they would accept help from us. And that's not to mention the violence we witnessed from others."

His mother's eyes had widened, but when he spoke, Malachi realized she'd gotten stuck on his first point. "Racist against what? Why?" she demanded.

"Does it matter? I guess because I have darker skin than some, maybe. I don't know. That's not really the point."

She rolled her eyes, still stuck on his previous comment. "That is the dumbest thing I've ever heard. You're as white as they come."

"Mom, you're missing the point. It would be dangerous for us to attempt to go into town and help survivors—me, you, Gretchen or Audrey or anyone."

"We can't withhold help because people have small minds," his mother answered quietly.

He shook his head. "No. This is different. Austin said the stuff him and Nash have been reading has been encouraging hate and racism. Encouraging division in general. We've seen how bad that is first-hand. There's no help to give. We couldn't get to those who'd accept help if we wanted to."

"What about the plans to scavenge goods and supplies?" Gretchen pressed.

"We can't go back." He knew it wasn't what they wanted to hear. None of them did. They wanted to do what they had been put on the earth to do—to help others and share the word of God. How could they do that if they were isolated on the mountain?

"You mean, this is all we have to live on for the foreseeable future?" Gretchen asked, her face paling.

He nodded, though his eyes were still on his mother, who looked shell-shocked. "Yes."

His mother looked at Gretchen and then met his eyes, and then she went back to focusing on the flatbread as she answered, "Well, it is what it is. We'll tell the others, and we'll find a way to get by. Honestly, I think most of them were hesitant to venture into the city anyway. Drew might not be pleased, but I agree that we can't risk our lives, not again," she said, surprising him with her acceptance.

He was about to ask her when she wanted to talk to the others when Austin came into the kitchen with Amanda behind him. They both looked rough around the edges, and judging by the bloodshot eyes and dark circles under their eyes, they had slept very little. Malachi exchanged nods of greeting with them, and then they all watched his mother and Gretchen work for a moment before Austin spoke.

"I trust Malachi has filled you in on what we encountered?" Austin asked, his voice grim.

"Yes, he did. Thank you for keeping him safe," Tonya said pointedly, smiling sadly as she met Austin's eyes. "I'm sorry to hear such devastating news. I'll be talking with the others today and letting them know the city is unsafe."

Austin nodded. Malachi could see the strain on his face, though; the little wrinkles at the corners of his eyes looked more pronounced than he'd seen in the past week. He looked rather relieved now that there seemed to be no argument from Tonya about staying away from the city, but Malachi knew that this new information would also mean he'd be more worried than ever about supplies.

"Can you talk with the others and let them know I'd like to have a meeting, the entire household, tonight?" Austin asked, his voice weary.

Malachi nodded. "I will. Before or after dinner?"

Austin turned to Amanda, as he tended to do. She shrugged. "I think after dinner would be better—people will be in a better mood to listen."

"After dinner it is. We'll need to eat in here. It looks like it's going to rain," Austin commented as they left the kitchen.

"Oh! I'll get the buckets and pots ready!" his mother exclaimed, hurriedly brushing her hands of flour.

"I'll help you, Mom," Malachi said, already moving into action.

It was something they had talked about during the last rain-storm. They'd realized they'd missed an opportunity to catch water, extending their supply. Now, he opened the lower cupboard and pulled out two large stockpots while his mother went for the empty buckets in the pantry. Together, they walked outside towards the edge of the house.

"This should be good enough," his mom said, placing the buckets on the ground under the corner of the roof.

"Should I put these next to the buckets?" Malachi asked.

"No, let's put those at the back corner. We'll get more water from the roof at the inside corner of the roofline," she said, pointing to the area where the roof formed a small L shape.

He placed the pots on the ground. "This should work. Do you think we'll fill them?" he asked.

She shrugged. "Depending on how much rain we get. Your father and I, back when we were first starting out on the road, we used to do this when we were dry camping. Every time we thought it was going to rain, we put out every empty pot and bucket we could find!" she said, smiling at the memory

"Why not fill up at a park?"

"They would charge us! Plus, we liked the idea of being resourceful. I never realized those hard times would actually pay off. I learned a lot back then," she said fondly, patting him on the shoulder as they headed back toward the house's entrance.

"What do you think he would want us to do?" Malachi asked, unable to shake the feeling he was letting his father down.

She sighed and came to a stop beside him, looked up at the sky and then into his eyes. "I think your father would want us to be safe and survive. I don't know if this is our future, but it is what is best for all of us right now. I think we need to pray on it and let God guide us."

Malachi nodded, not feeling all that confident in this guidance system. It seemed to be quiet as of late. He felt stranded at sea, floating adrift with no real plan.

"How will we know?" he asked after another moment.

She smiled. "We won't know. We let our hearts lead us. Malachi, I want you to know that while I believe you are the true successor to your father's ministry, I am by no means putting the weight of the future on your shoulders. I do not expect you to make decisions for all of us. The others— Gretchen, Drew, Audrey, and the rest of them—they can make up their own minds. Some of them have relied on your father for a long time and are still looking for that guidance. You and I, we'll make decisions together, but you can in no way feel responsible for everyone. You remember that, alright?"

He let out a breath, and then leaned in to give her a tight hug. "Thank you. I want to do right by Dad. I want to make him proud."

"You do, and you will," she assured him, patting his back. "Put this in God's hands and let's worry about today and maybe tomorrow," she said as she pulled back from him, meeting his eyes so that he could see the familiar serenity he was used to observing in her slowly coming back.

He smiled at the sight of it, thrilled to finally feel sure that his mother was healing from her grief, to the extent that she could. He'd been worried she would give up altogether and leave him all alone in the world. She was coming back, though, and he sensed she was a little stronger than she'd been before. Together, the two of them could take over the ministry and hopefully continue to spread the Word, even if it was more dangerous than ever to do so.

19

The kitchen and dining area were packed, with some of the household even sitting on buckets of freeze-dried food. The news about what they had seen had spread, and everyone was waiting to hear a plan for what happened next. And Austin knew what he thought should happen, but he wasn't a one-man army. The decision had to be left to a democracy if they were going to avoid frustration all around.

Ennis was barely talking to him since their last confrontation, which had made things more than tense. He glanced to his right as everyone settled, catching eyes with Ennis as he stood next to him, making sure his place as the leader of the house was well-established. The two of them would be a united front in leadership, at least, though Austin felt sure everyone in the room could read the lasting tension between them. And it wasn't as if they agreed on what needed to happen next—they only agreed that it was the two of them who had to step up and force the group to plan for the future.

"I'm sure you've all heard what happened on our trip last night," Austin started, looking at the faces around the room.

"Right, but what does it mean for us?" Harlen asked.

"It means we need to do everything we can to hide up here," Ennis replied.

Austin looked at him. "That's one option."

Ennis raised his eyebrows. "Don't tell me you really think we can fight against the multitude of forces present in the city?"

Austin shrugged. "I don't know about all of them, but we do know there's one driving force behind what's happening there."

"I think hunkering down, keeping our heads low, and avoiding any trips to the city is the best option," Wendell said, having the nerve to actually stand up as if that would make his opinion more valuable.

Ennis nodded. "Exactly. We have what we need right here. We don't need to mess with the city."

"I don't want to go back to the city, but we don't have everything we need," Austin argued, looking around to meet everyone's eyes and make sure they were taking in the whole of the situation. "We need medicine. We'll need more clothing, supplies to build housing, a sustainable food source, and everything else required for day-to-day living."

"I thought you said we can't go back," Malachi said, confusion on his face.

Austin took a deep breath. "I don't think it's safe, but I've been thinking about it some more, and I think we could go back to the outer suburbs or head south to some of the smaller towns. That first trip we took, to the luxury suburbs, we didn't run into any issues."

"It would take a day or two to get to any of the towns south of here," Ennis replied.

"We have the horses," Amanda replied.

Ennis shook his head. "That's stupid and dangerous. You could lead people right back to the front door."

"You think we should hide up here and never leave?" Harlen asked, one bushy brow raised.

Ennis nodded, though his hesitation was clear. "I'm not saying never, but why leave? Why tempt fate?"

"I don't know if I can get on board with that. What if I decide to leave?" Harlen asked.

Austin looked at Ennis to see what his response would be. Ennis actually turned to Wendell, which infuriated Austin. He didn't see Wendell as a leader. He didn't even think the guy was a valuable member of the household—he certainly had yet to prove himself as such.

Ennis cleared his throat. "Obviously, you are free to leave at any time. My only request is you not tell anyone about this place. And if you think to come back, you'll need to be careful you aren't followed."

"How is that fair?" Ezra asked.

Austin traded looks with his brother but could see that he was just as confused as he was. "Fair?" he questioned.

"If he leaves, and we all stay and build the cabins and do what it takes to make this place better, why does he get to come back in after the hard work is done? I think there should be a vote about who gets let in after they've left," Ezra argued.

Austin took a moment before he nodded. "He makes a good point, assuming someone left for more than a day or two."

"Well, it isn't his house and he doesn't get to make the rules," Wendell snapped.

"And you do?" Amanda shot back.

"He's my guest," Ennis replied, shooting a glare at Amanda. "And... yeah, that makes sense. We can decide on some time frame. If someone disappears for whatever amount of time we decide on, then they're considered out. We'd all have to decide to let them back in."

Austin shook his head at the debate—they were assuming this place was safe. He raised his hand to stop the discussion and met his brother's eyes. "Back up for a second. What if we use the information we have on this group to shut them down?" Austin asked, looking at Nash as he finally brought up the idea that had been festering in the back of his mind.

"How could we use information?" Drew asked.

"There has to be some member or organization of our old government in place somewhere. We find them and give them the information about the tactics this NWO is using. There's more information to be deciphered in the files. The answer might be there," Austin reasoned.

The expressions on the faces of the people sitting around the room told him well enough that they didn't like the idea. He could admit it was an idea lacking any guarantees, but it had merit. He turned to look at Amanda, expecting her to have his back.

She only shrugged. "I think you have the right idea, but we'd have to find those people and then we'd have to hope they have the resources to fight back against this group. And we'd be putting ourselves in danger to do it."

Austin let out a sigh. "I just hate the idea that we sit back and do nothing. We know what they are planning to do. We've seen the death and destruction they're causing. Are you all really okay with letting it happen? Some of you were very adamant we go into town to help people. What if we could help the entire world by shutting this thing down?"

"I don't think we're a strong enough group to do anything to stop it," Tonya commented in a soft voice.

Gretchen looked at her and smiled, reaching out to put her hand on Tonya's. Then she faced Austin, and although she spoke gently, it was clear she spoke for most of the revivalists. "I agree. You all know how much we wanted to do something to help, but we have talked about this, and we believe there will be a time to help those who have survived… but that time isn't now. We cannot be of any help spreading the gospel if we are dead."

"I'm not talking about helping a few individuals or preaching to anyone," Austin told her flatly. "I'm saying we need to do something to stop this whole thing—to literally bring light back to the world."

Ennis made a choking sound. "Oh, you're going to save the world single-handedly? You always did think of yourself as a hero."

Austin made a move towards Ennis, but Amanda stopped him, reaching out and grabbing his arm.

"I don't think Austin wants to be a hero. We all want a chance to go back to a normal life, right?" Amanda asked.

"Yes, but how we can do that?" Tonya asked.

Austin shrugged, ignoring his brother for the moment. "I don't know, but I know sitting up here with our heads in the sand isn't the way to get that done. What about the future? Do we want to leave this mess for Malachi and Savannah to inherit? We're not going to live forever, and I for one do not want to leave my daughter in this world to try and survive with the way things are looking now. We're talking about the end of freedom. Our kids will be forced to be indentured to that group or killed. Do you want Malachi to be forced to be one of their soldiers? He would be commanded to kill or be killed."

"That seems a little dramatic," Wendell scoffed.

Austin turned to glare at him. "Really? And what about supplies? Let's talk about what you care about, huh? What do you think happens when we run out of booze, Wendell? Are you going to go into the city and find some or are you going to dry out?"

Ennis gave him a dirty look but didn't say anything. Wendell snapped his mouth closed, his lips forming a tight line. His dirty little secret wasn't really a secret at all. Everyone in the house knew he'd been hitting the bottle hard, whether Wendell realized everyone was aware of it or not.

Tonya held up her hand as if to stop the in-fighting, and met Austin's eyes. "Of course, I don't want to imagine a future that involves Malachi killing others, but we cannot be the only ones who've survived and are in hiding. Our military has to be around, somewhere."

Austin smirked. "Yes, I'm sure they are. I'm sure we met some of them, too; they were wearing a different uniform and pledging allegiance to a different leader."

"We can't change the world, Austin," Ennis snapped.

"Why can't we?" he shot back.

Wendell made another scoffing sound that nearly pushed the last button of Austin's already frayed nerves.

"I think it makes sense to wait it out," Harlen chimed in again.

"For how long?" Austin asked in all seriousness. If they were going to put a hold on acting, then he wanted a date—something to work towards.

"As long as it takes. We'll hunt, we'll fish, and we'll trap and build new shelters," Ennis said. "If the pioneers could do it, we can!"

There were a lot of nodding heads and smiles around the room. Austin took it all in with a pit opening up in his stomach. They had this romantic notion about the pioneer days. Like this was a new start instead of a dangerous ending. He felt like finding a history book and reminding them all about how hard it had been in those glorious pioneering days, and just how many people had died while trying to survive. And they'd been prepared.

"That is one way to look at it. I'm hopeful we can do it," Gretchen replied with a hopeful smile on her face.

Fine for her, but it was hope Austin didn't feel. He didn't want to spend the rest of his life in the house. He didn't want his daughter to have to spend the rest of her life looking over her shoulder, waiting to be kidnapped or killed by the soldiers. He didn't want her to worry about getting a cut that could become infected and kill her because she had no access to medicine.

"How long do you think it will be before they start searching the mountains?" Austin asked, looking at his brother.

"I don't know, but I guess we better figure out how to defend this place a little better."

"I agree," Harlen chimed in.

"Me, too," Drew added.

From there, it was a resounding yes to Ennis's plan to try and hide in the prepper house for as long as possible. Austin had to content himself with the fact that, at the very least, nobody was arguing that defense was unnecessary. But as the group broke into clusters of people talking hopefully about what could be done to safeguard their little piece of heaven, he couldn't even bring himself to participate. It felt, to him, like welcoming in danger.

"Alright then. I'm going to bed," Austin muttered, walking out of the kitchen.

He half-expected Amanda to follow. She didn't.

Alone, he headed upstairs, exhausted from the long journey and the lack of sleep the night before. He was ready to crawl into bed and sleep off the irritation at the situation. It felt wrong to him.

He couldn't remember whose turn it was to take the bed in the room, and opted for one of the beds on the floor. He was tired enough that it wouldn't bother him a bit to sleep on the hard floor. A soft knock on the door followed by the door opening grabbed his attention. He looked up and saw Nash coming in. He looked as tired as Austin was.

"I'm with you," Nash blurted out, stripping off his jeans and climbing into another one of the set-ups on the floor.

"Really? How so?" Austin asked.

"I think we have information that could shut this whole thing down. Do I think we'd be saving the world? No, but I do think we would stop these people from taking it over, and maybe give the good guys a chance to fight back," he said.

Austin felt relieved to know he had at least one person on his side. "So, what do we do? How do we get it into the hands of someone who could do something about it?" Austin asked.

"I don't know—yet. I'm going to keep digging into that information. There has to be something that will reveal their Achilles' heel. Once we find it, we exploit it."

"When Callum gave it to me, he told me to give it to someone in Washington. That's a long way away," he muttered.

"Yeah, but we aren't far from Cheyenne Mountain. Maybe we get there and see if it's been overrun. There's a chance our government and military are still operating, but that they've been pushed underground. The information might help them understand what they're up against," Nash explained. "Maybe your friend only told you to take it to Washington because that was the closest option where you could find major government he felt could be trusted. Or because he thought your contacts were there."

Austin thought about it. "You could be right, and I think that's a better idea than sitting around and waiting for the other shoe to drop. They have to realize we can't sit here and wait for something good to happen. This place isn't that secure, and doing nothing will result in nothing."

"We'll figure out a plan soon. For now, we keep this to ourselves and go on like nothing is different," Nash said, his voice revealing his exhaustion.

"I'm glad you're on my side, Nash. Get some sleep," Austin replied, leaning back and closing his eyes as Nash said goodnight. He tried to stop his mind from thinking about everything. They were both too tired to do more thinking or working now. Whatever came next would wait for the next day.

For now, he needed sleep in order to think clearly. He'd get one of the maps tomorrow and start plotting a route to the Cheyenne Mountain Complex. There was no way he could sit around and do nothing but hope for the best. Having the USB and the knowledge about the NWO's plans made it his responsibility to do something. He could never live with himself if he sat back and watched the world implode. He had to try, even if he failed.

20

When Austin awoke the next morning, he felt restless. He couldn't stay at the house. He needed to get out and do something. He didn't know what that was, but he wanted to be proactive. He'd go south, he decided. They knew what was to the east. The south was what they needed to explore if his and Nash's plan to reach the Cheyenne Mountain Complex was going to become a viable option.

He'd do a little scouting and clear his head. This in mind, he got up with more hope than he'd had the night before, noticing that Nash was still asleep, as were a couple of the other men who crashed in the room. There'd been a bit of a musical chairs situation when it came to the sleeping arrangements. It turned out that a couple of the men were serious snorers, which made it difficult for anyone in the room to get some sleep, leading to more frustration and tension. Harlen and Drew were the worst offenders, but it looked like everyone slept peacefully at the moment. A symptom of the night before's stress and exhaustion, maybe.

He quickly pulled on his jeans, glad he could sleep in his underwear now that they had closed doors to sleep behind. He walked out without turning the light on or making any real noise, doing his best to shut the door as silently as possible. It sounded like the whole household was still asleep.

After a quick glass of water, he headed outside, careful not to disturb Malachi where he lay passed out on one of the couches. Inhaling the fresh air after the rain yesterday, he started on his way to the horse shelter.

He heard her before he saw her. "Amanda?" he asked when he found her brushing Raven, with Charlie keeping a close watch nearby.

"Hey! What are you doing up so early?"

"I could ask you the same thing. What is that?" he asked, pointing to the brush in her hand.

She smiled. "It's a curry brush I picked up on our trip to the suburbs—I don't know if they used it for a big dog or what, but I couldn't resist grabbing it. So, what's up? What brought you out here?" she asked.

He'd been busted. He cleared his throat. "I was hoping to take a little ride," he confessed.

Her eyebrows raised and she stopped brushing the horse. "A ride? Where?"

"South," he said quietly.

She eyed him. "South. That's vague."

"I want to do some scouting. We haven't been in that direction yet. It's away from the city. I want to see if there's any rural homes we could scavenge. Maybe there are some farms or ranches we could do some trading with," he explained.

She was staring at him like she didn't believe him. Spending twenty-four hours a day with someone, seven days a week, had made her able to read him well. It made him a little uncomfortable about finessing the truth, too, and reminded him a lot of his wife.

"Austin, I thought we agreed to stay here, to stay close and avoid any chance run-ins with anyone," she said.

He shook his head. "I didn't agree to that. Everyone else did."

She nodded in understanding as she turned back to Raven. "I see."

He frowned at her tone, tamping down frustration. "I won't be gone long."

"I'm going with you," she said, putting the brush in a small plastic grocery bag and hanging it on a tree branch.

"You are?" he asked with surprise.

"Yes, I am. We'll need to get them saddled," she added.

"I need to grab another gun," he said. "I only picked up one for myself on my way out the door."

"You do that, and I'll take care of getting them ready. Maybe we'll find a nice green pasture for them to graze on," she said.

He grinned, suddenly glad she'd be going along for the ride. He felt isolated enough after last night's discussion. Traveling with Amanda again wouldn't be a bad thing. "I'll be back in a few," he promised, heading back down the small hill towards the house.

Malachi woke when he came through the door. Austin looked at him but didn't say a word. He headed for the kitchen instead, grabbing two of the empty water bottles they had saved and quickly filling them with water from the tap. He'd grabbed two for himself, but now that Amanda was going, he wanted to make sure he had enough for her. On top of the water, he also filled a couple of sandwich bags with trail mix from the large can in the pantry before heading towards one of the closets where they had guns stored, not wanting to keep the entire armory in one place.

He'd only taken the Glock with him when he left the house that morning and decided to keep it light on the guns. He grabbed the Beretta as a second weapon, along with two concealed carry holsters Ennis had stashed. His brother had been a huge proponent of concealed carry, but Austin couldn't imagine Ennis being the guy who saved the day in an active shooter situation.

With everything he needed for the quick trip, he walked into the kitchen to find Ennis standing there. Ennis simply looked down at the holsters and pack in his hand and raised an eyebrow. "Going somewhere?" he asked.

"Yes. That a problem?"

"Austin, where are you going? Didn't we decide it wasn't safe to leave the area?" Ennis growled.

Austin smirked. "You don't get to decide what I do and don't do."

Wendell walked into the kitchen with Savannah right behind him. Austin's plan to make an escape without having to talk to anyone was gone.

"What's going on?" Wendell asked, as if it were any of his business.

Austin walked to his daughter and gave her a brief hug, ignoring the man's question. "I'm going out of a bit, but I'll be back tonight," he told her.

She gave him a rather chilly return hug and stepped away. "Where are you going?"

"Out," he replied with a glance toward his brother. He'd be damned if he'd answer to his brother over every little move he made.

"You're being a fool," Ennis snapped.

"Because I don't want to sit around here and wait for someone to find us? Or because I don't want to be the guy who has the ability to stop what's happening, but does nothing because I'm too afraid?" Austin demanded. "Besides that, this isn't some half-cocked mission. I'm just going out to look around."

Ennis stepped towards him. "I'm not afraid of anything. I'm thinking about survival. You don't go out picking a fight you'll lose if you want to survive."

"Dad, please don't do anything that could get you hurt," Savannah said in a quiet voice.

"I'm not doing anything dangerous! Amanda and I are going for a ride, and that's it," he said, meeting her eyes. The last thing he wanted to do was worry Savannah.

"Of course, Amanda is going with you," Wendell snapped.

"Excuse me?" Amanda asked, walking into the kitchen behind Wendell.

Wendell spun around, clearly surprised to see her. Austin smiled. Wendell deserved every awkward moment he found himself in; the guy was constantly in Ennis's ear about Amanda and himself. He didn't like either of them, and didn't miss a chance to try and complain to Ennis about something they'd done, and Austin knew it. Seeing him caught in the act was the only good part about being held up this morning.

"I only meant, the two of you are always running off together," Wendell said, looking at Ennis.

"Running off?" Austin echoed.

"You aren't going to let this USB thing go, are you?" Ennis asked.

Austin shrugged. "Maybe not. That's my decision since it was entrusted to me."

"Not if it affects me!" Ennis growled as he stepped forward.

"Trust me, I don't want to do anything that might help you,"

Austin sneered, even as that voice in his head told him he was going too far again, all things considered.

Ennis shook his head. "You never do. It's all about you. You were always the popular one, the one Mom loved the most. You think any of that matters now? No! It doesn't! I'm the boss here! This is my house! You're not the one who calls the shots anymore!"

Austin clenched his teeth. Vaguely, he was aware of Savannah frowning and disappearing out of the room—he knew she hated to see them fight, and it only added to his frustration that they were upsetting her. When she was gone, he stepped into his brother's face. "You've never had the courage to make a single decision in your entire life. You need me or you'll sit up here and die."

"No, he won't. Ennis, you don't have to take this. This is your house," Wendell said, moving to stand beside Ennis.

Austin glared at him. "Shut up, you weasel."

"Don't talk to my friend like that!" Ennis near shouted, stepping closer to Austin.

The two brothers faced off, and Austin looked down at his little brother just like he had many times before when they'd been younger. Ennis had always been a hanger-on, and only stood up for himself and wanted his way when it made sense to him. Otherwise, he'd always relied on Austin, and it was getting old.

Austin pushed him backward. Not hard, but enough to send Ennis back several inches. Ennis glared at him. Austin stared back, daring him to say a word or to try and push back. Austin outweighed him, and they both knew it; he was physically stronger, and he'd outmaneuver him, too.

"Back off, Ennis," Austin hissed, even as he heard Amanda make a disgusted sound as she leaned up on the kitchen counter. Maybe they were acting like boys, but this had been a long time coming.

"Ennis, don't let him get away with disrespecting you. Everyone will laugh at you and take his side," Wendell whispered.

"That's enough, Wendell. This is between Austin and Ennis," Amanda scolded him loudly.

"Shut up!" Ennis and Wendell said in unison.

Austin watched the smile spread across Wendell's face as he turned to look at Ennis. The guy had a serious crush on his brother. It made him sick to think that Ennis was so easily manipulated. He was so desperate to be liked that he'd buddied up with a snake like Wendell.

"You need to get rid of this guy," Austin commented, eyeing the smaller man whose clothes smelled of alcohol.

"You need to get rid of that girl," Ennis snapped back.

"Fight back!" Wendell encouraged him.

Austin was about to tell the man to shut up when Ennis shoved him hard in the chest. Austin shoved back, sending his brother into the bar stools lined up under the center island. Ennis lost his balance, but quickly righted himself, glaring at his brother with such animosity that the room felt electric. Even Wendell finally backed off.

"Don't even try it," Austin warned.

Ennis swung out, clearly trying to hit him. Austin moved to the side, dodging the weak punch. Ennis, encouraged by Wendell, swung again, this time landing a rather soft punch against Austin's cheek.

Austin saw red. Weeks of anger and frustration erupted, and he swung his own fist, hitting his brother in the left eye. The feel of bone and flesh under his knuckles was exhilarating, and he reached back, ready to strike again when Amanda stepped in front of him, using her body to push him backwards.

"Dad! Stop!" Savannah screamed from behind him.

"Get out, already, you wanna put yourself in danger! Do what you want!" Ennis shouted. "I'm sick of this."

"Ennis, please," Amanda said in a gentle voice.

"I'm trying to do what's best for all of us, and you'd see that if you opened your eyes for two minutes!" Austin spat.

Amanda bodily pushed Austin several feet backward until he was at the door to the pantry. She held up one finger, looking him dead in the eyes. "Stop. It's over."

Austin nodded, finally, seeing the look on his daughter's face and realizing it had gone too far. She looked heartbroken, and now that the brothers had separated, tears erupted from her eyes and she fled the room. He'd screwed up.

Before he could figure out what to say to his brother, or even to Amanda, he watched Wendell push Ennis out of the kitchen, whispering in his ear the entire time. The sight made him gag. He pushed Amanda out of the way, ready to go after Wendell; things wouldn't have gotten nearly so violent if Wendell hadn't been there to egg his brother on. He was sick of the guy interfering, and wanted to show him just how angry he'd made him. Wendell had clearly encouraged the fight and wanted the brothers at each other's throats. Austin could see that even if Ennis was too blind to notice just how he was being manipulated.

"Austin, stop! Don't let him win. He's trying to provoke you," Amanda said, grabbing him by the arm and tugging him back.

"He needs to be taught a lesson about interfering!" Austin growled.

"Yes, but not now. Come on, let's go for that ride," Amanda said, gently pulling him out of the kitchen.

He took a few deep breaths, but then he nodded. He caught a glimpse of Wendell and Ennis heading into his brother's bedroom before the door was slammed shut. Malachi was standing off to the side of the living room with Savannah and Gretchen, who had her arm around his daughter's shoulders. He whispered a quick apology to her before he and Amanda left the house, but she barely nodded in return. He wouldn't linger, though. A couple of the other revivalists in the house had come downstairs and witnessed the aftermath of the war between the brothers, and they were all looking at him with a mixture of contempt and fear. He'd been made the outcast in a matter of minutes.

Following Amanda outside, he was a little embarrassed, ashamed that he'd lost his temper, but it was too late. The damage had been done.

21

Austin glanced over at Amanda sitting high on Raven's back as the two of them rode at a leisurely pace away from the house. They'd been riding for thirty minutes or so without saying a word. It was a warm day, but with the shade from the tall trees and the relaxed gait of the horses, the ride was very comfortable. He could hear birds singing and the occasional rustle of leaves as the birds flitted around between branches. He knew Amanda was giving him time to cool off. Things had been tense. That fight had been brewing for some time. He was sure the rest of the house had been feeling the tension between the brothers for days. Wendell's manipulations had only made things worse.

"Maybe he'll leave," she blurted out.

"What?" Austin asked, turning to look at her.

"Wendell. Maybe we can get him to leave. I think things would be so much more relaxed if he was gone. I caught him talking to Harlen yesterday, trying to fill his ear with a bunch of nonsense about things you and Nash were saying. He's stirring the pot, Austin. He has a purpose, and I'm not sure what it is, but we'd be better off without him."

Austin rolled his eyes at the idea of what Wendell might have been doing to rile everyone up. Nothing would surprise him. "The guy's a weasel. That's the only word I can come up with. He's one of the main reasons I don't want to live at that house indefinitely. He has some weird obsession with my brother, I'll tell you that; guy's going to end up killing us all one of these days so he can have Ennis all to himself."

Amanda chuckled. "I agree."

"I shouldn't have hit him," Austin muttered.

Amanda nodded, catching his eye. "No, but I don't think it was all that bad. You two have been circling each other since we got here. I'm guessing this rivalry goes back a lot longer than a few weeks."

He scoffed. "He's always been jealous of me. I don't think Mom liked me better, but Ennis sure thought so. It's just Ennis that has always been a little different, more needy of her attention and affection, and that fed into it. We have a hard time when we're together for any length of time, but it's nothing new."

"I don't have brothers or sisters, but I don't think a little sibling rivalry is all that rare. I'm going to venture a guess and say having a house full of strangers and trying to survive the end of the world as we know it has created a fair bit more stress than anyone is accustomed to dealing with. We'll take some time today and maybe tonight, and the two of you can talk—alone. Without me or Wendell around. This is between you guys," she advised. "Us being there only made it worse, I think, but maybe this morning will have eased some of the tension when we get back. I don't know if you could see it, but he saw things had gone too far, too."

Austin swallowed. "I hope we can work things out. If he wants me gone, I can't really argue with him. It is his house. But I will do my best to soothe things over for now, for Savannah's sake."

"Did you see that?" Amanda asked, pointing up ahead.

Austin squinted, looking in the direction she'd pointed. They'd passed the area they were familiar with and were now heading into a combination of younger trees and more brush. They'd been following an old dirt road that looked like it had been used by ATVs more than actual vehicles.

"I don't see anything," he whispered, his guard already up.

"I swear…" She pointed up ahead again, off to the left of the road.

Austin nodded, seeing the movement and guiding the horse into the thicker treed area about twenty feet off the road.

"We'll leave them here and check it out on foot," he whispered.

She slid off Raven and wrapped the reins around a branch as he did the same with Charlie's. They crossed the road again, moving into the area where the trees were thinned out with trunks that weren't quite as big, offering less cover.

"Voices," Amanda mouthed to him.

He nodded in understanding, dropping low behind some brush and straining his ears. He detected at least two men, maybe three. They were doing their best to talk in hushed voices, as well, making his and Amanda's spying all the more difficult.

"We'll meet back here in an hour," one of the voices said.

"I'm sure I can get my guy to agree."

"If we see any more guns than you've got out now, any talks of working out a trade are off," the first man stated.

"One hour," the other man said in a gruff voice.

There was some snapping of branches and the sound of footsteps over crunching foliage. Austin ventured a look over the bush he was hiding behind and saw two men heading into the forested area just south of them. The sounds of a person walking in the opposite direction told him there had been at least three people involved in the exchange, though they'd only heard two voices clearly.

"What do you think that was about?" Amanda asked.

Austin shrugged. "I don't know for sure. It sounds like two surviving groups setting up some kind of trade deal, right?"

She looked back at him with a smile on her face. "That's a good sign."

"Possibly."

"Are we going to stay and watch?"

"I don't know if that's wise. If they catch us, they're going to want to know who we are and what we have."

She grimaced. "Good point. We better get through here before the meeting happens then."

They carefully walked back to the horses, choosing to walk them through the thicker trees to avoid the overgrown dirt road.

"Stop!" a voice called out.

Amanda and Austin froze in their tracks, turning to look into the trees that ascended up toward a rocky hill.

"We're passing through," Austin said, hoping to keep the peace.

"Are you one of them?" a bodyless voice called out from somewhere up high.

"One of who? We don't want any trouble. We're only passing through," he repeated.

"Why are you trying to hide?" the male voice shouted.

Amanda scoffed. "We're not the only ones hiding. You know why we're hiding as well as we do."

Austin scowled at her before turning to face the trees. "We're not part of any other group. It's just me and my wife. We were out hunting and now we're moving on," he lied.

Amanda looked at him, one eyebrow raised. He shrugged a shoulder in response.

A young man, probably no more than eighteen, crept out from behind a few trees with an old twenty-two rifle aimed at them.

"My dad doesn't want anyone out here," the kid said.

"We aren't trying to encroach on anyone's territory. We were hungry and we thought we'd come up here and do a little hunting," Austin told him, keeping his voice even.

The kid must have believed their story, as he lowered the weapon. "Where are you guys livin'?" he asked.

Amanda smiled her friendliest smile. "I don't think we're *living* anywhere. We've been kicked out of everywhere we've tried to set up home," she lied.

The boy nodded. "Us, too. We finally made camp. My dad and uncle are going to try and work out a deal with some of the folks that are living down the mountain a little way. He says they're good people, just like us, but trying to survive."

Amanda smiled. "I think there are a lot of people up here trying to do that. Were you in the city when things happened?"

The kid nodded. "Yep. I was at a baseball game and everything went dark. My family's house was burned down a few weeks ago."

Austin shook his head. "I'm sorry to hear that."

"Trace! Trace! What are you doing?" the man from earlier

shouted as he emerged from the trees, a newer Remington rifle in his hand.

"I'm just talking to these guys, Dad, no big deal."

The man eyed Austin and Amanda carefully. "What are you doing out here?" he demanded.

"We were hunting. We came through here last night and camped out, hoping to get some food," Austin said.

"You didn't have any luck?" he asked.

Austin shook his head. "Not even a squirrel."

The man nodded, sympathy on his face. "That seems to be the way of it."

"We're on our way. We don't want any trouble," Austin reiterated.

The man looked him up and down as Austin did his own study of the man, determining he must have been a white-collar worker, like one of those guys who drove a Mercedes and golfed on the weekend.

"We're about to go into a meeting with another group of survivors. They live closer to town and have access to a warehouse. We're going to work out some trade deals. You're welcome to join if you'd like," the man offered.

Amanda looked at him, her eyes wide as she nodded. "Yes! That would be great! Thank you! Are you sure the others won't mind?" she asked.

He shrugged. "They're a little shady, but I'm sure they'd be open to trade. Everyone's best interests and all that. You have horses, and I think that's more than a lot of people have."

"I'm not trading my horses," Amanda immediately replied.

The man smiled. "You trade what you can. I'm John, by the way, and you've met my son, Trace. We're not so good at this living off the grid and surviving thing. I know we're supposed to be a lot meaner, but I can't help but think there are people just like us around here. You seem like good people."

Austin smiled. "I'm Ted, and this is Janie," he lied easily, feeling it was important to try and hide their real names.

"Well, Ted and Janie, we should get down the hill. I don't want to be late to our first trade deal. I'm a lawyer by trade, specializing in negotiations and settlements. This feels good, normal," he said with a smile. "We aren't supposed to have guns more than one a'piece, so if you do, I'd suggest you keep them hidden.

Austin nodded, doing his best to appear friendly and nonthreatening. He was glad they'd worn the concealed carry holsters under their shirts; these men wouldn't know they were armed at all if he had it his way.

"Excuse me," a new man said, the smile of a snake oil salesman on his face as he came up the dirt road.

John immediately pulled up the rifle, aiming it at the man wearing khaki pants and a black t-shirt with a baseball cap on his head.

"What do you want?" Austin asked, his voice low as he

thought how crowded this little area of the forest was getting all of a sudden.

The man smiled bigger, and it sent a chill down Austin's spine. The guy was bad news, that much was obvious.

The guy winked. "I heard your voices and thought I'd come say hello. I'm here to make a very generous offer," he replied. "My name's Hank Finlay and I can see you are all sorely lacking in firepower. I think I can change that."

"We do fine," John replied.

Hank laughed. "Fine against what, a rabbit? You need something a little bigger and a lot more powerful if you want to survive."

"And you have that?" Austin snapped.

The man, still grinning, nodded. "I do. I'd like to make you a one-time offer you can't refuse."

"And what's that?" John asked, clearly not as leery as he should have been.

"Don't shoot the messenger, or should I say, my helpers," Hank replied, putting his fingers in his mouth and whistling.

From further down the road, a horse emerged from behind a rock outcropping, dragging a cart behind it. Austin watched in silence, a feeling of dread coming over him. Something was off. Hank was too clean, and too well-fed to be a typical survivor. On top of that, this was all far too casual. He had to be attached to those other men John had been talking to, or else he'd been watching them and waiting for an opportunity.

Either way, this wasn't good. The horse came closer before Hank called for it to stop. Two other men, who were wearing all black, stood alongside it, guarding whatever it was they had in the cart.

Hank gestured for Austin and the rest of them to walk over. They followed, observing every move as Hank pulled back a heavy green tarp to reveal a variety of guns, all nestled nicely in another tarp.

"What's all this?" Austin asked.

Hank smiled. "My boss and I, we want you all to survive. We know how important it is to arm the people who are trying to make it up here. Let's face it, good folks like you are a rarity. There are gangs and bandits running wild, killing the good ones. We want to help."

"Why?" Austin asked, glad to see that John and his son were also keeping a few feet back—suspicion finally getting to them also, it seemed.

Hank eyed him carefully. "You're a cautious one, but that's good. That'll keep you alive. Trust no one."

"So, why would I trust you?" Austin replied evenly, telling himself to keep calm. No matter how suspicious this guy was, they didn't want a gun battle. Not when it would put all of them and the horses in danger, and when they were clearly outgunned.

"Because I'm offering you help. We don't have to be friends and we don't have to have tea together," Hank joked.

Austin looked at the two men in all black; they might be making an effort to hide it, but from those outfits, he had no doubt they were part of the NWO.

"Your *helpers* look like the men in the city running everyone out," Austin pointed out.

Hank shrugged. "We are a part of the New World Order, if that's what you're asking. We had some bad eggs within the organization and things got a little out of hand. We want to make up for all that, though, and are offering weapons to those good citizens trying to survive as we work to make the city—no, the world—a better place."

"You're the ones in control?" Trace asked.

Hank nodded. "I am only a lowly agent, but my boss, he's a generous guy, and he feels awful for what happened. We never wanted anyone to get hurt. The gangs, well… they're being dealt with, but for now, it's probably best you all stay out of sight. These weapons can help."

Austin knew the man was lying but wasn't quite ready to show his hand. And he didn't understand the endgame here, either. He wanted to know why the NWO was suddenly trying to make nice and arming the citizens. They weren't handing out the automatics and bigger fire power the soldiers carried, but the assortment of shotguns, rifles, and even what looked to be a few ARs in the pile were definitely useful weapons—if they worked.

"We're not one to look a gift horse in the mouth," John replied. "How many can we have?"

"Take what you need. I've got a couple more stops to make, though, friend, so don't take them all," Hank said with a wink.

Austin didn't like the guy. He was dirty and up to something. John reached in and handled a few of the guns, handing one of the ARs to his son before picking up a Smith and Wesson forty-five and a twelve-gauge shotgun. Austin doubted the guy knew much about guns from the way he was handling them. Off to the side, Hank looked at Austin and then Amanda when they made no move to take a gun. Austin didn't want to look suspicious, though, and so he quickly reached for another nine-millimeter. Amanda did the same. He didn't want to be encumbered by one of the larger, longer guns if they had to make a run for it, which seemed to be a common thing whenever they encountered the NWO.

"Thank you," Amanda replied.

"Of course. We better get going. Good luck to you all," Hank called out as he made a wide turn with the horse and cart, and headed back the way they'd come.

"That was nice of him," Trace said.

Austin nodded. "It was."

Amanda gave him a look that said she was highly suspicious of the free guns, as well.

"Let's go meet our new trading partners," John said, clearly buoyed by the gift.

Austin and Amanda walked behind the father and son, leading the horses downhill. Trace talked about baseball and all the things he missed as they walked. Austin wanted to tell him to stop talking so they could listen, but didn't want to be rude. At least they wouldn't be accused of sneaking up on anyone.

"Stop!" a voice screeched.

They all froze.

"It's us!" John called out.

Three men emerged, pointing guns at them. "Why are you carrying more guns?" one of them demanded.

Austin fought the urge to roll his eyes. "You're carrying guns," he pointed out.

The man looked down at the rifle in his hand as if he'd forgotten it was there. "We said not to arm yourselves more than you already were. And now we've heard you're planning for a fight. Sure looks to be the case from where we stand."

"What?" John said, his voice full of confusion.

Austin was already moving away from the confrontation, realizing what had happened. These were the men who'd been on the other end of the trade, and John and Trace had forgotten what they'd told them about having no extra guns. Now, things were about to go bad, and they were in the middle of it. He stepped backward, aiming to look as nonthreatening as possible. Amanda followed his lead, casually moving the horses away from the direct line of fire.

"A concerned citizen gave us a couple weapons, told us we better arm ourselves. Said you were planning to take what we have," the other man said, his eyes darting around the area.

John shook his head. "No, no. That's not true. Must have been the same guy who gave us these guns, but that wasn't our reasoning. Hard to turn down guns, the way things are now," he pointed out, his voice starting to shake.

"Sure seems suspicious," the man said.

He was making Austin nervous, too, what with the way he was moving his eyes around, his hands shaking on the gun he held. It was clear the man had little familiarity with the weapon and was uncomfortable in general.

"Let's calm down," Austin said quietly. "We're only here to talk about some trades. No one wants to hurt anybody, right?" he asked, lowering the gun he had in his hand.

His hope for a peaceful solution vanished when someone fired a shot from the woods, and it was followed by another. Before Austin could tell the opposing groups that the shot had come from down the road, the guns were up and the novice gun handlers were pointing their guns at one another. Things were about to get ugly. He swirled to Amanda and shouted a word of warning even as she lunged off the road, the horses in tow. Austin jerked his head to the left, watching the action as he moved. They couldn't risk the horses getting injured, and needed to get as far from the impending gunfire as possible.

Another shot rang out, and in a flash, John pulled the trigger, missing his target but setting off a round of shooting.

"Now!" Austin shouted, skillfully mounting Charlie as they moved with speed he hadn't known he possessed as Amanda did the same. Together, they kicked the horses into fast trots and sped away from the scene, going as fast as they could while maneuvering around small trees and bushes to leave the gun battle behind.

They made a wide circle back to the dirt road and headed down, on the same page without speaking and not wanting to bring the fight to the prepper house. The echoes of gunshots accompanied the sound of the horses' hooves pounding against the solid ground as they broke into a canter on the now open roadway. And then, the shooting stopped. Austin slowed Charlie and looked over at Amanda. Her eyes were wild, and he could see her breathing just as hard as Raven.

"Where did those shots come from?" she gasped.

"I have a feeling our good friend Hank set that whole thing up," he growled, irritated that more innocent people had likely been killed at the hands of the NWO.

Amanda was shaking her head, though, pointing up ahead to where Hank had just emerged from the trees with his comrades, and was now staring them down, guns pointed directly their way.

Amanda groaned. "This never ends."

"Follow my lead," Austin said in a low voice.

"What?" she asked, but Austin was already moving forward.

"Hey, good job back there," Austin said, congratulating Hank.

"Good job?" Hank asked, seemingly surprised by the congratulations.

Austin nodded. "We were sent up here to go undercover. We've been rooting out survivors the past few weeks. We didn't know anyone else was on this operation."

Amanda gave him a look but quickly went along with the plan. "You're lucky we didn't shoot you. You're not in uniform."

Hank smiled. "I never wear the uniform when I'm working the crowd."

Austin felt sick to his stomach at knowing this guy had been playing people against each other for a while. It shouldn't have surprised him, but to see it in action was disgusting.

"Why the change in plan? We've been doing fairly well in this area," Austin said, feigning irritation at having his operation interrupted.

Hank shrugged. "Our wires may have gotten crossed. When's the last time you reported in?" he asked.

Austin looked at Amanda, pretending to think about it. "I don't know—more than two weeks, maybe going on three. We've been slowly making our rounds up the mountain, ferreting out surviving groups and continuing the mission," he said, looking down at the three men from his position on top of Charlie.

Hank studied him, then Amanda. "I'm surprised you've kept the horses this long. These vagrants have been stealing from us left and right."

"That's because you guys don't blend in," Amanda teased, her voice light.

"That's for sure," Hank replied with a chuckle.

"We could use more of the semi-automatic rifles and ammunition," Austin commented.

Hank looked between them, one eyebrow raised. "Why?"

"Because, we've already given away what we had, trading for food and whatnot. If we don't act like them, they won't trust us. All we've got left are the handguns. We need ammo," Amanda replied a little angrily.

Hank nodded. "I've emptied what I brought, but I can take you to the cache we have not far from here."

"Thanks. You can let HQ know we're making good progress up here. Most of the groups we've encountered have since moved on," Austin said, leaving the words open to interpretation. So far, they hadn't been asked about a commanding officer, but the only name they had was Zander's, and he was gone. Maybe it wouldn't be suspicious if they dropped the wrong name, but Austin didn't want to take the chance. Who knew if he'd been the one in charge of this area, and whatever ongoing operations like Hank's were ongoing?

Hank chuckled as he turned away, and it was such a sleazy sound that it made Austin's skin crawl; he felt like his face might crack from holding the false smile.

Still, they followed behind the three men walking alongside the cart, and Austin wondered how many guns had been handed out that day. How many more groups were at war with each other, and how long before those groups found Ennis's supposedly isolated home?

They'd gone less than a mile when Hank pointed to what looked like an abandoned out-building left over from the pioneer days. The thing was barely standing, its wood rotting and the door held on by old, rusty hinges.

"Here," Hank said, looking at Austin and Amanda expectantly.

Austin took the initiative and slid off of Charlie. Amanda followed suit. The idea that they were walking into a trap crossed his mind, but Hank seemed to have bought his story pretty easily. Maybe a little too easily.

"Good spot," Austin commented.

Hank gave him a look of contempt. "It's served me well. I suppose you have somewhere better?"

Austin shrugged. He didn't want to appear too soft. "Maybe."

Hank turned to one of the men. "Grab one of the boxes—that's all they need."

Amanda looked to Austin, her eyes revealing her unease. He smiled, trying to tell her to relax. They had to play it cool.

"We'll take whatever you can spare. We'll be checking in sometime next week per our orders," Austin said, hoping he sounded like one of them.

Hank nodded. "Things are heating up down there. They'll want to know about your progress."

"We'll have a full report," Amanda assured him.

"Clint, help me out with this!" the man in the rundown shack hollered angrily.

Austin didn't think much about what he was going to do next. He only reacted to the situation. They were standing in front of a building housing a cache of weapons and ammo that could give him and the prepper house dwellers a real advantage.

He reached for the Glock in his concealed holster. The movement was fast, but not fast enough. Hank dove behind the horse pulling the cart at the same time Austin fired. The bullet slammed into the rotted wood of the cart. Amanda pulled her gun, ready to shoot the men who were bound to come out of the out-building.

The first one, Clint, appeared in the doorway, confusion on his face. He wasn't confused for long. Amanda's excellent targeting dropped him where he stood. Austin dashed to his right, taking aim at Hank and firing again. Hank was proving to be a wily moving target and began rolling over the ground, just making it behind the building as Austin shot up the ground where he'd been a moment before.

The second man shot through the hole Austin's bullet had created in the wood shack, narrowly missing Amanda.

"Go!" Austin shouted at Amanda.

She dashed to Raven and jumped on, firing at the building at the same time in a move that would have made John Wayne proud.

"Gun!" she shouted a second before Austin caught a glimpse of the rifle pointing around the back of the building.

Hank had managed to get his hand on a weapon. Austin moved with speed he didn't know he had, once again mounting Charlie in a single fluid movement as Amanda laid down cover fire for him. They headed downhill into the trees as Hank unloaded a clip into the forest. Austin winced when he was slapped in the face with a low-hanging branch. Another branch scraped against his arm as they continued their breakneck speed through the heavy trees. The horses were proving to be incredibly agile as they raced away from the sound of the gunshots, or else they were just as frightened as their riders.

"Whoa," Amanda called out, slowing Raven as they broke through the trees into what was a park of some sort.

Austin pulled Charlie to a stop beside her, his heart pounding as he looked around the area, making sure no one was waiting to take them out.

"What in the world were you thinking?" Amanda scowled at him.

He shrugged. "I was thinking we could really use that stock-pile of weapons."

She rolled her eyes. "Next time, talk to me. We could have gone back for it!"

"Sorry. I saw an opportunity and I took it."

"That wasn't an opportunity. That was stupid!" She glowered at him, clicking her tongue and spurring Raven into a slow trot.

"We need to take a very long way back in case they try to follow us," Austin warned her.

She shot him a look. "You think?"

She was mad, and he didn't blame her. He'd nearly gotten them both killed, and now Hank knew they were there. He'd be looking for them.

Surviving two gun battles in the span of a couple hours was enough, though. He was ready to get back to the house and figure out what to do next, though he wasn't entirely sure he'd be welcomed back to the house.

He couldn't let his emotions rule him anymore, he realized. He needed to think, plan, and strategize if he wanted to keep them and his daughter safe and alive.

"I'm sorry," he muttered after they'd traveled in silence for nearly an hour. "I wasn't thinking, and it was stupid of me. It won't happen again."

Amanda looked back at him, and he saw some of the tension had left her face as she nodded back at him. "It's fine. I think we need to keep this to ourselves for now, though," she advised.

He nodded his agreement. "But the house isn't safe, Amanda; do you see that now?"

"I get it. You can't blame any of us for wanting to believe it was, though. I don't know how you're going to convince Ennis, either."

"I don't have to convince him. He can stay if he wants to, but I can't sit back and wait for Hank or one of the other teams to find us, and we both know it's only a matter of time."

"I know. I get it," she said tersely. "And we'll tell them about this before we all split up. I just don't think it needs to happen tonight. Things are going to be difficult enough when we get back."

She was right, and he dropped the subject. He knew she wanted to settle in and enjoy the home Ennis had built. He didn't blame her, honestly. It was human nature to want to settle down and feel safe. Unfortunately, they were too close to the heart of the New World Order. They had no choice but to move, and they needed to do it soon.

22

Savannah was tired of all the tension and fighting. Her dad had come back late yesterday, still angry and not really talking to anyone. She'd never seen him so angry. The tension between him and her uncle had infected everyone, it seemed, and she didn't know what to do about it.

She'd tried to talk to Malachi after the fight yesterday, but he'd told her to mind her own business and let the adults handle things. That had made her madder than ever. She was tired of waiting around for Malachi to be her friend again, and what made things worse was that he acted like he was an adult, and she a child. One way or another, she needed him to take her seriously, and decided to do something she hoped would make him see she wasn't some silly kid who was always in the way.

That in mind, she took a quick look in the mirror, making sure her hair was perfect and that she didn't have anything in her teeth. A new outfit would have been nice, but she wasn't going to dwell on the fact that she had limited clothing options.

Ready as she'd ever be, she walked downstairs and found her target. "Hi, Nash," she said, hoping she sounded airy and light.

He looked up from the laptop sitting on his lap, where it always was. "Hey, Savannah."

She smiled and moved to sit beside him on the couch. "What are you doing?"

He gave her an odd look. "Working on reviewing the information on the drive, just like I do every day," he said, somewhat sarcastically, though she supposed she couldn't blame him after that question.

"Do you want to go for a walk?" she asked.

He stared at her for a moment, and then shook away whatever he was thinking. "Why? Don't you have chores or something to do?" he asked, his eyes going back to the screen.

She let out a dramatic sigh. "I already did my part. Come on, Nash. It's a nice day, and I could really use some time out of the house."

"Then go," he mumbled.

"I can't go anywhere by myself! Remember, my dad said everyone had to stick close and stick together," she reminded him.

Nash took a deep breath and turned to look at her. "You want to go right now?"

She grinned. "Yes!"

He tapped a few buttons on the keyboard before closing the laptop. "I should probably put this thing on the charger anyway," he muttered, standing up from the couch.

Savannah couldn't stop smiling. Her plan had to work. She stood and waited for him before following him out the door. As they moved into the yard, she scanned the area, looking for Malachi. If he wanted to ignore her, that was fine, but she was going to show him exactly what it felt like to be ignored all the time.

"Let's go up the hill a bit, over to the stream. We could get our feet wet," she said happily.

Nash looked at her as if she were crazy. "Get our feet wet?"

She tugged his elbow forward in the direction of the stream and walked ahead, turning back to speak to him in a way that she hoped would look flirtatious to anyone watching. "Come on. You've had your nose in that laptop for almost two weeks. You're pale. When I first met you, you were tanned, and I could tell you were a guy who liked the outdoors," she added sweetly.

He looked at her suspiciously, but followed along. "I have been stuck inside a lot lately," he agreed.

"See," she said, looping her arm around his and tugging him along.

He willingly followed her around the side of the house. They were all doing their best to avoid making obvious trails, which meant they had to brave the brush and the thistles that grew wild all over the mountain.

"I did a lot of cave exploration and hiking before all this. I'd planned to spend my whole summer in the mountains," he said on a sigh.

"You technically are in the mountains," she said with a giggle.

He laughed. "I guess that's true."

A sound to their right grabbed her attention. She glanced over and saw Malachi watching them. He was shirtless, an ax hanging beside him. Clearly, he'd been chopping more wood. It was all he did. Every single day.

"Where are you two going?" Malachi asked in a gruff voice, stepping out and catching their attention so that Nash paused.

"We're going for a walk," Savannah answered simply, smiling up at Nash even though she could see he was uncomfortable. She'd find a way to make it up to him later, she told herself.

Malachi looked at their intertwined arms, and then at Nash before he looked back to meet her eyes. She detected the tiniest bit of jealousy, which was exactly what she'd been going for.

"A walk? You don't have chores?" Malachi snapped.

"We've finished with ours. Let's go, Nash," she said, pulling him up the hill and away from Malachi.

She could practically feel his eyes boring holes into the back of their heads.

"You better be careful, Savannah—there are soldiers around!" Malachi called out from behind them.

Savannah turned to look over her shoulder at him. "Nash will protect me!"

Malachi clenched his jaw before spinning around and disappearing back into the trees.

"What was that about?" Nash asked after another moment had passed.

"What?" she asked innocently.

"Malachi, Savannah," he said simply. "What was that about?"

"I don't know what's up with him. He's the one who chose to volunteer for extra duties. He didn't have to," Savannah said.

Nash remained quiet as they walked through the trees until they found the anemic creek flowing down the mountainside. It was barely a couple of inches deep.

"I don't think that'll do much to cool us off," Nash said dryly.

"We can still get our feet wet," she replied.

He didn't look as excited as she was, but she found a rock to sit on and quickly untied the sneakers she'd been wearing.

"Savannah, we should be down there at the house, helping. I'm sure there are more chores that need to be taken care of," Nash said. "There's always more to be done."

"Nash, come on, we deserve a break."

He sat down beside her, not moving to take off his shoes. "Savannah, what's this all about?" he asked bluntly.

"What? I wanted to get away, and everyone else at the house is so old and boring," she pouted.

"You mean besides Malachi?" he asked.

She shrugged, a sudden lump appearing in her throat. "Malachi is busy."

"I might be the third youngest in the house, but I'm eighteen. I don't think your dad would be happy with us hanging out—alone," he stressed.

She chuckled, knowing he was right. "We're not doing anything."

"Savannah, I'm happy to hang out with you, but I really don't want your dad getting the wrong idea, or you. I'm pretty sure he'd shoot me," he said. She looked up at him to make sure he was joking, but couldn't quite tell. She certainly hoped he was joking.

Looking back to her feet in the water, she shook her head. "Nash, I have to confess something."

"What's that?"

"I'm not into you. I don't like you that way. I mean, you're cute and all, but you're too old for me," she said.

He chuckled. "I get it, Savannah. You like Malachi. Everyone knows you two had a little thing going."

She groaned. "Not really. I mean, I thought we did, and then everything happened, and his mom and dad were really against him stepping outside his faith or whatever, and now he doesn't want to have anything to do with me," she explained.

"So, you're using me to make him jealous," he grumbled, irritation clear in his voice. "I figured, but that's a lousy thing to do."

She suddenly felt guilty, hearing the clear annoyance in his voice. Put like that, it was pretty lousy—she'd only thought about affecting Malachi and hadn't considered how it might upset Nash. "I'm sorry. I hope I didn't hurt your feelings," she added more quietly.

He scoffed. "You didn't hurt my feelings, but I don't appreciate you dragging me into this. I think you should just tell him how you feel. I'm not a pawn."

"I can't tell him how I feel, Nash! I tried, but he doesn't want to talk to me," she whined. "I didn't know what else to do."

Nash looked at her with open irritation. "Savannah, is he worth the trouble, or is this just because he's the last guy on earth your own age?"

She grinned, and felt a little better when he smiled back. "I don't think he's the last guy on earth. You don't think that's a little over-dramatic? I liked him before everything happened and I think he liked me."

"I'm the one who's being dramatic—ha. Seems to me you're the one building up drama. What, are you one of those girls who thrives on drama?" he asked.

Her mouth fell open. "No! I don't thrive on drama. I'm sorry…" She stared at him another moment, and then looked back to the creek. "Just forget about everything. Forget I said anything."

"Savannah, don't you think we have bigger things to worry about?"

"Yes, but what good does it do to worry about everything and not have a little fun? I mean, does worrying change anything?" she asked. "I want to be a normal teenager for a day."

"You are a normal teenager. The world isn't normal," he replied.

"I'm going to get wrinkles if I sit around worrying all day like everyone else."

He shrugged. "I don't think we're all sitting around worrying and not doing anything. Malachi is ensuring there's enough wood to keep the house warm all winter long. We can't rely on the propane. We'll need that for cooking. I'm reviewing the information on the USB to see if there's anything that might help us end all of this. You've been putting in a hand, too, I know, but the chores don't stop."

She rolled her eyes. "Like you or my dad or even all of us together can actually stop the apocalypse."

"It doesn't hurt to try, or to arm ourselves with knowledge at the very least," he reasoned.

After a moment, she nodded. "I suppose."

They sat in silence for a few minutes more. She wiggled her

toes in the cold water, doing her best to try and forget about everything else happening in the world. She tried to imagine herself back home, sitting by the stream near their house.

"I'll go along with your little game, but I don't like it. It's kind of immature," Nash finally said on a sigh.

She put her head back, looking up at the sky. "You're right. It is immature, and I'm sorry I brought you into it."

"I wouldn't mind having a friend, though. I don't want to be your friend to make Malachi jealous, but it would be cool to hang out sometimes," he added quietly. "We're pretty close in age. I could use a friendship with both you and Malachi, you wanna know the truth."

She nodded, looking back to him with a smile. She knew he was a nice guy—maybe something good would come of her dragging him out here if they could start a friendship from it. "I would very much like to be friends. I wasn't lying when I said there's really no one else to hang out with."

"I get it. It's cool, but if you don't mind, I do want to get back to the computer. Thanks for dragging me out of the house, though, even if it was only for a little bit," he said with a friendly smile.

"Anytime. Thanks for being a good sport about all this, too," she offered.

He handed her her shoes and waited until she had them on before he helped her up. Then they headed back towards the house and were met by Malachi again.

"Did you have a good time?" Malachi asked, glaring at Nash.

Savannah looked at Nash, watching him bristle under Malachi's stare. Before she could figure out how to respond, though, he'd stepped forward to reply.

"Yes, we did. Maybe you should take a break, too," Nash said.

"Some of us have real work to do," Malachi shot back.

His tone had been hard, and suddenly she knew that this had been a horrible mistake.

"Some of us have to use our brains rather than our brawn to work," Nash replied easily. With that, he stalked past Malachi, and Savannah was left stunned and staring after them even as Malachi whirled away to go back to his log-splitting. Somehow, she'd made things even worse.

Good one, Savannah.

23

It was late, or else early in the morning—Nash wasn't sure which. All he knew was that he couldn't sleep. He was sick of the fighting and the alliances he could see being formed in the house. It reminded him of some of the reality shows he'd used to leave on for white noise while he did schoolwork. If only there were cameras in the house that he could use to spy on his roommates and maybe get a handle on how to cool it all down. He felt like everyone was plotting against one another. No one was really working together. The drama with Savannah and Malachi had been so trivial and irritating, too, and he couldn't believe he'd let himself get involved. Savannah was close enough in age that he hadn't seen it coming and had thought she might be broaching friendship, but he should have known better.

He'd volunteered to take a couch last night, almost feeling desperate enough to sleep outside in Ennis's defunct SUV just to get some extra privacy. Anything for a little time away from the darkness he felt in the house. Suddenly, he sat up, rubbing a hand over his face and resting his eyes on the sleeping form on the other couch, Wendell. Talk about drama.

Nash curled his lip with repulsion. The guy was always around. It seemed like he could be in twenty places at once, talking to everyone, stirring the pot and making the tensions so much worse than they had to be.

"Can't sleep?" Wendell's voice cut through the thick darkness in the room.

"No."

"Still thinking about all that stuff you were reading last night?" Wendell asked.

Nash stared through the dark room, a little disturbed that Wendell was awake, like he'd just been waiting for the right moment to start a conversation. It was flat-out creepy.

"Yeah, a little," he muttered.

"Are you still mad about last night?" Wendell asked.

Nash shook his head, thinking back to the demeaning job Ennis had foisted on him. "I'm not mad, I just don't understand why I was the one chosen to clean the toilet."

"Because Ennis saw you sitting in here," Wendell replied.

"I wasn't *sitting*. I was reviewing one of the files," Nash retorted.

"I think he thinks you're not carrying your own weight," Wendell said, but in a way that made Nash suspect it was Wendell who truly thought that.

Nash took a deep breath. "I found some information that I think could help us. If anyone would listen to me, I could explain it," he said, feeling the familiar frustration brewing. The last person to confide in was Wendell, but it couldn't hurt to talk since they were both awake. Not about this, anyway.

"I'm listening," Wendell replied.

Nash stared at the shadow still lying on the couch. "I think there's something in that cave, something valuable. I've talked with Austin, though, and he thinks it's a waste of time. That we have more important stuff to worry about."

Wendell scoffed. "Austin is not the king, despite what he might think. Why are you letting him dictate what you think and do?"

"He doesn't dictate what I think and do," Nash shot back.

But then he thought about what Wendell said, and realized the guy was right about this, at least. Austin was the one telling him not to follow the cave lead.

"Listen, I think you're a smart guy," Wendell commented. "You're the one who's been reading all that stuff and you understand it. The rest of us, well, we're not going to get it. You're going to have to make us understand. Maybe visual aids would help," he added.

"Visual aids?"

"You think there's something in the cave. Is it something tangible? A computer? Weapons?" Wendell pressed him, rolling over on the couch and leaning up on an elbow to face him.

"I don't know. I can't say for sure, but I have some ideas," Nash said, not quite ready to tell Wendell of all people what he believed might be hidden behind the second door in the cave.

"Why are you letting us keep you from doing what you think is right?" Wendell asked.

Nash knew he shouldn't trust Wendell, and knew the guy was probably manipulating him, but he couldn't help but agree with him.

"I think there is something there, but whether it's important is debatable. I don't want to take an entire day walking and exploring when there are things to do here. I know that's Austin's hang-up, along with the fact that the soldiers are probably out there combing every inch of the forest," he explained.

Wendell chuckled, the sound oddly eerie in the dark. "As if he isn't going out on his secret missions all the time."

"I'm not an idiot, Wendell. Going out alone is stupid. I don't have a death wish," Nash grumbled.

"I'm not suggesting you do. Maybe your new buddy Malachi would like to go with you," Wendell said, taunting him.

Nash could hear the underlying laughter in the man's voice. Malachi had made it very clear at dinner last night that he had an issue with Nash. He'd supposedly tripped and spilled his glass of water on Nash's head as he'd passed him in the outdoor eating area. It was a bunch of crap and everyone knew it. Malachi was mad at him because of Savannah's stupid little game. She'd have to solve the problem, though—he refused to be involved any longer, even as a mediator. It just wasn't worth his time.

"Whatever," Nash growled.

"You know it's that little girl that's got him all worked up," Wendell said.

"I don't know and I don't care. I don't have the time or energy to play high school games," Nash replied.

Wendell's disgusting laugh, filled with malice, permeated the quiet space. "You're a minute out of high school yourself."

"I'm going out," Nash said, feeling around the floor and finding his shoes.

"It's dark—there could be predators about," Wendell offered, but in a way that was more a dare than a warning.

"There are predators everywhere. I'll take my chances," Nash said, carefully navigating the room as he moved towards the closed door.

He pulled the heavy cord, sliding the door up enough for him to crawl under and out. They'd started closing the door at night, just in case. Just in case soldiers or other survivors attempted to come in. The steel door with the cable on the inside was as good as the best lock on the market.

Outside, Nash saw the first slashes of orange and pink in the sky, and suspected it was around four in the morning. He stepped into the front yard and stretched his arms high before arching his back, sucking in fresh air. His conversation with Wendell played through his head as he stretched out the stiffness left from trying to sleep on the couch.

He was an adult. He didn't need permission to do anything. It was time he followed his instincts. Okay, so Austin didn't understand what Nash saw—that meant he had to make him understand. He and his brother were the leaders around the house, and Nash respected the both of them, however much they might argue. That meant he had to convince them to his way of thinking. With his mind made up, Nash went back into the house, heading into the kitchen to grab supplies. Wendell never said a word, but Nash knew he was awake, listening to his every move. That was fine—he could tell the others where Nash had gone if they cared to ask. No doubt, he knew perfectly well what was happening: the guy was a jerk and a weasel, but he wasn't dumb.

Silently, Nash grabbed his backpack, which he kept stored in the pantry, and stocked it up with his supplies before he quietly walked out of the house once again. He was going to find out what was in that cave. His curiosity wouldn't be satisfied until he did, and whether Austin realized it or not, he sensed it was important.

The sun was barely peeking over the horizon, providing just

enough light for him to see where he was going. He knew how dangerous it was to go out alone, but he'd borrowed one of the handguns which had been hidden in one of the emptied cans of freeze-dried hash browns. He'd stumbled across it a few days before. He didn't know who had hidden it there, but it was snug in the back of his jeans now.

24

Amanda looked up from her spot on the couch when Austin came through the door. She'd been taking a turn at deciphering the information on the USB. With the heat of the day, it had seemed like a good time for a little downtime in the house, where it was somewhat cooler than outside. Proving her point, she could see sweat dripping down Austin's face now, and his blue t-shirt had a dark V of a stain on the front from where he'd been sweating.

"You'd better get some water," she told him.

He nodded, wiping his brow with the hem of his shirt and baring his stomach as he did. She noticed he'd lost weight since she'd first pulled him from the water that fateful day which lately seemed so long ago.

"It's hot out there today," he complained as he headed into the kitchen.

"Which is why everyone is taking it easy," she pointed out.

She heard the tap come on in the kitchen and knew he wasn't answering because he was gulping water. The tap turned on again before he came back into the living room and flopped on the couch, holding a glass of water.

"Everyone is being lazy," he complained.

"They're being *smart*. There's no chore worth your life, and that is exactly what you're putting on the line if you work too hard in this heat," she said.

"I was working on the security, setting traps on the east side of the property," he replied, slightly out of breath.

"What kind of traps?"

"I strung the fishing line across the ground. It's connected to a branch. The branch is supporting a good-sized rock. When the branch triggers and the rock drops, it's going to land on someone's head, hopefully," he said with a small laugh. "If it doesn't catch a human, it might get us a deer."

"That sounds very Mousetrap-like," she said with a smile. "You put out warnings for everyone?"

"It is, and I did. That old game's kind of where I got the idea from. I put up the red flags on our side, too, alerting our people to the trap, and I'll make sure to point it out to everyone this evening. I got some other traps with just fishing line and cans up, too—they'll make plenty of noise if someone comes traipsing in to surprise us."

She nodded. "We've told everyone to watch for the flags, too. They know that's the perimeter and not to go past it."

"Has anyone seen Nash yet?" he asked casually, though Amanda knew he was worried.

"No. I asked Savannah and she had no idea," Amanda replied.

"Why would you ask Savannah?" Austin replied, confusion on his face.

Amanda took a deep breath—she really hadn't wanted to be the one to tell him this, though it seemed everyone else felt the same. "There was some drama between Malachi, Nash, and Savannah yesterday," she said. "It hasn't quite worked itself out yet, so my best guess is that he wanted some space."

"Drama?" he asked, one brow raised. "Like what kind of drama? Did he do something?" he asked, suspicion sounding in his voice.

"No, no," Amanda said. "You know Nash better than that. You also know Savannah likes Malachi, but he doesn't seem interested. I think Savannah was hoping to make Malachi jealous by buddying up to Nash yesterday."

Austin groaned and leaned back on the couch, shutting his eyes. "The water last night," he said, shaking his head.

"You got it. I overheard Malachi talking with Ezra, complaining about Savannah being too young for Nash. Ezra and Malachi seem to be good friends. I noticed some tension after dinner last night, and it was Ezra and Malachi making it clear they did not care for Nash."

"Where's Savannah?" Austin asked, his voice tight.

"I think she's upstairs with Gretchen."

Austin got up, walked to the foot of the stairs, and shouted his daughter's name. A few seconds later, the teenager came downstairs.

"Sit," Austin ordered her.

Savannah looked confused, but walked to the couch and flopped down, crossing her arms over her chest. "What? I didn't do anything," she said, scowling.

"What's this mess with Nash and Malachi about?" he asked, not bothering to be tactful.

Amanda cringed, already guessing how Savannah would respond.

"This mess? There is no mess!" Savannah retorted.

"Where's Nash?" he asked next.

She shrugged. "How should I know?"

"I don't know, weren't you the one who instigated a fight between Malachi and Nash, which has now turned into Ezra and Malachi against Nash?" he demanded.

Savannah's mouth dropped open, then snapped shut. Guilt spread over her face before her shoulders slumped. "I didn't mean for that to happen," she said in a quiet voice.

Austin had his hands on his hips, staring down at his daughter.

His eyes met Amanda's, and she gave a slight shake of her head, telling him to take it easy.

"Savannah, Nash is a nice guy. It isn't cool to play games with him," Austin said, now speaking a bit more gently.

Savannah looked up at him. "I know, and I told him I was sorry. He said he understood, and just not to do it again."

"Did you tell Malachi what you did? It wasn't right to pit the two of them against each other. Nash doesn't know anyone, not like Malachi. How would you feel if people were teaming up against you, if you were the odd man out?" Austin asked, his voice a little accusing.

Amanda had sat through a similar lecture from her own parents when she'd gotten in trouble for picking on a girl at school. It was a lesson that had to be taught, she knew. Kids, even teenagers, didn't always understand the consequences of their teasing or jokes at another's expense, and there was no question that Malachi had a support system in place here, whereas Nash clearly didn't. Everyone liked him well enough, herself included, but he hadn't gotten close to anyone as of yet.

Across from her, though, Savannah looked to be near tears. "Dad, you don't understand. I'm the odd man out!" Savannah protested.

At that moment, Ennis strolled out of his room, his eyes moving to Austin and Savannah, and then to Amanda.

"What's going on?" he asked.

"None of your business," Austin snapped.

Savannah's eyes were glistening with unshed tears, and Ennis, being the doting uncle, moved to sit beside her on the couch, wrapping an arm around her shoulders.

"What happened? Why are you yelling at her?" Ennis asked, looking up at his brother.

Amanda grimaced, dreading another confrontation between the brothers. Things had been tense, but they hadn't tried to kill each other again. She'd been hoping the whole fight would be allowed to blow over.

"I'm not yelling at her. Like I said, it's none of your business," Austin seethed.

"Dad, I don't have any friends," Savannah whined. "Malachi was my only friend and now he doesn't want to talk to me."

"Shh, he's a stupid boy," Ennis soothed her, though he met Amanda's eyes and rolled his own now that he understood what was happening—it was enough, Amanda noticed, to make Austin back down a notch, at least. "Don't let him get to you," Ennis added.

Austin paced away and leaned on the island, and then turned back to her. "Savannah, you being upset about Malachi does not give you the right to throw Nash under the bus."

"I didn't throw him under the bus. I already told him I'm sorry. He said he was okay with it all and then, last night... I don't know why Malachi did that," she said, the tears sliding down her cheeks.

Amanda took a deep breath. "Why don't I get Malachi and we can clear all of this up now?"

Austin looked at her and nodded. "That's a very good idea."

"Dad, no!" Savannah nearly shrieked. "You don't have to do that! I promise, I'll tell him to stop!" Savannah pleaded, looking from her father to her uncle.

Ennis looked confused. "Why is Malachi being brought in?"

"Why don't you ask your niece?" Austin shot back.

"I didn't mean for it to get so out of hand," Savannah said softly.

"I'll be right back," Amanda said, and with that she headed upstairs, knocking on the room Malachi tended to hang out in when he wasn't out working on chores. The fact that he'd come inside was itself testament to how unbearably hot it was at the moment.

A few minutes later, she walked downstairs with a trepidatious Malachi trailing behind her. Amanda gestured for him to sit on the other couch, away from Savannah and Ennis.

"What?" Malachi asked sullenly.

"Malachi, this thing between you and Nash, it needs to stop," Austin said firmly.

Malachi shrugged, staring at the floor like a true teenager. "There isn't anything between us."

"Savannah wants to tell you something," Austin said, looking at his daughter.

Her eyes went wide. "Dad!"

"Savannah," Austin said, in a tone that left no room for argument.

Savannah looked at Malachi, finally. "Nash was only being my friend. Please don't be mad at him."

"I'm not mad at him!" Malachi snapped back.

Amanda took a deep breath, leaning back against the wall. This might fix things, but it was certainly uncomfortable.

"Do you know where he is?" Austin asked.

Malachi shrugged again, more defiantly. "Don't know and don't care."

"Listen, we're all living here, and we all have to get along," Austin said, his irritation showing in the lines around his eyes again.

"Oh, like you and your brother?" Malachi replied.

Amanda couldn't help being shocked to hear him talking in such a disrespectful tone, and saw that Ennis had even gone rigid with the comment. Malachi was usually a very silent, humble kid—Savannah's behavior had really gotten to him.

"That was wrong, and Ennis and I will deal with that. This thing that's happening with the three of you, and now Ezra, it needs to stop," Austin told him.

"Malachi, it wasn't Nash," Savannah blurted out. "I did it. I wanted to make you jealous because you won't talk to me. I practically forced Nash to go for a walk with me. He's not interested in me. He told me I was too young. It was stupid, and I'm sorry. You guys have to be nice to him."

Malachi looked disgusted. "I have to go. I'm in the middle of a card game. Is that all?" he asked Austin, getting to his feet.

"That's it, but I want your word you're not going to keep bugging Nash and making him feel like an outsider."

"He's welcome to hang out with us anytime he wants," Malachi said.

The words lacked feeling. Amanda had a feeling Malachi was going to take his anger with Savannah out on Nash—assuming the kid even came back—but there wasn't much to be done about it. Being in the house was a lot like being inside a volcano being shaken by earthquakes. Eventually, it was going to blow, and when it did, it was going to be disastrous.

25

Austin looked at Amanda as she sat watching him. Ennis had just escorted Savannah outside to talk. Apparently, his little brother was the only person Savannah wanted to talk to, but considering the chat they'd just had, it wasn't surprising. He couldn't lie to himself and try to convince himself it didn't hurt to see her buddying up to Ennis, though. She was in a weird place in her life, and although Austin was sure it was part of the teenage thing, it was difficult to deal with when everything else in their lives was so much more important. Worrying about boys seemed trivial in his mind, but then again, he wasn't a fourteen-year-old girl.

"Was that bad?" he asked Amanda.

She smiled at him, shrugging one shoulder. "Honestly, I don't think it was bad or good. I'm glad you confronted her on the matter, though. All that needed to be said. I don't think she was trying to be mean or hurtful at all, but it was wrong, and now Nash is the one paying the price."

Austin moved to sit beside Amanda on the couch, leaving a few inches between them because of the heat. "Where do you think he is?" he asked, growing more worried about the kid as he continued thinking about it. Disappearing wasn't like him.

She shrugged. "I have no idea. Wendell said he didn't hear him leave, but he was gone when I got up this morning."

"Hopefully, he's just clearing his head. We've all been there before," he muttered.

"Exactly. I don't think we need to worry, yet. If he's not back by dinner, we'll start looking," she assured him.

Austin nodded, leaning his head back on the couch. He could hear the tapping of keys on the laptop, though, and sat forward upon realizing that whatever had flashed into his sight hadn't been anything he'd seen before.

"What's that?" he asked.

She turned the laptop so he could see the screen better and read the previously unseen heading. "I found this file Nash has been trying to open. I used some of my ancient knowledge from my computer class back in college and managed to get it unlocked. I guess smarty-pants Nash isn't familiar with the old-fashioned way of doing things," she said with a grin.

"Wow, good job. Nash will be impressed," Austin said, his eyes scanning what appeared to be a letter.

"Your buddy, Callum Barker, he locked these files. See here."

She pointed to a line in the letter written to a Dr. Sarah Bastani. "He's the one who encrypted those other files that Nash is certain can't be opened by anyone except for the person with the encryption key."

"Who's this Dr. Sarah Bastani?" Austin asked.

Amanda clicked over to another document. "She's a cryptologist who used to work at the NSA with Callum. He must have planned on your contacts reaching out to her."

"Callum wrote this letter to her, but did he send it?" Austin asked, not really expecting an answer.

"I don't know, but look at this," Amanda said, pulling up another document from one of the files Nash had been fighting with.

"What's that?" Austin asked, looking at what appeared to be a Google map with a pinpoint on it.

"I think that's where Dr. Bastani is."

Austin shook his head. "How do you know that?"

Amanda sighed. "Nash was organizing the information into files based on what each document contained. Alone, they don't make a lot of sense, but when you start combing through them, you'll see a trail of breadcrumbs so to speak. There's one more file I'm working to unlock. I'm hoping that will be another piece of the puzzle," she explained. "But looking at all this… if this doctor worked at the Cheyenne Mountain Complex, which is what I'm thinking, it makes sense she'd live in this area. It's not far from us," she added.

Austin nodded. "You're getting a lot farther than I did. I got sucked into that propaganda rabbit hole."

"That information is important. It outlines their plan, or what I think they referred to as Phase One," she said, her eyes back on the screen as her fingers flew over the keyboard.

"That part of the plan is disgusting," he said, curling his lip.

"Callum didn't tell you anything else about this?" Amanda asked again, pausing her fingers above the keyboard.

"Honestly, I wasn't paying all that much attention. He'd sent a few emails, but you have to understand that the guy was kind of out there. He saw a conspiracy on every corner. He saw hidden messages in everything and was convinced it was a secret society communicating in plain sight. I figured he'd tell me more when we met, but he didn't get the chance," Austin said, his voice going quieter with the memory.

"I think your friend was right. It's too bad no one listened to him."

Austin flinched. The truth was, he should have listened. "Callum was a good guy, but way, way out there. It was really hard to take him seriously."

"I understand, Austin. I didn't mean—" She stopped talking and suddenly turned to look at him with a huge smile on her face.

"What? What is it?" he asked, turning the laptop towards him.

"It's for you," she said, handing the computer to him.

Austin's mouth dropped open. It was a letter written to him from Callum, dated two days before they'd met on the bridge.

"He says he wants me to get to Washington and make sure the file's safe, and then contact this doctor to get her into Washington to see the drive and open up what he's encrypted," Austin paraphrased.

"Why?"

He shook his head, still reading the letter. "That map you found—it's the location where she's most likely gone into hiding if she's not in Washington, according to him. We have to hope she's there and not on the other side of the country, I guess. She is the only one who can open those encrypted files. He insists I need to get the information to her."

"Does he say why?" Amanda asked.

"He says the files are the way to stop the EMP from happening. He thought I would have time to get to Washington and do some digging with the help of some of my old contacts. It happened too soon. I never got the chance," he told her, feeling dread wash over him as he re-read the letter.

"Your old contacts?"

"Fifteen years ago, I did a lot of stories on government corruption and scandals. I still have some contacts there, but I haven't seen or spoken to them in years. I told Callum that, but he must have thought I still did. In the letter, he's asking me to find out why billions of government dollars were being siphoned off and put towards a secret facility," Austin explained, his blood running cold as he read the last paragraph.

"What? What is it? You just got very pale, and with your skin tone, that is not easy!" Amanda exclaimed, though the joke fell flat even as it left her lips.

Austin's mouth was dry as he processed the information. "Crap."

"Austin, if you don't tell me what is going on in the next three seconds, I'm going to hit you!"

"Nash," he whispered.

"What? Nash? Nash is involved? Oh no, don't tell me he's a mole—some secret agent? I knew he was too smart for a typical eighteen-year-old; he's probably thirty and a Russian spy," she groaned, falling back into the couch beside him.

Austin put a hand on her knee. "No. Slow down. Nash isn't a secret agent. The mine where Nash and I got the cables from, the place he kept trying to tell me we needed to investigate further, that's the same place Callum names as the underground facility that was being built." Having said it out loud, Austin went silent and allowed himself to stare into space, trying to put it all together. And, more than that, trying to tell himself he shouldn't feel so guilty for not listening to the kid. There was no helping it, though. He should have listened, and now he couldn't help worrying that Nash had gone out there on his own to investigate. It wasn't like him, but...

Amanda broke into his thoughts. "The government built a

secret, underground facility that Nash found?" she clarified. "That's what we're talking about?"

"The old mine, where we got the cables. Nash had found a door, like one of those nuclear blast doors. He kept telling me we needed to check it out," Austin explained.

She grimaced. "He mentioned something to me about it, as well. I just assumed it would be more computers and stuff."

Austin turned his attention back to the letter, putting Nash's whereabouts out of mind for a moment. He wasn't so stupid to have gone out there on his own—there was no way. "Maybe it wasn't really our government that built the facility. With all the secrecy and the siphoning of funds from the defense budget, this could be the work of some covert operation, one meant to overthrow the government."

"You mean an inside attack? Someone working for the government is part of all this?" Amanda demanded.

He shook his head, his brain spinning. "I don't know. I guess it's possible."

"Maybe the government was preparing for an attack like this, and the facility in the mine is their base of operations," Amanda suggested.

"Then why aren't they doing anything?" he asked.

She grimaced. "I don't know."

"We need to find Nash and go back there. We need to find out what's in there," Austin muttered.

"Austin, if that mine or cave, or whatever it is, is truly an underground bunker built by the government, I'm guessing they're not going to lay out the welcome mat for anyone. And, if it is the bad guys using that place as a base, we definitely can't go waltzing in there like we're tourists looking for a photo op," she pointed out.

He gave her the laptop back, rubbing his face with his hands, trying to think. Callum had known about the mine. The fact that they just happened to be nearby was coincidence or dumb luck—or really bad luck—but it was what it was.

"I need to find Nash," he said, getting to his feet.

"What are you going to do?" she asked him.

He looked down at her, saw the worry in her eyes, and shook his head. "I don't know, but sitting here is not an option, especially if we're this close to ground zero. We're in danger here. We thought the city was bad, but we could very well be neighbors with the group that outlined that plan. Maybe we were wrong and what's happening in Denver isn't happening to this degree everywhere. Maybe this is the worst of it, and it's looking to spread. The very people who've been orchestrating mass murder in the streets could be below our feet at this very moment."

"Oh God, is this ever going to get easier?" she groaned.

He let out a long sigh. "I don't see how it can. We haven't seen the worst of it yet."

Her chin dropped to her chest. "This sucks. This absolutely

sucks. I hate that I thought my life had bad days before. I would give anything for those bad days."

His heart went out to her and to everyone else suffering through the mess created by a selfish group of people, but he also felt real fire in his gut for the first time in days. An inner voice inside his head refused to be quieted. It was demanding justice. It demanded that he take action. He only regretted the fact that he'd waited so long. Part of him had been hoping someone else would fix the problem, and that same part of him kept telling him he was only one man. He couldn't possibly be the one to make a difference. But Callum had believed he could. He'd given him the key, and died to do it; now it was up to him to do something with it.

26

Z ander looked around the table, staring at the people he'd been put in charge of. He'd clawed and killed his way to get to his elevated position in the organization, and there was no way he was going to let anyone take it all away from him now, which meant these people needed to be the best.

His gaze moved to Hank Finlay. The guy was older than Zander and had always harbored a grudge against him. Zander had climbed the ranks much faster than Hank even though they'd joined around the same time. Hank was a sociopath, though, and not a very smart one. Zander disliked him in general, but up until yesterday, he'd been valuable. Ruthless, he had no qualms about killing women and children—unlike some of the other dedicated soldiers.

"Tell me what they looked like," he said, his eyes mere slits as he stared at Hank.

Hank only shrugged, clearly not understanding how angry his

boss was. "The guy was tall, dark hair and blue eyes. Had a couple tattoos on his arm, beard, kind of scruffy looking," he said nonchalantly.

Zander could feel his anger rising. "And the woman?"

"Petite, dark hair, looked Mexican or Italian or something like that," he replied.

"You idiot!" Zander shouted, pounding his fist against the table and tearing open the still healing wound in his arm in the process.

Hank, unperturbed by Zander's outburst, raised an eyebrow. "It isn't like they got more than a couple guns. What's the big deal?"

"The big deal is that I have a search party out there right this minute looking for those two!" Zander screeched.

Hank's mouth dropped open. "That's the guy who busted out of here?"

Zander closed his eyes, counted to five before opening them and looking at Hank again. "Yes, that's the guy who busted out of here, along with his little girlfriend, that brat kid, and a couple other guys!"

"I didn't know, man. I'll go back up there and ferret them out," Hank said, still not understanding the gravity of what he'd allowed to happen.

"You'll do no such thing. I can't trust you to get it right!"

"Hey, they didn't get the weapons cache. I've already taken

care of moving the guns to a new location. No harm, no foul," he said with a smile that pushed Zander's last button.

Without hesitating, he reached for the Beretta in his side holster and aimed and fired a shot that landed right between Hank's ugly, evil eyes. The hole in his head bloomed red before his body slumped in the chair.

Zander looked around the table at the other men, none of whom moved. They were the smart ones. They knew not to try his temper, and that failure wasn't an option. Those who failed died. Zander would not be the guy sitting at the table with the main bosses and getting a bullet between his eyes because he'd failed to retrieve the information on that stupid flash drive.

"Now, who's got the map?" Zander asked, feeling much calmer.

"I do, sir," one of his captains said, pushing a large map of Denver and the surrounding areas into the center of the table.

"Get that cleaned up. He stinks," Zander sneered, not bothering to look at the body five feet to his left.

Two men jumped up from the table and quickly hauled Hank from the room.

"I think we can divide the area into four search grids," Captain Davis said, using his finger to draw invisible lines. "We know they're in the mountains to the west."

Zander nodded. "Where are the search teams now?"

"They're packing up their go-bags and getting ready to head back out there," Davis replied.

"Good. I want them to shoot all except for Merryman. I need him alive," Zander ordered.

"Got it, sir."

"And if he is killed, bring me every person that survives. Someone will know something," he said firmly, looking at each of the six men still sitting at the table.

"Yes, sir. Will you be joining us?" Davis asked nervously.

"No. I've got work to do here," he said, though the reality was that he knew he wasn't strong enough to trek through the forest.

"We'll report back when we find them," Davis said confidently.

"You'd better find them, or don't bother coming back," Zander snapped.

The men all took that as their dismissal and quickly filed out of the room. Watching them go, Zander smiled. He loved that they were afraid of him. Fear led to respect. He would kill any man who failed him and they all knew it. It made them try harder. And those who did try to run away would be killed by the others who were loyal to him.

27

Nash had made it to the mine faster than expected. He'd gotten a little twisted around, but once he'd gotten himself back on the right path, he'd made good time. The time alone had given him plenty of time to think about everything happening back at the house, too. He felt like he was completely alone now—the only thing really keeping him around was the mystery on that USB and the idea of making a difference in what was happening with the NWO. Austin had once been his friend, yeah, but lately the man had been too busy to talk to him much at all.

He wasn't being taken seriously, either. He knew there was something beyond that door, and no one would listen to him. It was a lot like being back in his college classes. No one wanted to listen to the kid. He was too young to know better than them. People were intimidated by his genius, so they tended to ostracize him right away, never giving him a chance to prove he could be a fun guy to be around. The same thing was happening all over again at the house.

It really was hard being the smartest guy in the class, or in his case now, the house. He intended to prove he wasn't wrong, though, and that everyone needed to start taking him seriously.

"There it is," he whispered when he crested a hilltop and saw the tiny parking area below the mine.

He bounded down the hill, anxious to discover the secret behind the door that had been haunting him since he'd first laid eyes on it. He stepped inside the mine without any real hesitation, not hearing any sounds outside of birds. The cool air was welcomed as he slid his hands along the wall by the light of a glowstick. He was confident he could find the first door in the darkness by feeling alone, but the glowstick wouldn't hurt.

Nash found the opening and stepped into the room. His eyes had adjusted to the darkness, and he could vaguely make out large shapes on all sides—the shelving from before.

But he only took one step more before he froze, the hairs on the back of his neck standing on end. He wasn't alone. He'd been so eager to get to the door, he hadn't stopped to check the room.

"Hello?" he whispered, his voice hoarse with the idea that he'd walked into a strange lair for a bear, or something far worse.

There was a flash of light followed by a muted pop and then

white-hot pain erupting in his thigh. Before he had a chance to register what was happening, a strobe light kicked on, followed by the horrible sounds of bullets slamming into the rock and shelving around him. A horrible, pinging sound came next as bullets hit the steel door to his right. Then, all was quiet, and he was left with ringing ears and more pain than he had ever endured in his life.

Hands gripped his upper arms, and his backpack was ripped from his body along with the gun he'd stashed in his waistband.

"Take him inside," a male voice growled.

Nash blinked, watching the door that had brought him to the mine silently open. It was bittersweet to realize he was finally getting to see behind the door, but would likely not live long enough to do anything about it. Dizzy with pain, he found himself unable to focus on much of anything as his body was dragged into a dark cavern. The steel door he'd been so desperate to get through was slammed shut behind him, and the soft glow of lights revealed he was in a tunnel, going deeper underground. Somewhere, in the back of his mind, he was smiling. He'd been right.

"Sit him down and bandage that leg—we need him alive," a man said from somewhere in the shadows.

Nash was pushed into a chair, his arms wrenched behind his back and his hands quickly bound. One of the men who'd dragged him into the underground room stepped in front of him, his large frame offset by the room that was filled with more technology than Nash had ever seen in his life. Nash struggled to see around him, staring at the huge flat screen monitors mounted on the far wall.

"Get a hemostat bandage on that leg; I don't want him bleeding out before I get a chance to question him," a man ordered.

Nash's vision blurred as he watched one of the men hand a bandage to the guy in front of him. Without any care, a bandage was stuffed inside the hole in his leg, bringing on a whole new level of pain. He screamed, and the sound echoed, but the men around him didn't react.

"Where are we?" Nash groaned when he caught his breath, only to be hit with the butt of a gun to the side of his head.

Tears rushed to his eyes as pain shot through his skull.

"Shut up! We'll ask the questions."

He felt dizzy and knew he was about to be sick. "I'm going to throw up," he moaned, only about two seconds before he turned his head to the side and vomited.

"I'm not cleaning that up," one of his captors grumbled.

"Quit crying. That bandage'll keep you alive, for now," the man who'd manhandled his leg stated.

"What do you want?" Nash asked, his brain foggy with pain and what he suspected was blood loss.

The man from the shadows stepped forward, the glow of the many computer screens in the room illuminating his face and giving him an eerie blue skin tone.

"I want to know why you're here and who you are," the man stated.

"I came into the mine looking for shelter," Nash lied.

"Try again," the man said.

Nash moaned, trying to clear his head and keep his thoughts straight. He couldn't tell them the truth.

"I've been living up here for a while. I was exploring the cave, I mean the mine; I figured there'd be coal and thought I could mine it and sell it to the people in the city," he said. He could hear himself slurring, and his lips and tongue felt thick, the words difficult to form.

There was laughter from the other three men in the room. "You were going to mine coal?" one asked incredulously.

Nash tried to smile. "Yep. I figured it'd be valuable, and I could get rich."

He knew it was a ridiculous story. He just had to hope they thought he was that stupid. Stupid might be the only thing that saved his life.

"You expect me to believe that story?" his interrogator asked.

Nash blinked, trying to focus his eyes on the man standing a few feet in front of him. The ringing in his ears was subsiding. He could hear muted voices in the background, behind him. He turned his head, looking towards the bank of computer screens, and realized the room was far bigger than he'd initially thought. The tapping sound he'd heard wasn't natural, either; it was the sound of keyboards.

"Where am I?" he asked, playing up the concussion he knew he likely had.

"Remind him where he is," the interrogator said in a quiet voice.

Nash looked up just in time to see the butt of the gun slam into the side of his face. He felt his cheekbone shatter, and then his eye went white with pain when he was struck again. Blackness hovered on the edge of his consciousness, ready to take him under, but he fought it. He couldn't pass out—he wouldn't let himself. He felt warm liquid pouring down his face, falling down his neck and soaking the collar of the t-shirt he was wearing.

"Now, tell me, why are you here?" the man asked again.

Nash moaned. "I was lost. I wanted coal." He could barely understand his own words, though.

It was becoming harder for him to talk, to think. That was their plan, he knew. They were going to beat him into giving up information. He had to be strong. He couldn't let them know about the house. Passing out would be a blessing, he realized. He had to stop fighting and give in to the blackness. He was almost looking forward to the next blow that would put him out of his misery.

"You were lost and wanted coal? I don't believe you. Do you want to live?" the man asked, bending over to look Nash in the one good eye he could see out of.

"Yes," Nash said, trying not to whimper.

"Then tell me why you're here. Who sent you?"

"Nobody. Just me," he managed to get out.

"You had a gun. Where did you get it from?"

"House," he mumbled, before quickly correcting himself. "My house. Denver."

In the distance, which sounded much farther away than he knew it to be, he could hear the low voices of two people talking. They were talking about something called the 'Blackdown Protocol.' The words danced through his mind. He knew they were significant, but his brain wasn't working. He couldn't find the puzzle piece that was somewhere in his mind. The voices continued to murmur, their words not making any sense. One of them kept referring to Blackdown. Nash held onto the word, tossing it around and tucking it away for safekeeping. If he survived the interrogation, that one word was going to be important. He could feel it.

"I don't think you understand how serious I am," the man said.

"I'm alone," Nash said, trying to remember what the man had asked him.

There was a chuckle from his right. "We got that, but why? No one is alone these days."

"I'm alone," he repeated.

The interrogator stood to his full height, looming over him. "I think it's going to take a little more persuasion to get this one to talk. This should be fun."

The evil grin on his face sent ice through Nash's veins, and he shut his good eye. Why had he been so stupid? Why had he run off on his own? He wanted to cry, to curl up in a ball and have his mom comfort him. His life couldn't end this way. It just couldn't.

28

Austin walked into the kitchen where dinner was being served. It had started raining a bit ago, forcing everyone inside. Personally, he'd heard a bolt of thunder and immediately made a mental note to prepare for a power outage. Thinking of it in this situation, he smirked. Old habits died hard.

The tension was still thick in the air. Everyone was walking on eggshells, worried one of the brothers would either try to kill the other or turn their anger on someone else, and he couldn't help being embarrassed to be at the center of the drama. He scanned the room as he got food, seeing Ennis sitting at the dining table with Savannah, Wendell, and Tonya. Ennis looked up, glaring at him.

"Here," Amanda said, interrupting the stare-off.

Austin looked away from his brother and took the glass Amanda was offering. "Thanks."

He quickly finished dishing up the meal of what was supposed to be chicken fajitas before taking his plate and moving to the living room. All of the seats were taken, so he moved to the stairs, away from everyone else, and sat down on one of the lower steps. Amanda joined him a minute later.

"Still haven't talked to him?" she asked in a quiet voice.

"Nope, and don't plan on it."

"You need to. Do you notice Nash isn't here?" she pointed out.

Austin looked up, surveying the living room, and did a quick mental rewind of the kitchen. *Damn.* She was right. "Has he been back at all?"

"Not that anyone has seen. He wouldn't be out in this weather, Austin," she said in a quiet voice.

He nodded in agreement. "Maybe he's mad and blowing off some steam?"

"What if he's not mad? What if they got him?" she hissed.

"He's a big boy. He knew what he was doing when he left," Austin said nonchalantly, though he was worried sick about the kid. He'd thought he'd be back by now. Once again, the idea that he could have gone to investigate the cave reared its head, but he shook it off. He wouldn't have gone alone. He knew better than that.

"You know things haven't been okay with him. We need to find him," Amanda insisted.

"Amanda, we have to get to the cryptologist's place. We're

sitting on a ticking time bomb. We have to get her this information," Austin said. "And if she's as close as that map suggests, there's no reason to delay."

"Are you actually suggesting we leave Nash out there?"

Austin took a deep breath. "I'm saying, our priority has to be saving all of us. Bastani might be the key to that."

He heard footsteps then, and looked up to find Ennis and Malachi moving towards them. He groaned inwardly, dreading another confrontation. Thankfully, Wendell wasn't glued to Ennis's butt at the moment.

"Malachi is worried about Nash," Ennis grumbled, not looking directly at Austin.

"So am I," Amanda replied.

"I may have said some stuff to him that I shouldn't have," Malachi confessed, looking as if he were carrying the weight of the world on his shoulders.

"I'm going to look for him first thing in the morning," Amanda concluded. "We've waited long enough for him to come back on his own."

Austin shot her a look. "We have to get that information to that woman."

"What woman?" Ennis asked.

"We found some information on the drive that indicates a cryptologist is hiding out nearby, assuming she survived the initial attack and the NWO hasn't found her. According to the documents, she's the only one who can decipher the encrypted pages. She might be able to figure out a way to shut this whole thing down," Austin explained.

"Seriously?" Malachi asked excitedly.

Austin nodded. "Yes, which is why I think we need to get to that cryptologist first thing tomorrow."

"But Nash may be hurt or waiting on us to find him," Amanda argued.

"Where's this magical woman who's going to fix the world?" Ennis asked.

"About twenty miles from here in some dense wooded area, way off the grid," Austin replied.

Ennis grimaced. "You're talking about steep terrain that's pretty rough. That isn't a quick trip."

"I'll go," Malachi immediately volunteered.

Austin looked at the boy's face. He understood why Malachi wanted to go. He was feeling guilty over the way he'd treated Nash, and getting away before Nash came back was one way to avoid the confrontation. But he was capable and smart—he'd be an able companion if it came to needing him.

"Okay," Austin agreed.

Amanda narrowed her eyes. "I'm going to look for Nash in the morning."

"Good. We'll split up. It makes more sense. There's enough

people in the house, we can divide and conquer," Austin replied.

Ennis shook his head. "The two of you are going to get us all killed. You can't go running around the mountain. You're bound to run into someone. What if they follow you or force you to tell them where the house is, where the rest of us are?"

"We'll be careful," Austin replied, not willing to argue the matter.

"Me, too," Amanda said.

"I'll need the horses," Austin told her, knowing it was a bold ask.

Amanda shrugged. "That's fine. I'm going to head towards the mine. I have a feeling that's where Nash would have gone. He's been talking about that place for weeks. Maybe he's staking it out. It'll be easier to look for tracks he may have left if I'm walking anyway."

"Amanda, Nash is a smart, capable guy. I think he'll come back on his own," Austin reiterated, though his gut clenched as he said it. Was he being realistic, or letting his hopes get the better of him?

"I feel like something's wrong. I won't be able to do anything else until I know he's okay," she said.

"I think you're all being foolish. I guess I'll stay here and prepare for an attack when one of you gives away our location," Ennis grumbled.

Austin grinned. "Good idea. Why don't you work with a few of the guys on their target practice?"

"Really?" Ennis asked with surprise.

"Yes. You're good at it, and they'll listen to you. I don't plan on bringing any trouble back, but it is out there, and we all know it's coming. Keep these guys sharp. Put someone on watch on the east and south sides. I'm trusting you to keep my daughter safe, Ennis," Austin said, looking his brother right in the eyes.

"And you know I will," he said somberly before turning and walking back into the living room.

Amanda turned to look at him, a small smile on her face. "Does that mean the two of you have officially made up?"

"We're brothers. We fight. We make up. In the end, we're still brothers," he said easily, hoping that was the case.

They didn't have time for old drama. They were facing something much bigger than their sibling rivalry and were going to have to stick together to survive. Austin looked through the stair rails and saw Wendell glaring at him. He shot his own look of malice right back at the man. Wendell looked away and went to stand by Ennis. The infatuation was disgusting. Austin only hoped his brother could see what was happening and keep his guard up.

"Malachi, we need to get the bags packed with supplies. We're going to need enough for three days, just in case the terrain is bad enough to slow us down," Austin instructed.

"Take extra water for the horses, just in case," Amanda added.

Malachi headed for the kitchen as Austin turned to Amanda. "You'll need to take extra supplies with you, as well."

She nodded. "I will. I can make the trip there and back in a day."

"I don't know if Nash took anything with him. Be prepared to give him food and water, as well," Austin said quietly.

"I will. And I will find him, Austin," she said, reaching out and putting a hand on his knee.

"He'll be fine," Austin said, more for his own sake than Amanda's.

29

It was dawn when Austin walked into the kitchen, grabbing one of the protein bars from the box and quickly tearing it open. He did his best to move quietly through the house, preparing for his trip to find the doctor. Malachi had already gone out to bring the horses around.

"Be careful," Amanda whispered, startling him and nearly making him choke on the food in his mouth.

"I will. You, too. Who's going with you?" he asked.

"Probably one of the younger guys."

"Keep your gun at the ready," he ordered her.

"You do the same," she said with a smile.

They stared at each other, a different tension than usual in the room. "I should get out there," Austin said with what he knew was an awkward grin. "Malachi is anxious to go. Truth be told, I think he's running from a certain teenage girl."

Amanda laughed. "She must be doing something right if she's got him running."

Austin stepped in and embraced her in a quick hug before stepping around her and heading out of the kitchen.

"See you in a couple days," he called back as he walked out, telling himself not to worry—she was more capable of defending herself than he was, really, and he knew it.

He slid under the front door and found Malachi petting Raven's nose, quietly talking to the big horse. Dawn had barely broken, washing the area in hues of orange and pink. Austin inhaled the fresh air, the scent of rain still lingering. He could feel the moisture in the air and hoped the weather held for both their sake and for Amanda's.

"You ready?" he asked Malachi, hoisting himself onto Charlie's back.

"Yep," the kid said, and quickly mounted Raven.

Austin had one of the Remington rifles in the saddle scabbard he'd crafted from one of the holsters in Ennis's stash. He had the trusty Glock in a holster on his side. Malachi wore a holster, as well. The kid had become very good at handling the smaller thirty-eight, impressing Austin with his willingness to learn and to direction.

They set the horses at an easy walk, making their way northwest up the mountainside.

"How far is it?" Malachi asked.

Austin shook his head. "Fifteen, maybe twenty miles. It's on this side of Apache Peak, which is not going to be an easy climb. I hope you're ready for thin air and cold. Did you pack the gloves and beanies?" he asked.

"I did. Do you think it will be cold even now?" he asked.

"I don't know for sure. I'm guessing the daytime temps will be mild, but the nights could be very cold. We'll probably be outside tonight. I don't want to deal with hypothermia," he explained.

Malachi nodded in understanding. "Got it."

"It's going to be above the tree line, which means we're not going to have anywhere to hide. I doubt the soldiers are going to be up that high, but we can't be sure. Keep your eyes open," Austin instructed.

"Do you think there might be survivors living up there?" Malachi asked.

Austin grimaced. "I doubt it. If I remember my geography right, it's pretty uninhabitable. There are no trees, minimal wildlife, and the weather would be rough. The options for finding shelter would also be limited."

"Unless they were to pitch tents or something," Malachi offered.

Austin nodded. "True. I guess we'll find out when we get there."

They travelled in relative silence, both of them listening for sounds of man or beast. The sun was high in the sky when Austin declared he needed to stop for a minute. He climbed off his mount, his leg throbbing with the lack of movement. He shook it out, trying to get the circulation flowing again before he made his way into the thinning, young trees to relieve himself. When he was done, he'd begun to turn already when the snap of a twig behind him froze him. He turned slowly then, hoping to see Malachi's face. It wasn't him.

"Don't move." The image of a young Grizzly Adams stood before him with his own rifle pointed directly at Austin. The implications of his accoster holding the gun he'd left on the horse was not good. Austin immediately worried for Malachi. He'd only been away from the kid for a couple of minutes, but Grizzly Adams must have been lying in wait, or possibly following them. He couldn't believe he hadn't noticed or heard. It was a serious mistake. He silently berated himself for not paying more attention. The man shouldn't have been able to sneak up on him.

"I don't want any trouble," Austin said, raising both his hands.

"So we heard," the man said with an ugly smile, revealing stained yellow teeth.

"I don't have much," Austin said, hoping the man would leave him be—not missing the part about a 'we.'

"Walk, back to the horses."

Austin sighed and slowly made his way back to where he'd left Malachi with the horses. The Glock was still on his side.

His captor clearly wasn't all that smart or skilled in the art of hostage-taking, which was a good sign. Austin only had to wait for the right moment and hope he could free his weapon from the holster before Grizzly Adams fired his rifle. Two other younger men were already rifling through the two bags Malachi had packed. Malachi glanced at him apologetically from where he stood off to the side. Austin noticed two of the water bottles had already been emptied and tossed to the ground.

"You're supposed to be watching him!" the old man shouted at his buddies, who were shoving the trail mix in their mouths by handfuls.

Malachi's thirty-eight was in the dirt next to one of the back-packs that had been emptied onto the ground. Austin stared at the supplies that were meant to sustain them on their journey. Then he looked at the boys—that's what they were in his opinion. They couldn't have been more than sixteen, and it looked as if they hadn't eaten in a while.

"We are watching," one of them replied without looking up.

"Look, you have our supplies. Let us go," Austin reasoned.

"Why would we do that?" the old man asked.

"Because what do you plan to do with us, make us slaves?" Austin snapped.

The old man laughed. "Now that you mention it, that sounds like a good idea."

Austin looked around the area, checking for signs of anyone

else lurking, standing guard. He didn't see anyone. The two boys greedily ripping open the protein bars Malachi had packed weren't paying attention. They were so overwhelmed with the food, it was their sole focus. Austin met Malachi's eyes, looked towards the horses standing about ten feet away, and then back towards him. Malachi barely moved his head, but Austin could tell he understood. Their captors were sloppy and not exactly threatening. It would be easy to escape, assuming Austin could get the rifle out of the man's hands and the two others didn't reach their weapons in time.

"We'll go. Keep our food," Austin said in a low voice.

"I'll take that gun at your side, too," the man commented.

Austin couldn't believe how bad this man was at the robbery business. He met Malachi's eyes, silently communicating that he needed to get ready.

"This gun, right," Austin growled, pulling the Glock from its holster and bringing it up to fire a single shot all in one smooth, fast motion. The old man's face twisted in shock and pain before his rifle fell to the ground, followed by the man screaming in pain.

Malachi raced for the horse, grabbing their reins and pulling them into the woods while Austin turned his gun on the two young men staring at him in total shock.

"We don't want any trouble," one of them said, holding his hands up.

"Kick my gun over here and I won't shoot you," Austin

ordered the kid, moving to take the rifle from the dying man's hands.

One of the young men, his mouth full, used the toe of his worn shoe to kick the gun across the rocky ground towards Austin. Austin, with his gun still trained on them, reached for Malachi's thirty-eight. He stuck it in the back of his pants, before slowly backing towards the horses.

"Start moving," he ordered the young men. "Walk away, now."

The young men nodded, holding their hands up as they walked backwards, in the opposite direction Malachi had headed. The old man was still writhing in pain on the ground. Austin looked at him, confirmed it was a gut shot, and knew he would die soon. He hated to have killed a man, but it was kill or be killed.

"Don't leave me here!" the man groaned.

Austin ignored him. "Go, now," he ordered the two young men who were taking slow steps backwards.

They both started running away.

He turned to Malachi, who'd reappeared without the horses. "Grab what's left of our gear," he grumbled, noticing most of the food was gone.

Malachi knelt as directed and did his best to scoop as much as he could into the overturned backpacks before he disappeared to retrieve the horses, their packs in hand. Austin's eyes scanned the area. They couldn't stick around. There could be more starving bandits that were far more capable at robbery, just waiting to take their turn.

When Malachi returned, already on horseback and leading Charlie, Austin didn't waste another second. He quickly jumped into the saddle, spurring Charlie to move immediately. The rocky terrain made it impossible for them to go much faster than a hurried walk, but he wanted out of the area now.

"That was close," Malachi mumbled after they'd ridden for a good fifteen minutes.

Austin nodded. "Too close. We have to pay attention. If they'd been soldiers or men who actually knew what they were doing, we'd be dead."

"I'll do better. I was drinking water and not listening to my surroundings," Malachi muttered.

Austin didn't answer him. He was just as much at fault as Malachi was. It was a lesson learned. He was only glad they survived it. They fell into silence, both of them hyper-aware of their surroundings after the close encounter. The trees were thinning out and the rocks grew much bigger the higher they climbed. There was no clear trail, which was both good and bad.

"We need to find water and refill our bottles since they drank our backups," Austin muttered.

"Seems to be a row of green bushes parallel to us, almost like an invisible line," Malachi said, pointing toward a row of shrubbery that had fewer brown leaves than the other shrubs dotted around the landscape.

"Water?" Austin asked.

Malachi slid out of the saddle, moving to some rocks and kicking them over. "It's moist here. You see the darker color of the rock from the topside?" he asked.

Austin got off his own horse and squatted down to inspect the area. "I see it."

"We can try digging a little or try to find a small pool in the shade of the brush," Malachi suggested.

Austin grimaced. "It's a good idea, but I don't think it's enough, and that could take time. We're fine now... let's just keep a lookout."

They both stood, surveying the terrain that had grown more and more barren.

Austin shook his head, doubtful they were going to find a spring or any other body of water. "I think we have to press on. I know there are some hiking trails around here. We can follow them to the state park. There might be water there."

"You want to approach a place there might be others?" Malachi asked.

Austin shrugged. "I think we have to, and people could be anywhere, truth be told. There's no way to guarantee avoiding them."

"Which way?" Malachi asked with resignation.

Austin took a few seconds to orientate himself, and then pointed. "That way."

Navigating without signs, GPS, or even a map of the area was tough. He'd memorized what he'd seen on the computer, but it wasn't exactly a clear snapshot image. Going towards civilization wasn't the smartest thing, but it was the lesser of two evils in his eyes.

It took much longer than Austin had anticipated before they finally saw what looked to be a ranger station in the distance.

"Keep your gun at the ready," Austin said in a low voice as they slowly approached the building.

A shot rang out from somewhere behind them. Austin spun around in his saddle, his eyes scanning the area, trying to find where the shot had come from. A woman wearing a pale, dirty pink jacket and khaki pants emerged from a copse of trees, a rifle in her hands.

"Turn around and go out the way you came," she ordered.

Austin immediately decided she wasn't a threat. "We need water, that's it. We won't bother you. We've been walking all day. We were robbed early on. They took our water and most of our supplies."

The woman eyed him closely before turning her gaze on Malachi. "You have guns," she stated.

Austin nodded. "We do."

"Why didn't you shoot the people who stole from you?" she asked skeptically.

"They caught us off-guard. They'd already drunk our water

and eaten what little we had when we managed to make our escape," Austin explained.

"But you kept your guns?"

"It's how we got away," he replied. "They weren't exactly skilled soldiers. They were hungry and desperate, and more interested in the food than the guns."

"He's telling the truth," Malachi added.

"Take off your guns and drop them to the ground. The rifle, too," she ordered them.

Austin looked at Malachi and gave a quick nod. They both did as they'd been told. Another woman emerged from the ranger's shack and approached, grabbing the guns. The women directed them to follow them toward the shack, and then stopped them when they were a few yards away.

"Get down. We'll give you water and that's it," the woman who'd first approached told them.

"Thank you," Austin said, knowing it was Malachi's presence that had persuaded her to help them.

She didn't want to hurt a kid. That was going to work in Austin's favor.

"Move down the trail," the woman ordered.

Austin turned around, surprised to discover two more women now, their guns pointed at him and Malachi as they stood to either side of the trail. He guessed they were hikers judging by the way they were dressed. They were all lean and looked to be in good physical condition, if not a little on the thin side. They watched him and Malachi as they passed on the horses.

The trail led into a makeshift campground complete with an outhouse. It would have been a basecamp for hikers making the long, challenging trek over the Rocky Mountains. He'd never understood the desire to want to hike hundreds of miles for the sheer joy of saying you'd done it.

They kept walking past the tents until he found himself in what had to be a park. A picnic table was positioned under a small wooden cover with a grill a couple feet away from where they brought the horses to a standstill and dismounted as directed. He remembered the many parks he and Savannah had stopped in on their travels across the country. This one was clearly a day-use park for those who wanted to escape the city for the day and enjoy a little nature.

"Sit," the woman barked out.

Austin was more than happy to take a seat at the metal table. Malachi sat on the opposite side of the table, facing Austin.

"Cara, get them water. Dana, take care of the horses," the first woman instructed.

"Thank you," Austin said again, turning his head to face the woman now standing at one end of the picnic table, the gun still pointed at him.

"Whatever. We're not killers. You know we can't have you stay, right?" she asked.

Austin nodded, studying the woman's features and guessing her to be in her early twenties. "We don't want to stay."

"How long have you been up here?" Malachi asked.

The woman stared at him, clearly sizing him up before she answered. "Since it happened."

"How did you know about it?" Austin asked.

She shrugged. "We met some people on the trail. They told us the world had gone mad. I didn't believe them at first. We hiked into the city and saw what was happening. We gathered what we could and came back up here. We don't see a lot of people this high up."

Austin nodded. "I can see why."

Another young woman, brown-haired and petite, delivered them two tin cups filled with water. Austin wasn't going to question whether it was safe to drink. He grabbed the cup and gulped it down. Malachi did the same.

"The horses are being given some water, as well," Cara said with a friendly smile.

"Thank you, truly, I appreciate it," Austin told them, glad to have run into them.

"It's going to be dark soon. We can offer you shelter for the night, but then you'll have to go in the morning," the leader announced.

Her offer of shelter took him by surprise. "Really?" he asked.

She offered a small smile. "Yes, really. We're not bad people. We're trying to live and let live, nothing more."

Austin looked at Malachi before nodding. "We'd appreciate that. We've been up since daybreak," he explained.

"You came all the way from the city?" the woman asked with shock.

Austin shook his head. "No. We've been moving for several days, camping out overnight and then getting up to keep going again the next day."

"Where are you going?" she asked.

He had to think fast. "Salt Lake, maybe. Anywhere, really. Denver is too dangerous, and we don't have the means to live out here," he lied.

That seemed to relax the woman a bit more. "I'm Tara, by the way. We'll get you guys something to eat and then turn in for the night. We get up early," she explained.

Austin nodded, exhausted and ready to close his eyes. He could tell their hosts were still wary and weren't giving them free rein of the camp. That was fine with him. It wasn't long before Dana appeared, carrying a plate of what looked like some kind of small cooked birds.

"It isn't much, but it's all we can offer," Tara said, putting the plate between Austin and Malachi.

"It looks great, thank you," Austin told the three women.

He wondered where the fourth was, suspecting she was probably keeping guard somewhere. They were acting nice, but he sensed they weren't quite as innocent and easygoing as they looked.

After their meager dinner, they were taken back to the shack they had first come upon and ordered to go inside. The space was maybe eight by eight, with no furniture at all, but there were a couple of blankets neatly folded in the corner. The windows had been boarded over—that was something that happened while they had been enjoying their dinner, which instantly put him on alert.

"I'm sorry, but you'll understand that, for our own safety, we have to have you stay in here tonight," Tara announced. "We'll let you out in the morning and you can be on your way," she said, closing the door and plunging them into darkness.

"This doesn't feel right," Malachi whispered.

Austin took a deep breath. "No, it doesn't. I don't think they have any intention of freeing us in the morning," he whispered, angry with himself for letting them be taken prisoner.

They heard the women outside and Austin pressed his ear to the door, listening to their conversation.

"It's him, isn't it?" one of them asked.

"I think so. Six foot, tattoos, blue eyes and dark hair. How many guys like that have you seen around here?" a quiet voice replied.

"Do you think they'll actually give us the reward?" one of them asked.

"We'll get the reward and then hand him over." He recognized that voice as Tara's.

It grew quiet, and he realized the women were walking away, still talking, but he couldn't make out the words. Their female captors weren't nearly as innocent and peaceful as they claimed.

"Were they talking about you?" Malachi asked, his breath washing over Austin's face.

"Certainly sounds like it. I guess I have a price on my head. That's new," he grumbled.

30

Amanda wasn't happy. No one had wanted to go with her to the mine. Ennis and Wendell had decided it was more important they work on the security of the house and set more booby traps, rather than go in search of Nash. Savannah had volunteered to go along, but that wasn't an option. Austin would kill her if something happened to his daughter. Some of the revivalists had looked like they were considering volunteering, but in the end they'd all opted to leave Nash to his own devices and work around the house, some of them openly assuming that he must simply have moved on and that looking for him was a waste of time.

She angrily snapped a branch that was hanging in her way as she stomped through the forest. "Selfish jerks," she muttered.

Wendell had almost seemed happy that Nash was missing or had chosen to leave the group. She couldn't help but think he had something to do with the disappearance. He'd had that look in his eye that made her distrust him in general.

She'd packed extra food and water, anticipating she would find Nash along the way. He'd be tired from staying out in the forest all night. She'd lecture him and then they'd go back to the house; no harm, no foul. That's what she was hoping for. So far, though, she'd seen no sign of Nash, and it was worrying her all the more.

She knew she was close to the mine, however. She'd been walking fast, wanting to cover as much ground as possible. The extended daylight worked to her advantage. She'd be able to make it back to the house before nightfall—she hoped.

"A-ha!" she exclaimed when she recognized the area. She quickly covered the remaining distance to the mine entrance, her legs burning after the long journey. She could feel sweat pooling at the small of her back and reached behind her to lift her shirt away.

She stepped inside the mine after taking a moment to sip her water, pulling out the glowstick she'd brought along and quickly snapping it, slapping it against the rock wall to make it glow bright. Her eyes adjusted to the dim glow, allowing her to see clearly. She walked along, remembering what Nash had told her about the door off to the side. He was either here or he wasn't, and if he wasn't, then she was back to square one, but at least she'd have checked the most obvious option.

She found the door in no time. It was hanging open, exposing the contents of the room. Cable sat coiled in a corner, and just beyond it, she could see the door Nash was convinced held more secrets. If the documents they'd read were factual, the door could be the opening to an underground lair for the bad guys.

"Please tell me you didn't get in there," she whispered, pulling the gun from the holster on her thigh and holding it in front her while she held the glowstick in her other hand.

She froze when she saw the pack on the floor. *Nash's.* She spun around, clearing the room before moving to the pack and lifting it up. There was a dark stain on the ground. She shone the light over it and determined it was blood. She stood holding the light in front of her, aiming at the solid door and trying to decide what to do. She could see indentions marring the smooth metal surface.

"Noo, no, no," she muttered, realizing the dimples were caused by bullets.

She focused on the ground and found brass casings scattered around the area. Someone had opened fire in the room. She focused on the small stain that was no bigger than the size of a fifty-cent piece, and then looked around. There wasn't a lot of blood. It could have been from a small cut, she reasoned. If Nash had been standing where she was and been hit by a bullet, there would have been more blood, she told herself, trying to make herself believe Nash was okay.

Out of pure curiosity, she tried to open the door, unsure what she would do if it actually opened. If Nash was right and the door led to some secret hideout, she didn't want to just waltz in like she owned the place. But the door didn't budge. She looked around the room again. Nash had to have been taken inside. He wouldn't have run without his pack.

She reached down and ran her hand over the dark circle she saw in the pack, only now realizing it wasn't a stain. It was a hole—a bullet hole. "I've got to get help," she whispered, heading back into the mine and walking towards the entrance at a fast clip.

When she broke into the bright daylight, she looked around, paying more attention to the ground. The rain the night before had washed away any footprints that may have indicated how many people she would be dealing with when she came back. And that's when it hit her—she already knew what she was going to do. She was not going to leave Nash in that hole, no matter what.

She jogged toward the house, knowing there was no way she could make it there and back before darkness fell. Still, adrenaline pumped through her veins, giving her a fresh boost of energy and driving her to move faster. They couldn't afford to wait. Nash had been gone a full day. He was being held prisoner and could very well be injured. They had to rescue him.

Amanda's heart raced, her breathing becoming labored as she pushed herself to keep moving. She couldn't slow down. Every minute counted. The heat was beginning to wane as the sun sank lower in the sky. She nearly walked right into one of the booby traps in her haste to get back to the house, narrowly avoiding a bucket of rocks being dumped on her head.

She found Ennis sitting on a stone, sharpening a branch into what looked like a spear. "They have him!" she exclaimed, standing in front of him and gasping for air.

"What? Who has him? Who's him?" Ennis asked.

"In the mine. They have Nash," she managed to get out.

"Are you sure?" he asked, lowering the stick and folding the blade back into his knife.

She nodded. "Yes. There're signs of a gun battle. I found his pack. It had a bullet hole and there was some blood on the ground. I think they took him through the door. We have to go back for him."

"What door?" he asked, looking around behind her as if someone might have followed her.

"The door!" she shrieked. "The same door he's been telling us about! The same door that's outlined in the documents Callum passed off to Austin!"

She felt frantic, and she wanted to shake Ennis until he listened and understood.

"Do we know he's alive?" he asked after a moment.

Her eyes widened. "I don't know, but we can't leave him! We've got to try and save him!"

"I'll go," Ezra said, coming to stand next to her.

Amanda turned to look at him. "You will?" she asked, knowing there'd been some tension between them.

"Yes. I'm a pretty good shot now. I'll go back with you," he replied. "I really thought he'd just left or I would have gone with you before."

"We'll need a few others," Amanda said, already planning the rescue mission in her mind. The more people they had on their side, the better the odds of a successful rescue mission.

"I'll talk to Jordan. Mike will probably go; maybe Harlen, too," he said.

Amanda was nodding. "Thank you. We have to leave first thing in the morning, earlier if we can. I don't think it's safe to try and move through the forest tonight, but we have to be ready early," she repeated, her hands shaking as the adrenaline that had fueled her return slowly ebbed.

"You need something to drink," Ennis said, putting an arm around her shoulder and guiding her toward the house's entrance.

It was the first kind gesture he'd shown her in a while. "Thank you," she said, her voice barely above a whisper.

Ennis walked with her inside the house, and they found Tonya cleaning up the kitchen.

"What is it?" she asked, her voice full of fear.

"I'll get you a drink," Ennis said, moving towards the pantry.

He returned a few seconds later, handing her a bottle of vodka. She took a swig straight from the bottle, letting the alcohol calm her nerves.

Then, Amanda collapsed onto a barstool and quickly retold

the story of what she'd found, leaving out some of the information about what might be behind the door. None of that mattered to her. They had to get Nash back, and if they were lucky, maybe they'd see what was worth hiding and trying to kill for.

"We have to get in that door. It's solid, but maybe a tire iron will work," Amanda mused aloud.

Ennis cleared his throat. "I might have something that can take care of the door."

"What?" Amanda asked.

"It's a little plastic explosive," he said, offering a small smile.

"C-4?" she asked with shock.

He shrugged. "Basically. It'll get the door open."

"I'm not even going to ask how or why you have it. That should definitely do the job, plus providing enough of a distraction for us to find Nash, assuming he's being held in there somewhere," Amanda said.

"I can go along," Gretchen volunteered.

Amanda looked at her. "Thank you. It might be dangerous. No, it *will* be dangerous, but I could really use your shooting skills."

"It's fine. I'm in. He's one of us, and I want to get him back," Gretchen replied.

"Then it's settled," Ennis declared. "We'll get things ready, and the five of you will set out as soon as it's safe to do so in the morning. The rest of us will stay here and guard the house," he said.

Amanda looked around the kitchen that was now filled with the revivalists. Wendell was hanging back, leaning up against a wall and watching it all. He hadn't volunteered to go along, which wasn't all that surprising. God forbid the man actually lift a finger to help anyone else, she thought to herself.

31

"When I say go, run—don't stop, don't look back. Don't worry about me, either," Austin whispered through the thick darkness in the shack.

"I will," Malachi answered.

"They want me. If you can get away, do it," Austin reiterated, regretting he'd ever allowed Malachi to come along. "Get back to the house and let them know they aren't safe. The reward on my head is going to make all of you targets."

Tonya would be crushed if something were to happen to her son, and Austin wasn't going to take away her only child. He simply refused to let that happen.

"Got it."

"I heard the horses, so they're close. I don't know how long we've been in here, but let's hope the women are asleep by now," he said, hoping their captors weren't all that skilled in the art of prisoner-taking and that they'd gone to bed with the falling night.

They had to get away before the soldiers showed up. Austin had no doubt in his mind that one of the women would set out with daybreak in search of NWO soldiers to fetch the reward for capturing him. But now that Austin had spent some time using his hands to push apart the slightly rotted wood that had been used to cover one of the windows, it was time to move. He pushed more, until he felt it give, and then worked the other side. He was confident he could break it free with some hard hits.

"Ready?" he asked Malachi, unable to see the kid, but feeling his shoulder brush against his lower arm.

"Ready."

"On the count of three," Austin whispered. "One, two, push!" he whispered loudly.

Together, the two of them pushed hard on the board, feeling it give way.

"Again," he ordered.

On the third try, the board hung off to the side. Austin gave it a good whack with his palm and pushed it all the way off before crouching and forming a step for Malachi to use to escape out the window. Malachi was thin and agile, and quickly jumped through the window. Austin never heard him hit the ground.

He waited, listening for sounds that would indicate their

captors knew they were making a break for it. They heard nothing.

"Clear," Malachi whispered.

Austin was too big to fit through the window, which meant Malachi would have to open the door. He hoped there wasn't a lock—if there was, Austin was going to be stuck unless Malachi could find some way to break in, but at least Malachi would be free.

Austin listened to the sound of something moving against the door. A second later, it swung open, Malachi's white grin barely visible in the dark of night.

He didn't hesitate a second. They headed in the direction Austin had heard the horses and found them standing in the shadows, still saddled as if they'd been waiting. Austin and Malachi hopped up and rode off, doing their best to be as quiet as possible.

When they had ridden at least a mile from the camp, Austin finally allowed himself to breathe a sigh of relief.

"Good job, kid," he said to Malachi.

"Anytime," Malachi said with a chuckle.

"I don't know what time it is or how long until daylight, but we need to keep going. The house should be close. I saw the park on the map. I think we're about five miles west of it," Austin guessed. "We'll rest some when we get closer and try to approach first thing in the morning rather than surprising her in the middle of the night."

"I'll follow you," Malachi replied.

They rode for a few hours, not daring to stop for a break until they were a good distance away from the campground. The going was slow as they had to carefully navigate the steep, rocky terrain. Finally, they stopped and rested, taking turns shutting their eyes against the night and getting some brief shut-eye while the horses rested. When dawn came, they were moving again.

"It's got to be around here," Austin mumbled, looking at the barren terrain after they'd traveled for another hour.

There wasn't a house in sight. There wouldn't be, however. It would be well-camouflaged, he realized.

"Look over there." Malachi pointed into the distance.

Austin looked in the general direction, not sure what the kid saw. He blinked several times, and that's when he realized that the hill, covered with tall weeds, was an odd shape. It was almost a perfect dome.

"Good job!"

They rode towards the house that had been built partially underground, grass grown over the top of it. It would be almost invisible from the air. As they got closer, it became a little more apparent. The brown spot was the door, disguised as a rock formation.

"Ready for this?" Austin asked.

Malachi shrugged. "I hope she's a lot nicer than those other women."

"Let's leave the horses to graze over here. I don't know what to expect from this woman. Be ready to run if I tell you."

"What if she isn't here?" Malachi asked.

"It's a possibility."

They walked towards the dome. Austin hated not having a weapon. It left him feeling vulnerable, but there was nothing to be done for it.

"Don't move." The deep voice had come from behind them.

Austin groaned. He was getting really tired of being taken by surprise. "We don't want any trouble. We're here to see Dr. Bastani," he said.

"I guarantee she doesn't want to see you," the voice replied.

Austin couldn't tell if it was a man or a woman speaking. He looked over his shoulder, catching a glimpse of a tall, scrawny woman with black curly hair and thick glasses. He had a strong suspicion she was the woman they were looking for. It wasn't like there'd be a lot of people living in the area.

"I'm unarmed," he said, slowly turning around.

"That's your mistake," the woman replied, the cocking of the gun a clear warning.

"We came here to talk to you about something important," Austin said.

"Who are you and how did you know about this place?" she asked, the gun still pointed at his chest.

"I'm Austin, and this is Malachi. Can we please talk?"

She spat on the ground. "I don't want to talk to anyone. The last couple of guys who came by to talk are providing fertilizer for my garden."

Austin's eyes widened at her bold threat. Callum could have warned him. She wasn't like any doctor he'd ever met.

"I was sent by Callum Barker," he said, and with the name, he watched the surprise come with recognition on her face.

"Callum? Where is he?" she asked.

"Dead," Austin replied.

"You killed him?" she replied, not sounding all that upset about the idea.

"No. We were meeting and a man open fired on us. Callum was shot and killed, but not before he gave me something I think you'll find interesting. He said to get it to you."

"You think I want it? What is it?" she snapped.

"It's a USB with some encrypted files on it. He left me a note saying you could open the files. The files have information about the EMP and who's behind it," Austin said.

She scoffed. "What good is a USB going to do?"

"I have a working laptop," he replied. His arms were growing tired.

"You have a working laptop. Well, shoot, do you want a prize?" she growled.

"Can I put my hands down? I'm not armed and we're not here to hurt you or rob you. We came up here because we're hoping you can open those files and tell us what Callum knew," he said.

She sighed, lowering the gun. "Fine. Come inside. I was about to have some coffee. You look like you could use some. You too, kid," she said, finally looking at Malachi.

They followed her in the small door, though Austin had to crouch down to avoid hitting his head. He was surprised to see how roomy the dome-style house was. There was a small kitchen area, a seating area, and a bed off to the side. A single door towards the back of the open space would likely be the bathroom, he guessed. There was a small pot-belly stove against the wall with a coffee pot sitting on top of it. He could feel faint heat coming from the area, evidence of an earlier fire.

Dr. Bastani gestured for Austin and Malachi to take a seat on the small sofa while she grabbed cups from her kitchen and filled them with the dark, fragrant liquid. Austin sipped the lukewarm coffee, appreciating the strength of it and waiting for the doctor to tell him what she knew—if anything.

She sat down in the wood rocking chair next to the stove. "I'm sorry you boys came all this way, but I can't help you."

"You have to help us," Austin insisted.

She guffawed. "I don't have to do anything. I've got the encryption software on discs, but it isn't going to do you any good."

"Can I have the discs anyway?" Austin asked, hoping Nash would know how to use them, or maybe Amanda.

"No. You won't know what to do with the program. Only a trained cryptologist will know how to decipher the information."

"Then come back with us," Austin insisted.

She shook her head. "I'll do no such thing."

"We can't sit on this information and do nothing. We need to know what they plan to do. That's the only way we can stop this," Austin hissed.

She shrugged. "You can't do anything. This is already happening. I tried to warn people and everyone ignored me. They all laughed at me, but I guess we know who's laughing now."

"You're right. They should have listened. But we need you now," Austin insisted.

"No. That's my final answer. Finish your coffee and get out of here. I don't like guests and I'm not going with you," she said, her voice firm.

Austin was tired, cranky, and sick of people telling him there was nothing he could do. His frustration had pushed him to the point of no return. He dropped the coffee mug and lunged for the woman. She shouted and tossed the cup of warm coffee at him, but he didn't stop his attack. He wrestled her to the ground instead, getting her belly on the floor so that he could sit on her back.

"Grab something to tie her up," Austin shouted at Malachi,

who was sitting on the couch, staring at him with a stunned look on his face even as Austin wrenched the woman's arms behind her back.

Malachi jumped up, looking around the room before he found a lamp. He yanked the cord, trying to pull it from the lamp, but it wouldn't give. Austin grew impressed with his ability to think on his feet as the kid raced into the kitchen area and grabbed a knife, slicing the cord.

"Here," he said.

"I have to hold her," Austin grumbled, barely able to keep the fighting woman restrained on the floor.

Malachi wrapped the cord around her wrists and tied a knot before Austin rolled off of her. She was still kicking and hollering.

"I'll get another cord," Malachi said, running to the other lamp in the room and quickly slicing off the cord.

"Stop moving," Austin growled.

"I'm not going anywhere with you!" she shrieked.

"Yes, you are. Where are the discs?" he asked.

"I'm not telling you anything!"

"Malachi, search the place. Trash it if you're so inclined," Austin ordered.

"No! Stop! Wait!" the woman screeched.

Austin had had a gut feeling the woman wouldn't want her

place trashed. Everything was in its place. It was all too perfect. He suspected she was a little on the OCD side.

"In the bottom drawer," she hissed.

Malachi rushed to the side of the room where a chest of drawers was pushed against the wall; he yanked it open and, after moving some clothes around, pulled out a small plastic case.

"This?" he asked.

"Yes, you little brat," she snarled.

"Good, let's go," Austin said, getting to his feet and easily lifting the slightly-built woman.

He tossed her over his shoulder in a fireman's carry and walked out the door. He was not in the mood to ask her to pack or if she needed anything else. It would take all day to get back to the house—hopefully, no longer than that. He was anxious to get back and finally find out what was on the drive.

32

It felt weird to be around the house with so few people about, but Savannah actually felt like a valuable member of the team while carrying the small pistol Uncle Ennis had given her to protect herself. Now, though, she walked along the perimeter Ennis had instructed her to patrol. Drew, Audrey, and Bonnie were on the opposite side of the house, putting in more booby traps and keeping their eyes and ears open for soldiers in the area.

"Are you supposed to be out here by yourself?" Wendell asked as he walked towards her out of the brush.

"I'm on duty. Uncle Ennis wants me watching for any intruders," she answered.

"With a gun, even. Your dad won't be happy when he sees that," he quipped.

"My dad knows I can handle a gun," she retorted. "What are *you* supposed to be doing?" she asked.

He shrugged. "I'm watching the house. Ennis took Harlen and Tonya with him to check the traps and make sure no one's been sneaking around the property. Apparently, Harlen is some excellent tracker now," he grumbled.

Savannah ignored his snide comments. She'd come to realize Wendell didn't like anyone except for Ennis and maybe her. She wasn't entirely sure he wasn't nice to her face and then turned around to talk bad about her to anyone who would listen, but she didn't have reason to think he disliked her yet. Her dad had told her not to trust him, though, and she was taking that advice.

"We all have to do our part," she replied.

"I suppose. Are you worried about your dad and your boyfriend?" Wendell asked with a grin.

"I don't have a boyfriend," she replied quickly.

"Good. I don't think your dad would allow it anyway."

She rolled her eyes. "It isn't up to my dad."

"Why would you want that kid anyway?" he asked as he fell into step beside her. "They're weird. All of the God squad is a little out there. Every time I turn around, one of them is praying for something."

"I don't think they're weird. They just have some strong beliefs. That's not a bad thing. They're nice people," she offered.

"Whatever you say. I don't trust them," he snapped.

She laughed. "I don't think you trust anyone."

He only shrugged. "You're right about that. Trust no one but yourself is what I always say."

"That's a rough way to live," she told him.

"What's with you and Malachi anyway? Are you trying to get with Nash? I heard there were some things said," he said.

She shook her head, knowing he was looking for gossip. "There's nothing with me and Malachi. His parents told him to stay away from me. They're convinced I'm the spawn of Satan," she said with a disgust.

Wendell threw his head back and laughed. "That's funny. The dad is dead, and the mom seems to be a little out of it most of the time. If you want that kid, I think you can persuade him. You're a pretty girl, but if I were you, I would hold out for something better."

She shuddered with revulsion at his weird compliment. "I—"

The wind was knocked from her lungs as she was tackled to the ground from behind. Her hands broke her fall, her palms cutting on the jagged rocks and sticks littering the ground as her knees slammed into more rocks before she dropped flat to her stomach.

Wendell actually shrieked and attempted to flee, but her attacker launched off of her and tackled him to the ground. Savannah tried to get to her knees, but her chest felt constricted, sending her into brief panic as she struggled to breathe.

Wendell was rolling on the ground, his arms and legs flailing as the man in a black uniform tried to restrain him. Savannah finally managed to suck in a gasp of air and lunge at him, knocking him off Wendell.

"Gun," she gasped as they fell sideways.

Her single word was lost on Wendell, who had scrambled to his feet and taken off running for the house. The man in black pushed Savannah away and went after him. Savannah staggered to her feet, looking around for the gun that had been in her hand when she'd been knocked to the ground.

She found it and raced towards it. Out of the corner of her eye, she saw the man coming back for her. He was fast on his feet —there was no way she could get the gun and shoot him before he was on her again. Instead of trying, she raced into the trees, dodging and weaving around massive trunks and going right through the thorny shrubs that seemed to be everywhere.

Savannah wasn't sure where she was going. She simply moved fast, without the time to orientate herself to her surroundings. She saw an opening in the trees up ahead and thought it signaled the road they took to go to the fishing hole. She raced towards it, realizing too late that it wasn't a clearing, but a ravine. She tried to stop, her arms flailing out as she fought to keep her balance.

It was no use—she was sliding, falling twenty feet down, her arms and legs bumping against rocks as she fell. She barely managed to keep her head protected as she slid down the side of the steep ravine. She hit bottom and looked up to see her pursuer on the edge of the ravine, looking for the best way down. Her body ached and her skin stung in the places that had been scraped on the way down as she forced herself to push away the pain and get up.

"Help!" she screamed, hoping Ennis or someone was nearby.

Her eyes darted around the unfamiliar area as she got to her feet once again, prepared to run for her life. There was a shout then, drawing her attention back to the man in the black jumpsuit. He was rolling down the hill, Wendell standing on the ledge above and looking very satisfied.

Savannah lunged, picking up a rock the size of a softball, ready to hit the man with it the moment he wasn't a moving target. The man stopped rolling and got to a sitting position. Savannah stood a few feet away.

"Don't move!" she shouted.

The man had blood streaming down his face. He looked up at her, his eyes glazed. She could see he was seriously injured, swaying where he sat, his hand covering the wound on his head with blood trickling out from between his fingers.

"Let me go," he muttered.

She scoffed. "Yeah, right! You nearly killed me."

"I was only trying to talk to you," he insisted.

"Do you normally jump on people you want to talk to?" she snapped.

"My name is Fabio. I don't want to hurt you. I'm looking for a man, Merryman. I swear, I only wanted to talk to you," he said, his words beginning to slur. "There's a reward."

Savannah felt fear running through her. They knew her dad and they were searching for him. If this man had made it that close to the house, the others wouldn't be far behind. She looked up and saw Wendell daintily coming down the hillside, over where it was less steep and a lot less rocky.

"I don't know anyone by that name," she lied.

He nodded. "Okay, I'm sorry. I'm going to go," Fabio said, holding up his hand and trying to smile.

She smirked. "I don't think so."

"Where's your gun?" Wendell asked, rushing to her side.

"Back there somewhere," she muttered. "Where's yours?"

"I didn't have one," he replied sheepishly.

"What do we do with him?" she whispered.

Wendell looked at her, apparently surprised she'd asked him. "I don't know. We can't leave him out here. He'll go back and tell his people."

She looked at the rock in her hand. "I can't kill him," she said, her gut rolling with the very thought of it.

"Well, I'm not going to kill him," Wendell said with horror.

"I promise, let me go and I won't tell anyone you're here," Fabio said, his voice growing weaker.

"I don't believe you, Fabio," Wendell replied.

"Please," Fabio said, swaying heavily before falling backwards into the ground.

Wendell and Savannah stared at him. "Did he faint?" Savannah asked.

Wendell moved to pick up a stick. He carefully approached the man, jabbing his side with the stick. The man didn't move.

"Maybe he's dead?" Wendell suggested.

"Check!" Savannah shrieked.

"No way! You check!" Wendell shot back.

"Oh my God, you're such a pansy. Move," she stomped towards him, keeping the rock in her hand. She stared at the man's chest, seeing it rise and fall. "He's alive."

"So, now what? Do we run?"

"Like you did earlier?" Savannah said, glaring at him.

"I was going to get help," he said, looking extremely guilty.

"Sure, you were. So where is it? Look, we can't leave him out here. When he wakes up, the first thing he's going to do is tell his people."

"Are you saying we're going to take him to—"

He stopped talking when she put her finger to her lips. "I'm saying, we tie him up out here. Somewhere no one will find him. We'll need to gag him," she said, nodding as the idea bloomed in her head.

"With what?" Wendell asked.

She sighed. "Go get some rope."

When it looked like he would protest, she gave him a look that she'd practiced on her father many times. Wendell nodded and headed off back up the hill, leaving her alone with the soldier. She stared down at his bloodied face. He was probably Nash's age, she realized. It was sad. He was so young and already doing horrible things. She stepped away from him, keeping her eyes on him and remaining ready to throw the rock at him if he moved.

It felt like forever before Wendell returned. He wasn't alone. Ennis was racing along behind him and nearly tumbled down the hill.

"Are you okay?" he gasped, holding her by her arms and looking her over.

"I'm fine, just a few bruises," she assured him.

"Help me tie him up," Wendell said.

"Tie him up? For what? Wendell told me you were going to tie him up and leave him in the woods. Why? We have to kill him," Ennis insisted.

"No!" Savannah near shouted.

Ennis turned to look at her. "Savannah, he's one of them. He'll kill us if given the chance."

"We can't kill him. He's unconscious and unarmed," she insisted.

Ennis turned back to look at the man still lying unconscious on the ground. "Where's his gun?" he asked.

Savannah rolled her eyes. "I don't know. I didn't stop to ask while he was chasing me."

"Is he out here all alone?" Ennis asked.

"I doubt it. He told me he was looking for a man named Merryman," she said quietly.

Ennis's mouth dropped open. "What did you say?" he whispered.

"Nothing."

"Are we going to kill him?" Wendell asked a little too eagerly.

Savannah glared at him. He was clearly okay with killing a man as long as he didn't have to do it. Ennis put his hand on the butt of the gun resting in a holster at his side. He looked at Savannah apologetically.

She shook her head. "No, you can't do that. Uncle Ennis, look at him—he's probably seventeen or eighteen. He's only doing what he's been told. He doesn't have a choice!" she pleaded.

Ennis put a hand on her shoulder. "I'm sorry, but if he lives, we won't be safe."

Wendell stood next to Ennis, his back to the unconscious man on the ground. "Sorry, kid, but I agree with your uncle. I don't care if he's fifteen or fifty. He was too close to—" He stopped himself before he blurted out what he'd clearly been about to, that they were close to the house.

"Shh," Savannah hissed, not wanting to say too much in case the guy was playing possum.

"Ow!" Wendell shouted, his hand going to the back of his head before spinning around. "He threw a rock at me!" he shrieked.

Their supposedly unarmed attacker was now holding a knife and staring at them. "I'm leaving," he hissed, as if talking hurt him.

"I'm bleeding," Wendell wailed.

"Shut up!" Savannah shouted.

Ennis reached for his gun, and Savannah wished she would have let Ennis shoot him when he'd been unconscious.

She screamed when Fabio threw the knife at Ennis. Ennis shouted, jumping out of the way of the incoming knife, pushing Savannah to the ground as he moved. The knife landed inches from where Savannah fell. Ennis was already up, the gun pulled from his holster. He pulled the trigger over and over again, trying to shoot Fabio as he stumbled off through the trees.

Wendell stood in shock, staring at Ennis and then Savannah. Ennis lowered the gun, running a hand over his face.

"Now what?" Savannah whispered.

"Now, we get back to the house as fast as we can. They're going to be coming for us, and it isn't going to be Fabio by himself," Ennis said, dread in his voice.

"My head," Wendell whined.

"You'll live. Let's go," Ennis ordered, helping Savannah to her feet.

Her mind was reeling. What would happen now? Would an army show up at the house? They couldn't possibly hold them back. She fought back the tears that were threatening to fall. She needed her dad. He would know what to do.

33

Amanda hoped the explosives worked. They could end up blowing themselves up and getting Nash killed, assuming he wasn't already dead. It was risky, but it was their only option. The five of them were doing their best to be as quiet as possible as they worked. They didn't want to alert whoever was beyond the door of their presence.

"What if they have a security system?" Ezra whispered.

Amanda shrugged in the darkness. They had a glowstick inside a sock, muting the light to keep from drawing too much attention to themselves while they carefully placed the explosive in the crevice around the heavy door. Amanda's hand was in a sock, too, protecting her skin from touching the explosive. She used her fingers to push the putty-like substance as far in around the hinges and the lock as she could before carefully placing one end of the detonator into the C4 and unfurling the thin wire as she walked backwards. There was no guarantee this would work. There was also no guarantee they'd find Nash beyond the door.

"Let's move out," Amanda hissed once the explosives were placed on either side of the door and they'd rolled out the cord leading to the detonator. "We wait in the main tunnel. Ezra and I will go back inside while the rest of you wait here, covering us. If Nash is in there, we'll bring him out."

"We don't know how big that bunker is or if it leads to another tunnel," Mike answered.

Amanda shook her head. "No, we don't. We don't know anything. This is all chance and luck. If you guys want to say a prayer right about now, I wouldn't mind," she muttered.

It was a huge risk, and the more she let herself think about the million different things that could go wrong, the more worried she got. She had to push all of that to the side. In her mind, they were killing two birds with one stone. They were rescuing Nash and finding out what was on the other side of the door. She could already hear Austin lecturing her. She only hoped she lived long enough to hear the real thing.

There was a shuffling of feet as they all moved out of the room, lining up against the smooth, damp walls of the mine entrance. Mike and Gretchen headed toward the entrance, prepared to be the surprise attack should NWO soldiers flood out through the exploded door. It would have made sense to have them deeper in the mine, hiding in the darkness, but for the possibility of a cave-in. In case that happened, they might be needed to dig the others out, if anything.

Amanda's heart raced as she held the tiny trigger in her hand. She wasn't big on praying, but she did it anyway. Ezra's rapid breathing on the other side of the opening told her he was just as nervous as she was.

"One, two—" she whispered before turning her head, shielding her body with the heavy rock wall and flipping the trigger.

The explosion was instantaneous. The sound echoed through her ears, vibrating her chest and shaking the mine around them, though the dreaded cave-in didn't come. She blinked several times before turning to look towards the door. She could see nothing through the rock dust and dirt that had been stirred up.

"Did it work?" Jordan asked.

"I can't see—where's that glowstick?" Amanda hissed, holding out her hand.

A second later, the area was flooded in a warm light. "Oh no," Ezra muttered.

The door was still in place.

"No!" Amanda gasped, realizing they had failed. The door was much more durable than she'd thought.

She didn't have time to be disappointed, however. The door was thrown open and several men in black jumpsuits started pouring out, reminding her of ants fleeing a drowning anthill.

"Now!" Ezra shouted, pushing Amanda out of the entrance.

She dropped to one knee, pulling up her rifle and beginning to open fire. Anyone that came out of the tunnel was the target. She used the wall both as a shield and a support as she fired the AR15. Ezra was on the opposite side of the opening doing the same thing. Jordan's knee was rubbing against the back of her head as he stood over her. They continued laying down fire until men stopped coming out of the tunnel. It had been a lot like shooting fish in a barrel.

Jordan's hand touched her shoulder. "Clear!" he shouted.

The sound of gunfire still echoed in her ears. The fight had probably only lasted thirty seconds, but it had felt like hours to her poor, throbbing eardrums.

"I'll check," Ezra said, stepping into the room and kicking weapons towards Amanda, who knelt on the floor, grabbing them and sliding them into the open tunnel to be packed up by the others.

Mike and Gretchen appeared from where they'd been waiting in the dark.

"What happened?" Mike asked.

"The door's open and there was some resistance. They're all down," Ezra replied.

"We have to get Nash," Amanda said, getting to her feet.

"There could be more soldiers waiting beyond that door," Mike pointed out.

"Then we go in guns blazing," she replied. "This is why we came, right?"

Each of them checked their weapons, picking up the weapons and ammo taken off the soldiers lying dead in the room and, in a single file procession, heading through the door.

"Do you feel that?" Jordan whispered.

Amanda nodded. "Fans," she replied.

There were small lights along the floor of the tunnel, much like one would see on a runway. The hum and air swishing around them told her there was a ventilation system running. The documents on the drive had been right—this was an underground lair of sorts.

They walked another fifty feet until the tunnel opened into a room with computer screens glowing on the far wall.

"Don't take another step," a male voice growled from her left.

She turned to find a gun aimed at her head. Another man all in black glared at her.

"We're here for our friend," she replied, not letting her voice reveal her fear.

"I don't care why you're here. Drop the gun," he ordered.

Amanda looked to her right, seeing Ezra beside her. She hoped Mike had hung back like she'd told him to. Her eyes scanned the room, noting that while there were a few men and women sitting at the computers, they were all looking at her with terror on their faces. She spotted only one other guard, his gun aimed at Ezra. Two guards, then. They could take them, if they could make the first move.

"Where's our friend?" she asked, not lowering her gun.

"Drop the gun or I'll drop it for you," he growled.

Amanda looked to Ezra, giving him a brief nod. Together, they lowered their guns to the floor, putting their hands in the air.

"There. Now, where's our friend?"

"The other two," he replied.

Amanda let out a breath of frustration, turning to look behind her at Jordan and Gretchen. "Do it."

They complied, and the four of them stood with their hands in the air. Amanda's attention was drawn to the computer screens. She could see what looked like a satellite network on one screen.

"Are we going to tie them up?" the other soldier asked, his voice full of hesitation.

Amanda looked from one guard to the other, then the slack-jawed computer geeks. She had a feeling their timing couldn't have been better. They were dealing with the C-squad.

"Look, we just want our friend and then we'll leave," she said, her tone soft.

"They've seen the systems!" one of the computer geeks worried out loud.

"I don't know anything about computers," Amanda said, shaking her head.

"Should I hit the button?" the geek asked.

Amanda raised her eyebrows, turning to look at Ezra. That sounded ominous.

"You don't need to alert anyone else. We don't want anything except Nash," she said.

"Alert," one of the geeks scoffed, as if the word *alert* was ridiculous.

"Not yet. If you hit that thing, we're all dead," the guard retorted.

Amanda's eyes jerked back to the man at the computer. It had to be some kind of self-destruct button they were talking about.

"We'll leave," Amanda said, knowing it was a long shot, but she had to try.

The first guard scowled. "Sure, you will."

She noticed Ezra out of the corner of her eye. He'd subtly moved his hand. When she met his eyes, he glanced behind her. She made no move, afraid to alert the guards to Mike's presence. Her heart was pounding so hard against her chest that she was convinced the guards would see it and know something was up.

"Down!" she heard Mike shout from behind her.

She didn't think twice, dropping flat on her stomach and reaching for the gun she had surrendered at the same time.

Ezra did the same. More gunfire echoed around the room. She was pulling the trigger immediately, not particularly aiming at any one person, but hoping to take out any others who may have been lurking in the shadows.

"Clear!" Mike shouted from above her.

Her heart was in her throat as she looked around at the mayhem. The two guards were down, as well as two of the geek squad. A third man was hiding under the desk, sitting in a puddle of what she assumed was his own pee.

"Grab him," she said to Ezra, getting to her feet.

"Is everyone okay?" Gretchen asked, coming to stand beside Amanda.

Amanda looked over at the redhead, her hands holding a gun that was literally vibrating in her hands.

"I'm good. Jordan?"

"Good," he called out as he stepped into the room, his gun leading the way with his finger hovering over the trigger.

One of the screens remained intact. Amanda slowly walked towards it, staring at the blip. "What is that?" she asked the man Ezra had just pulled up from under the desk.

The guy swallowed, his thick, black-rimmed glasses sitting askew on his face. Amanda guessed him to be in his early twenties. He was scrawny, pale, and looked like the epitome of a computer nerd.

"It's a satellite," he replied in a shaky voice.

"Why are you watching a satellite?" she asked him.

"We have to get out of here," his voice squeaked, ignoring her question.

"Why?" Ezra snapped, yanking the young man's arms up higher behind his back.

Amanda watched his gaze move to a small red button attached to a panel. Her heart sank. "You didn't!"

The kid shook his head. "I didn't, but he did," he said, nodding towards the dead nerd lying on the ground.

"What is that?" Ezra asked.

"Over here!" Mike shouted before the kid could answer Ezra's question.

"What is it?" Amanda called out.

"I've got Nash. He's in bad shape," Mike replied, fear sounding out in his voice.

"The button, what is it?" Ezra asked again.

"It's the self-destruct sequence. This whole place is going to go. No one can access this information," the kid replied, putting his chin up defiantly.

Amanda stared at him, and debated taking him hostage and questioning him further, but she was sure it would be pointless. Everyone in this room had died trying to protect whatever was happening in that bunker. He wouldn't talk. He'd be too afraid of the people behind the madness.

"Let's go," Amanda said. "Tie him up to his chair and let him have a front row seat to his actions," she ordered Ezra, rushing to where Mike had picked up Nash from what seemed to be the next room over.

She gasped, looking at Nash's bloodied face; his eye was swollen closed. He'd been beaten. He looked at her through his one eye, glazed and bloodshot. She wasn't even sure he was really looking at her.

"We've got you," she said softly, reaching her hand out to push aside a clump of his shaggy blonde hair, which was crusted with blood.

His cracked lips moved, and there was moaning, but no words. Her heart ached seeing him suffer. Mike apologized before tossing the man over his shoulder in a fireman's hold and heading towards the tunnel.

"Go!" Ezra shouted.

Amanda glanced back and noticed a red digital clock in the corner of the working screen. They had less than a minute. Without another word, they rushed back down the tunnel and out of the mine; they were in the parking lot when they heard a rumble below their feet. The earth moved, the cars abandoned in the makeshift lot vibrating.

"Go!" Amanda shouted as they ran as fast as they could away from the mine's opening.

The mine exploded behind them into a huge plume of dust, rock, and smoke. The group didn't stop running. Mike's brute strength combined with adrenaline kept him going under Nash's weight as they raced into the trees. Amanda checked to make sure they weren't being followed as they ran, but anyone in that mine had been killed. That was something.

34

Austin had grown tired of listening to the good doctor and her litany of complaints. The day had been long. They'd stopped only a few times to give the water they'd taken from Bastani's house to the horses. The horses were doing the heavy lifting and needed the water more than the riders. Malachi had chosen to walk part of the way, doing what he could to get away from the cranky doctor. Austin had walked for brief intervals, as well, just to give the horses a break from carrying three people.

He'd actually considered knocking Bastani out to make the ride a little quieter, but was worried his tactics would be too effective. He needed her awake and ready to get started with the process of opening the files as soon as they made it back to the house. They were making good time, though, which was about the only highlight of the annoying day.

"How did you know where I was?" she asked again from her place in front of Malachi.

Her hands were bound, and Austin had made it very clear he'd shoot her if she tried to run. He would, too. He was getting that tired of her.

"I told you. Callum. He had a Google pinpoint with your house's location," Austin said, his jaw clenched.

"This is not good. How many other people did he tell? There could be people crawling all over this area, and my place," she said.

"Which is why we need to get back to the house, where it's safe," said.

"Nowhere is safe. Don't you understand that?" she hissed.

He rolled his eyes. "Safe enough. It's safe enough for you to get to work on those files."

"Why? What's the point?" she spat out.

"The point is to try and fight them," he retorted.

She angrily shook her head. "These people are ruthless. They've killed and will continue to kill. We don't have what it takes to stop this."

"We have to try," he replied.

She scoffed. "You and a single computer are not going to be enough."

"We have you, and you can access those files. You can tell us how to combat them," Austin said, trying his best to keep his temper in check. "Callum wrote in his letter that the secret to defeating them is in the files. It's why he safeguarded them. He didn't want the wrong people to find the loophole and fix it."

"You don't understand. This thing has been building for years. They have underground dens, computers, satellites, and more weapons than the military," she said.

"What's that?" Malachi asked, pointing to the east.

Austin stared at the trail of smoke rising into the air. It was too close to be in the city. "I don't know. It could be a forest fire. It could be the NWO trying to burn people out."

He kicked Charlie, spurring him on, anxious to get back to the house. He guessed they were still at least three to five miles away.

"They're evil," Dr. Bastani whispered.

He nodded. "Yes, they are."

As they got closer to what he considered their safe haven, though, he heard the echo of gunfire. His mind raced with possibilities about what was happening. He wanted to believe it was only an echo, and that the gunfire was happening some-where far away from the house, but he couldn't.

"Is that gunfire?" Malachi asked.

Austin nodded. "Yes."

"Could they be target shooting?"

"No," Austin replied, knowing Ennis wouldn't waste that much ammunition on training. This was the real thing.

They kept up their pace, knowing it was risky to the horses to move this fast now that they were on rocky slopes again, but a sense of urgency drove him on. When they got within a mile of the house, it became clear the shooting definitely came from around the house.

"We need to go in slow," he said, slightly out of breath as he slowed Charlie.

"Is this what you call safe?" the doctor demanded.

"Shut up!" Austin snapped, fear for his daughter at the forefront of his mind.

The *tap, tap, tap* of repeated gunfire was becoming clearer as they rode closer. He glanced over at the doctor and realized he couldn't take her any closer, however. He couldn't risk her being killed, and he also wasn't about to arm the woman with the guns they'd taken from her place.

"Austin?" Malachi asked, looking at the back of the doctor's head.

"Over there," he said, nodding towards a stand of trees with several large rocks around the area. It would provide good cover for her while they went on.

"What are you doing?" Dr. Bastani asked frantically.

"We're leaving you here," he snapped, sliding off Charlie and walking the horse into the trees. "With the horses. We'll come back for you."

He reached up and pulled the doctor from the back of Raven, pulling her behind one of the rocks and using the cord in his bag to tie her to a tree.

"You can't leave me here!" she shrieked.

"Trust me, it's safer for you here than where the fighting is," he growled.

"Take me with you! I can help!" she cried out.

"Let's go," he said, ignoring her and walking the horses over to some trees, winding their reins around a branch.

"We leave the horses," he said, cutting off Malachi's protest. "They're too loud and too big. We need stealth."

Malachi caught up with him as he began moving toward the house at a cautious jog. "Are we really leaving her?" he asked.

"Yes, we need to reach one of the caches and arm ourselves with better weapons. The house is under attack," he said, looking at the landmarks and remembering where they had stashed some of the guns.

He was already moving toward a tree with a faint red X on it. Malachi sprang into action from beside him, his young, nimble body going up the tree and quickly pulling the guns from where they'd been stored inside several black plastic garbage bags.

They quickly loaded the weapons, Austin taking the AR they had taken from the NWO while Malachi took the twenty-two. Austin also checked the handgun that had been stashed in his holster, taken from Bastani's place.

"Watch for the traps we set," Malachi whispered as they started to move down the hill towards the house. The occasional sound of gunfire told him the battle was being dragged out. That was a good thing. It meant whoever was at the house was holding off the NWO.

Austin nodded, watching every step, which slowed his progress, but it was necessary. He caught a glimpse of the roofline of the house, an occasional gunshot followed by what sounded like firecrackers going off, cutting through the normally quiet forest.

"They're attacking from the front," Austin whispered. "We need to split up."

Malachi's eyes widened with fear. "What?"

Austin looked him in the eyes. "You can do this. We don't know who's in there. We need to get an idea of what's happening down there. We'll meet back here in, say, fifteen minutes if I don't see you down there. Take out as many as you can. Don't hesitate. This is life and death, Malachi," he said sternly.

"How do I know when it's been fifteen minutes?" he asked.

Austin sighed. "I don't know. Just get down there, look around, and then get your butt back here. If you see soldiers, take them out."

Malachi looked solemn as he nodded. "Okay."

Austin glanced back once, hating the idea of sending the kid off by himself but knowing they didn't have any other options.

They were stretched thin. He had no idea who was in the house. Part of him even hoped the house was empty. It was better than the alternative.

He approached one of the booby traps with great care. It was pointless. The trap had been triggered and the man who had triggered it was lying face first on the ground, knocked out cold. It had definitely been effective. He checked to make sure he wouldn't come to anytime soon, and reminded himself to come back and shoot him later. For now, he wanted to keep the element of surprise on his side.

"One down, and how many more to go?" he muttered, skirting the perimeter of the house as he moved around to get a better view of what was happening.

He heard a shout of pain followed by more shouts. The booby traps were proving effective. Then came more shooting and the acrid scent of smoke in the air. It didn't smell like the typical campfire or burning wood. There was something different about it. Tear gas, he realized. It was a smell he'd encountered before while overseas. The bangs he'd heard were probably flash-bang grenades. There was only one reason those would be used—the soldiers were trying to get someone out of the house.

His heart raced, knowing in his gut that that someone would likely be Savannah and some of the others. He couldn't very well take out an army, but he was sure going to try. He picked up his pace, moving closer to the house to avoid the booby traps that were on the outer perimeter.

He passed the makeshift barn and saw it had been ripped

apart. The sound of men's voices and the occasional crack of gunfire kept him moving down the hill, crouching low and doing his best to stay behind the trees. He strained his eyes to see through the trees, wanting to know exactly how many soldiers he was dealing with.

He could see the east side of the house now, but needed to move around to the front. From where he was positioned, he could see five of the NWO standing in a semi-circle in front of the house. He looked further down the driveway and could see a few more moving about. The sound of gunfire on the far west side worried him. That's where Malachi had headed.

Suddenly, the cold metal of what could only be a gun barrel was pressed against the back of his neck. "Peek-a-boo, I see you," a man said in a sing-song voice.

Austin groaned, cursing himself for not paying attention to his surroundings once again. He dropped his gun to the ground before putting his hands up.

"Up, slow and easy. Try anything and my friend will shoot you," a voice growled.

Austin rose to his feet and slowly turned to face the man who'd caught him unawares. "You got me."

The man raised an eyebrow. "You're him. Holy crap, you're him!" he said, a smile spreading over his face. "Look, Gary! I got him! We win!"

Austin shrugged. "I am *a* him."

The guy shook his head, turning to look at his buddy. "It's him. We got Merryman. Zander's going to love this."

"Zander?" Austin asked, dread coiling up in his gut.

"You didn't think you actually killed the guy, did you? He's immortal, like the undead. He's too mean to die," the man said, smirking.

Austin looked around, trying to find an escape route. There was no way he was going to go easy. He'd fight and take out as many of the soldiers as he could. If Savannah was in that house, he was going to do all he could to up her odds of surviving.

"Get Zander," the man ordered.

His partner scurried off into the trees while the first man held the gun on him, his finger on the trigger, making Austin a little nervous. If he slipped or sneezed, Austin would be shot. He made no attempt to escape now, though. He'd get his chance.

"Who's in the house?" Austin asked.

The man scoffed. "Your people."

"I have a lot of people, and I can guarantee you they're not all in that house. One could be walking up behind you right now," he said, hoping to get the man to lower his guard for a second —that's all he needed to make a move.

"Not going to work. Good try, though. I think it's your kid that's in there, to tell you the truth. Zander is pretty upset with her."

Austin didn't let his reaction show. He wouldn't give the man the satisfaction.

"He's mad he got outsmarted by a young girl. Understandable," Austin said easily.

"She didn't outsmart me," a voice replied, approaching through the trees.

Austin looked up and saw the man who'd nearly killed Savannah coming towards him. Hatred boiled in his blood as he sneered at Zander. He was going to kill him, and do it right the second time. Somehow.

"From where I stood, she did," Austin said, doing his best to play it cool.

"Search him," Zander ordered, ignoring his jibe.

The second man stepped forward, patting down Austin and removing his guns before reaching his hands deep into his pockets and finding nothing more than a lighter and some tinder he always carried around.

"Looking for anything in particular, or do you have a crush on me?" Austin asked with a smile.

The man stood up and looked at Zander, slowly shaking his head. "It's not here."

"Where is it?" Zander snapped.

"What is it that you're looking for?" Austin asked, knowing very well what it was.

"The USB. Give it to me now and I might let you live," Zander growled.

Austin guffawed. "We both know that isn't true."

"Where is it?" he snarled. "Tell me, and I'll think about letting that brat out of the house before we torch it."

Austin shrugged, not letting fear for Savannah show on his face. "I think I lost it."

"Shoot him in the knee," Zander ordered, as casually as if he were ordering a hamburger.

Austin didn't flinch. He wouldn't give Zander the satisfaction. He stared directly into the evil man's eyes instead, waiting for the shot that would leave him permanently crippled, assuming he lived at all.

35

Amanda dropped to one knee, aiming the Glock at her target. She released her breath and pulled the trigger. The look of shock on the man's face before he fell backwards in a dead drop was satisfying.

"Now," she said, her voice calm.

Jordan was standing next to her and took the next shot, but it was too late. Zander was already on the run, along with his lackey. Austin turned, looking in their general direction with an expression of surprise on his face. She stood and moved forward, watching as his face erupted into a smile.

"Thanks," he said, grinning. "Your timing is always spot-on."

She shrugged. "I seem to always find you in the worst situations. You're not allowed to hang out with that man anymore. It seems like he's always trying to kill you."

Austin rolled his eyes before turning to pick up the guns he'd been relieved of. "Someone's in the house."

"I know. I'm guessing it's Savannah, Wendell, and Ennis. We found Drew on our way back."

"What about the others?" he asked.

She shook her head, weight pressing on her. "I don't know for sure. They'd split up."

Austin looked up, hearing the stress that had come back into her voice. "What aren't you telling me?" he asked.

"Drew was with Audrey and Bonnie. They got taken by surprise."

Austin froze, his mouth opening and then shutting before he asked, more quietly. "They're both dead?"

She nodded. "Yes. Drew was shot in the upper arm, but it wasn't bad. I'll take care of it once this is all done."

"I hate that we lost them. They were good women."

She sighed. "It's sad, and I know the others are going to be devastated."

"Did you find Nash?" he asked.

She simply nodded and turned toward the house, not wanting to give him the specifics of Nash's condition. Not yet. Right now, they had to focus on saving Savannah and whoever else was trapped in the house. They'd decided early on that, if they were ever attacked, they'd all rendezvous a mile or so up behind the house, where the spring was. But they had to make sure everyone was out.

"I've heard some flash-bangs and I can smell what I think is either tear gas or pepper spray. I haven't been able to get close enough to see if the door's closed," he said, returning his focus to saving his daughter.

"The door is down; it has to be or they would have already gotten in," Amanda assured him. "They wouldn't be out here shooting if they could get inside."

"Which way did you come in from?" Austin asked.

"Southeast."

"Smell that?" Jordan asked.

"Fire!" Austin shouted, remembering what Zander had said.

"Wait! Amanda said, reaching for his arm. "I've got a group on the west side and some watching the south. We've got the east. We've got them surrounded. We take them out and then we worry about the house," she said.

"I'm not worried about the house, I'm worried about Savannah," he snapped.

"I know, I understand," she told him, holding his eyes with her own. "We'll get to her. They've probably got at least twenty guys down there, though. We need to be smart or they'll win this."

She watched him sag, relenting. "Okay," he grumbled.

"We need to move. Zander is probably already moving back up here with a small army."

"I really want to put a bullet between that man's eyes," Austin snapped, already stalking down the hill towards the house and moving toward the open area up-front, where she knew he'd be seen and shot if he didn't slow down. She rushed in behind him, ready to provide cover fire.

The smell of fire grew stronger as they moved, and Amanda suddenly worried they'd be too late. All she could do was hope the others had escaped the house. Harlen had said the trio had been inside, last he checked. Amanda had also left out the part about Savannah being banged up after a fall. Austin didn't need to know that just yet, either.

"Down!" Amanda hissed, seeing a contingent of men about twenty feet in front of them, their backs to them.

Austin dropped to his knees, Jordan beside him. There were few trees close to the house. The wild shrubs and plants weren't great cover and did little to actually hide them. Amanda knew that, if the men turned, they'd be seen.

"Now," Austin whispered, raising his gun and mowing down the men where they stood outside the burning house.

Amanda covered him, firing at the same time, unsurprised by his ruthlessness; the man was back in daddy-mode. He'd walk through fire to save Savannah.

"Ten o'clock," Jordan said, his voice steady as he used his own AR to start shooting the reinforcements.

The echo of gunfire from around the area made it hard to determine which way the shots were coming from. Amanda hoped her friends were doing the shooting. She'd had little time to give them direction about what to do except to move towards the house and kill every soldier on sight.

"Go, go, go," Austin said, making his way into the area just outside the house.

Amanda could feel the heat from the flames eating up the wall of the house. Ennis's SUV was also burning. She wasn't sure how much gas was left in the rig, but it would likely blow up. The soldiers who'd been in front of the house were all either dead on the ground or gone. Swirling at the sound of more gunfire, she watched a few more soldiers run down the driveway as others fell mid-step, with the ones who made it down the drive getting around the house only to be taken out by the team on that side of the property. There were more smatters of gunfire, shouts of pain, and then silence.

"I think they're on the run," Amanda said, a little shocked by the notion. She wasn't even sure any were left standing to run, at the moment.

At the thought of it, she couldn't help but smile a little, proud of the little army that had been born out of desperation. Then she looked over and saw that Austin was focused on the house, which was now fully engulfed by flame. She moved to stand next to him in the open area in front of the house, staring at the flames which had become tinged blue in places as the heat intensified. Jordan was at their backs, watching the driveway and surrounding trees with his gun at the ready.

"I can't—" Austin choked out the words.

Amanda wrapped her arm around his waist, pulling him against her. There was no getting into the structure now—they just had to hope the others had gotten out somehow. The lack of gunfire and shouting told her the soldiers had cleared out. Turning to look around, she noticed the others coming up from the driveway and emerging from the other side of the clearing where they'd eaten dinner and spent nights under the stars.

Everything was gone.

"We need to get back," Amanda whispered, pulling Austin with her. "Maybe they're out, waiting for us," she tried.

He was as stiff as a stone statue, his feet seemingly glued to the ground. "I can't," he said again.

She wasn't sure what he was trying to say. They had fought so hard together the past few months, and all of it had been to keep Savannah alive and safe. Her face felt hot as she turned to watch the devastation. One side of the house collapsed, the roof dropping into the burning inferno. She heard Austin gasp and felt his knees buckling.

"Jordan, help me," she said softly.

Jordan quickly put down his gun and went to Austin's other side, moving him back another twenty feet. Austin dropped to his knees there, his face twisted up in grief and pain that nearly tore out Amanda's heart. She looked around the group of people, noticing a few faces were missing.

There were tears streaming down some faces, looks of shock

on others. She could see a few with wounds that would need tending, but all of that could wait. None of them could pull themselves away from what was happening before them. The crackling fire with the occasional hiss and high-pitched squeal of something burning was mesmerizing, and the heartbreak in the air was palpable—no matter what she said, she also couldn't believe that the others had gotten out. Not with that steel door down and the NWO all around, just waiting to fire on it.

She knew they should be making an escape. The soldiers would be back. They'd regroup and be back for revenge.

In this moment, though, none of that mattered.

36

Austin stared at the flames that were just slowing down with little else to burn. He had no idea how long they'd watched the house burn. It felt like a lifetime. His mind was reeling, refusing to believe what he was seeing in front of him. He looked to his left, expecting to see Savannah standing there, horrified by the loss of the house and all their supplies. She wasn't. He looked to his right, seeing more faces, but none of them were his little girl.

There was a disconnect from it all, as if he were watching it all from somewhere else.

Savannah wasn't gone, though. She couldn't be. Life wasn't that cruel. He'd already lost enough; fate couldn't be so horrible as to take the one thing he had left in the world.

"Austin." Amanda's soft voice from beside him drew his attention.

He looked into her eyes, saw the sorrow, and reached for her. She held him close, her hand moving through his hair, murmuring words of comfort as she held him in her embrace. He let her hold him, letting her absorb some of the pain that was paralyzing him. He closed his eyes, trying to block everything out, but the heat, the smell, and the sounds of the fire refused to allow him the reprieve.

"I have to go get the doctor," he mumbled, suddenly remembering he'd left the woman tied to a tree.

"The doctor?" Amanda asked.

He could see the confusion in her eyes. So much had happened in the last forty-eight hours, he'd forgotten she hadn't been with him. He was so used to her always being there.

"Dr. Bastani," he clarified, his throat raw with grief.

"Where is she?" Amanda asked, not letting him go.

"On the hill behind the h—" he didn't finish the word. There was no longer a house.

"I need to check on Nash. I left Mike with him. He's in bad shape," she whispered.

Austin pulled away, looking at her face. "What?"

She nodded, slowly, regret clear on her face. "It's a long story, but we got him. He's badly beaten and wasn't able to walk. We had to make a stretcher to get him back here. He was unconscious and barely holding on when I left him. He'd been shot and lost a of blood. He also has what I suspect is a serious brain injury. He's not going to make it, Austin. I don't have the skills or equipment to save him," she said, her voice low as she admitted defeat.

"No!"

She nodded, visibly swallowing down tears. "Austin, I'm surprised he's still hanging on. So many times on the way back here, I thought we'd lost him. He's a fighter, but…"

"I have to see him!" he told her, Dr. Bastani forgotten.

Austin wanted to scream and rage and kill Zander with his bare hands. He wanted to make the man suffer in pain before he ended it. Nash had had his whole life ahead of him and hadn't deserved to die such a horrible death. Neither had his daughter, but he couldn't allow himself to think about that now. He wouldn't.

"He has said your name a few times. Your name and the word 'Blackdown,'" she said. "I think he wants to say goodbye."

"Blackdown? What's that?" he asked.

She shrugged. "I have no idea. It could be anything. He could be hallucinating."

"Austin!" someone shouted his name.

He looked up and saw Gretchen, a huge smile on her face. His initial reaction was anger. How could she smile, now of all times? And then he looked closer. There were tears streaming down her face, but she was smiling. He'd always thought the woman was a little off, but now he knew for sure. She was probably going to tell him they needed to pray, he realized, and he might shoot her if she did.

"Oh my God," he heard Amanda gasp.

"What's wrong?" he asked, reaching for his weapon, almost looking forward to killing someone.

Amanda pointed to the trees where they had often eaten their dinners. A bench had been pushed over, and Wendell was standing beside it, mouth agape as he stared at where the house had been. Just behind him, he saw Savannah's head appear out of the ground, from within a hole beneath where the bench had sat.

He jumped to his feet, his mind telling him it wasn't possible, but his heart demanding it to be real. He crossed the gravel driveway, reaching Savannah where she stood beside Wendell staring at the fiery scene.

"Savannah!" he croaked.

She looked up and saw him, and shoved Wendell out of the way as she ran to him. Austin jogged towards her, pulling her into his arms, finally feeling her solid form and knowing it was real. Savannah was alive.

"Dad," she sobbed into his shoulder.

"Shh, I've got you, you're okay," he soothed her.

She cried in earnest for several minutes while he held her. He looked up then and saw Ennis watching him, a small smile on his face. Wendell was swaying beside him. Austin couldn't be sure, but the guy looked drunk.

"The escape tunnel," Ennis said. "It took some time for us to get out, but it had closed on the other side, shutting out the fire. Sorry it took us so long to break out."

"The tunnel," he echoed. "I forgot about it…"

Ennis grinned, nodding, and Savannah hugged him tighter.

Amanda was beside them then, her hand resting on his shoulder. "I've got to go," she whispered.

He nodded. "I'll go with you."

"Where are you going?" Savannah asked.

Amanda and Austin exchanged a look. "To get Nash."

"You found him?" she exclaimed, wiping the tears from her cheeks, a smile on her face.

Amanda grimaced. "We did. I need to tend to him, though. Maybe you should stay here," she said softly.

Austin watched Savannah's face fall. Fresh tears appeared in her eyes. "Oh no," she whispered, covering her mouth with her hand.

Ennis wrapped an arm around Savannah's shoulders, looking at Austin. "I'll take care of her. Go."

Austin nodded before following Amanda and Jordan back across the driveway. He ignored the smoldering ruins as he passed. Savannah was okay. It seemed unreal, but his daughter was alive and well.

"Just up here," Amanda said as they climbed up the hill, past the rock he had taken to calling his own little quiet place.

Mike appeared out of nowhere, his face grim. Amanda rushed into the small cave created by a couple of fallen trees. It was an excellent hiding place. Austin followed behind Amanda, wincing when he saw Nash's battered body lying on a bed of pine needles.

"Nash," he whispered, dropping to the kid's side and taking his hand in his.

The kid was grossly pale, almost gray. Austin understood what Amanda meant. It was nothing short of a miracle that the boy was still breathing.

Amanda was busy checking his eyes, opening one and then the other. The look on her face told Austin it wasn't good. His heart clenched in his chest. Suddenly, he almost wanted Nash to pass. It was clear he was suffering.

"Hang in there, buddy," he forced himself to say. "Amanda is going to fix you right up. I'm sorry it took us so long to get back to you. We were a little busy," he tried to joke, the words all lies. He wanted to tell Nash to let go, that it would be okay, but he couldn't quite make himself. Not after he'd fought this hard to remain alive.

Nash's cracked, bloodied lips moved, as if he were trying to smile. "Get 'em?" he asked.

"We did," Austin lied.

Amanda moved to put her fingers on Nash's wrist. Her facial

expression was telling. Austin met her eyes and saw the sadness. She gave a slight shake of her head. His heart sank as he turned to look at Nash's face.

"Black," Nash mumbled.

Austin leaned closer, putting his ear just above Nash's mouth to try and hear the faint whisper. "Say it again. What are you trying to tell us?" Austin asked gently.

"Black—down," he said, pushing the word over his lips with a great deal of effort.

"Blackdown?" Austin asked, clarifying what he thought he'd heard, and what Amanda had told him.

Nash gave a weak squeeze to Austin's hand, confirming he'd heard correctly.

Amanda held Nash's other hand in hers, using her other hand to gently stroke his arm. They sat with Nash for several long minutes, listening to his breathing slow.

"You can go, Nash," Austin finally whispered. "You did well. I heard your message, and trust me, I am going to figure out what Blackdown is. You're an amazing kid and I will never forget you," Austin said, his throat closing as he spoke, staring into Nash's ghostly-pale face.

Amanda offered him a small smile, still stroking Nash's arm, lulling him into a peaceful sleep he'd never wake up from.

It wasn't long before Nash's breathing stopped, but Austin couldn't let go of his hand. He'd been there when his wife had died, and remembered the moment vividly. He knew what death looked like. He'd hoped to never see it again, but he'd never forget this goodbye, either.

Amanda gently lowered Nash's wrist before moving to place two fingers on the side of Nash's neck. Austin held his breath, waiting for the verdict. Amanda's shoulders slumped forward as she pulled her hand away. Austin stared at the now relaxed features of the guy he'd come to consider a close friend. The loss hit him hard then, much harder than he could have anticipated, and he fell forward over him.

He shook his head. "I'm sorry, Nash. I'm so sorry. I should have gone after you. I should have listened to you," he whispered, the lump in his throat growing painful.

"He waited for you," Amanda whispered, "to say goodbye."

Austin nodded. "I'm glad I got to say goodbye."

Amanda was openly sobbing now. Austin couldn't shake the guilt weighing on his shoulders. Amanda had known something was off. She'd done everything in her power to save him, and he'd died anyway. Austin hated that he hadn't himself been there to help Nash when he'd needed it, like Nash had been there for him to help save Savannah after she'd been kidnapped. He'd never forget that.

"We should get back," Amanda said suddenly, wiping her face and clearing her throat.

"Amanda, take a minute," he told her.

She shook her head. "No, we need to get back. We need to be ready in case those soldiers come back. We know they will.

We have the caches of supplies. We need to get those," she said, getting to her feet, hunched over and walking out of the natural shelter, back to her all-business self.

Austin took one last look at Nash before he followed her out. Mike was standing there, silent tears streaming down his face. Austin knew Nash's death was going to be hard news to pass on. The group was tight-knit, and Nash had been liked, despite some of the drama that had been going on the past few days. He'd been young and energetic, and an easy guy to be around. An easy guy to care about and befriend.

"I'll stay with him," Mike said in a somber voice.

Amanda nodded. "I'm sure everyone will want to pay their respects. Fire off a shot if you see or hear anyone coming," she said.

"Yes, ma'am," he replied.

Austin walked behind her, impressed by the new respect Amanda had clearly earned from the revivalists. They'd initially been hesitant to follow her commands, none of them willing to be trained fighters, but that had clearly changed.

Austin reached for her hand, not caring what anyone thought about the public display of affection. It wasn't necessarily a romantic gesture anyway. It was about him being there for her, supporting her in what he knew was a difficult time. They might have won this small skirmish, but he knew it wasn't over. As long as Zander was alive, he was going to keep coming for them.

37

Ennis stared at what remained of his house, at what had once been his pride and joy. He could hear the soft murmurs of the revivalists consoling each other over the loss of Audrey and Bonnie. While it was sad to lose anyone, he'd been left reeling at the thought of having nothing. He had prepped and stored for years. He'd always had an abundance of the things he needed to survive. Now, he had nothing. He couldn't believe it was all gone.

"All the alcohol is gone," Wendell said from beside him.

Ennis turned to glare at him. "You drank most of it before it had a chance to burn!" he seethed. "You did nothing! Nothing to help us escape! I don't know what's wrong with you, Wendy, but you've got some serious issues."

"I'm sorry. I thought we were going to die," he mumbled.

"We would have."

Wendell gave a drunken smile. The guy was three sheets to the wind and barely functioning. "I couldn't stand the thought of it all going to waste," he said.

"You mean you couldn't stand the thought of dying and thought you'd drink yourself into oblivion first, leaving me and Savannah to figure out how to save your sorry butt!"

"Hey, I tried," he mumbled.

Ennis shook his head with disgust. Wendell had shown his true colors, and Ennis didn't like what he'd seen. Austin had been right all along. Ennis had seen the way Wendell had reacted when they'd realized the house was under attack. He'd run for the pantry, leaving him and Savannah to drop the steel door down, but not before one of the stupid flash-bangs had been tossed inside. They'd barely been able to function enough to lower the door.

"Dad?" Savannah called out.

Ennis looked to where Savannah, Malachi, and Tonya Loveridge had been huddled together in a happy reunion. Savannah was staring into the trees where Amanda and Austin had disappeared earlier. He looked up and watched Austin, holding Amanda's hand, come into the clearing, passing the hunk of metal that used to be his SUV and then standing in total silence.

He could see Amanda had been crying. Something was very wrong—more wrong than the complete loss of the house and supplies—and it was more recent than the loss of Audrey and Bonnie, which he'd been informed of already.

"What's wrong now?" Wendell blurted out.

Ennis turned to glare at him. "Shut up!" he hissed.

Jordan and Ezra, along with Gretchen and Harlen, had been scouring the perimeter, making sure the soldiers were well and truly gone. They moved back towards the rest of them, waiting to hear what Amanda had to say. Tonya, who had been tending Drew's arm, got to her feet.

Amanda looked around the group, her eyes going to Savannah. "Nash didn't make it," she said, her voice so low that Ennis almost convinced himself he hadn't heard her correctly.

Savannah put a hand to her mouth, shaking her head. "No," she sobbed. "No!"

Austin dropped Amanda's hand and went to Savannah, wrapping her in his arms again. Malachi stood behind her, his face pale as he stared at Amanda. Ennis knew of the drama, knew of Savannah's role in all of it, and knew it was likely the stress and anger of that drama that had driven Nash to leave the house alone in the first place, at least in part. The guilt that Savannah and Malachi would be carrying would be tremendous. His heart broke doubly thinking of it, and knowing that wasn't what Nash would want for them.

"We'll bury him here," Ennis spoke up.

Amanda nodded. "I think that's a good idea."

"Where is he?" Ezra asked.

"Mike is with him. If you'd like to say goodbye, I'll take you there," Amanda said.

Everyone except Wendell walked towards Amanda. Austin, with his arm wrapped around Savannah's shoulders, began to head back into the trees. Ennis could hear him whispering comforting words, telling her it was best if she didn't see him. As expected, Savannah insisted. She was a stubborn, brave girl, which Ennis admired.

One by one, the residents of the house went in to say their goodbyes. When it was Ennis's turn, he took a deep breath, preparing himself. He'd seen the looks on the faces of the others as they'd come out of the shelter. He knew it was bad. He'd tried to think of an excuse to avoid seeing Nash, but nothing valid came to mind. He had to face the death of someone he'd called a friend.

Nothing could have prepared him for what he saw. Real tears ran down his face as he looked at the body that had once been so full of life. Nash had saved his life. There was no way Wendell would have figured out how to open the door to that house. He closed his eyes and thought about the teenaged boy with the big smile and the surfer-boy good looks. He'd been too good for all of them, Ennis couldn't help thinking.

"I'm sorry, Nash. I'm so sorry. Thank you for saving me," Ennis whispered before taking a few deep breaths and rejoining the others.

Some of the men were already scouting out a place to bury his body and those of the women who'd been shot down. Without tools, digging in the rocky ground would be difficult, but he could see the determination on their faces.

"I need to get the doctor," Austin said, pulling Ennis to the side.

"You got her?" he asked with shock.

Austin nodded. "We did."

"I'll go with you," he offered.

Austin looked back at him, a slight smile cracking his lips as he nodded. "Thank you."

After speaking with Amanda and Savannah, Austin started the walk up the hill, Ennis beside him. There was a lot that needed to be said, but it wasn't the right time. Ennis was content to accept the peace between them.

"Savannah is one tough girl," Ennis said, interrupting the silence.

"I want to know every detail of what happened while we were gone, including the part about Savannah getting beaten up," he commented, a slight growl in his voice.

"She didn't get beaten up. She fell down a ravine when Fabio was chasing her," Ennis said.

Austin stopped walking. "Fell down a ravine? Who's Fabio?"

Ennis quickly filled him in, finishing up simply. "We made it back to the house and were just about to go back out on watch when we heard gunfire. It didn't take long to figure out Fabio had made it back to the others and told them where to start looking for us."

"We should have been better prepared," Austin muttered.

"Yes, we should have, but we weren't. Savannah and I realized we were surrounded and had nowhere to run. We shut the front door, dropping the steel barricade, and locked ourselves in the house. We thought we'd ride it out at first. We hoped the soldiers would realize they couldn't get in and retreat. Instead, they tried to burn us out," Ennis grumbled. "That's when we went for the tunnel."

"Try? They did burn you out! Speaking of that tunnel—you said before that Nash saved you," Austin said, choking some on the kid's name. "Why not use the tunnel then? I'd forgotten you'd had the damn thing."

"There wasn't enough juice to get it open when the house froze up," Ennis replied simply, remembering how angry he'd been when even his escape hatch had seemed to be faulty. It had come through in the end, though, that was for sure.

"And Wendell?" Austin inquired.

Ennis scoffed. "He was in the pantry downing as many bottles of vodka as he could."

"Ennis, I know we've talked a lot about this, but that guy is bad news," Austin said again.

"I know. I agree. I'm not sure what to do with him," Ennis admitted. "My conscience won't let me send him away on his own. We both know he'll die."

"At least we know he has to be sober for a while. It's about time he had to face life head-on instead of living in that bottle," Austin muttered.

"I did talk to him about the drinking, but obviously he ignored me."

"We'll figure it out. She's up there," Austin said, pointing to a large rock on the hillside.

The horses were casually chomping grass nearby. When Austin had told him they'd left the horses, Ennis had expected them to be gone, stolen by whatever soldiers had survived. Seeing them was about the only bright spot in what had turned out to be one of the worst days of his life.

"Are you sure?" Ennis asked, not seeing anyone.

"Dr. Bastani?" Austin called out.

"It's about time! Why would you leave me up here to die! Do you actually think I'll help you, especially after the way you've treated me?" a woman's voice floated over the area.

Austin rolled his eyes. "Yep, still here."

Ennis chuckled. "She sounds pleasant."

"Maybe we can send her and Wendell off to live together," he mumbled, heading for the rock.

Ennis smiled. "Just as soon as we save the world, we'll ship them off."

38

Dusk was falling fast. Austin looked around the circle of people sitting around the small campfire they'd made. Everyone had the same look of sadness and despair. The losses they'd endured that day had been severe—more than enough to break their spirits. Even he was struggling to stay focused on the goal.

Dr. Bastani sat up against a rock, her hands and ankles still bound. He wasn't sure what to do with her. They'd just finished burying the dead and were all lost in their own thoughts. Savannah had barely spoken since she'd seen Nash. He hated that she'd insisted on saying goodbye, knowing the image of his beaten face would stay with her forever. He had warned her, and tried to prepare her, but it hadn't been enough.

"You may as well let me go," Dr. Bastani snapped.

Austin looked at her, realizing she was right. There was little she could to do to help them now. Amanda had told him the mine had been destroyed along with all the electrical equipment. He'd had the USB tucked safely away, buried in a plastic container under a few rocks, but without the laptop, what good was it? He'd decided to hide it before he'd left to get the doctor, just in case he was captured. He also hadn't trusted Wendell not to take the thing and try to use it as leverage or sell it to the highest bidder. But now…

"You're right," he grumbled. "You'll have to walk back to your house. We can't let you take a horse," he told her.

"You can't let her go," Ennis protested.

Austin shrugged. "What's the point of having her? She doesn't want to be here, and there's nothing she can do without the laptop."

Ennis got up and walked back to the hole in the ground, disappearing inside before emerging a few minutes later carrying the laptop bag.

"What's that?" Amanda asked.

"Savannah insisted on taking this stupid thing. I told her to leave it, but she grabbed it anyways," Ennis said with a grin.

Austin turned to his daughter to congratulate her for her fast thinking, but the words died on his lips. She wasn't paying attention. She had a dead look on her face as she stared at the flames. She was thoroughly traumatized. He'd seen the look before on the faces of soldiers who'd seen their buddies die in front of them.

"She's a smart kid," he said softly, moving away from the crowd to retrieve the buried USB.

He returned with the drive in hand and he stopped in front of the doctor, holding it up.

"What do you want me to do with that?" she snapped.

"I've already told you," he said, his tone surly.

She looked away. "I won't do anything until you untie me."

"Don't untie her, not yet," Amanda said.

Austin turned to look at her. "Why not?"

"We need to figure out what we're going to do first," she said, her voice revealing her exhaustion.

"I agree," Ennis said, taking his seat once again, the laptop tucked against his side.

Austin moved to sit down, looking at the somber faces around the fire. The devastation smoldering behind him was hard to look at.

"We can move on," he started, looking at Malachi and knowing he was essentially the leader of the revivalist group.

"Where?" Mike asked.

Austin shrugged. "I don't know. I do know these mountains are littered with hunting cabins. We might be able to find one to take for our own."

"What if they keep looking for us?" Tonya asked.

"They want us because of that USB," Gretchen stated.

Austin nodded. "That's true. They want the USB, and their leader Zander has a personal vendetta against me. He'll keep coming for me. If you want to leave and go separate ways, I don't blame you a bit."

"Mom, we're family now," Malachi said in a hushed tone.

Tonya took a deep breath before speaking. "He's right. We're a family now. All of us, we've gotten this far together. I think we stay together."

Austin gauged the reactions of the others, waiting to see if they would stay or go. He had no real personal connection with any of them, but he knew they'd die if they all tried to go it alone. He didn't want anyone else to die.

"Personally, I'm willing to stand behind you," Wendell said.

Austin turned to look at the man's face. "Really??" Austin asked, knowing the guy was only trying to be nice now because he knew he'd pushed Ennis too far.

"Yes. I'll fight for you," he said, his chin raised.

Austin rolled his eyes. "Thanks," he said sarcastically.

Ennis was shaking his head, clearly disgusted by the sudden display of butt-kissing. Wendell had sobered up and realized his mistakes, but he'd burned the last bridge he'd had standing with Ennis. He had no friends in the house.

One by one, though, the others had begun nodding, and Austin realized they were truly in this together now. He found he was glad for it.

"Do we stay here tonight?" Malachi asked.

Austin looked up at the sky and nodded. "I don't think we have a choice. Everyone, sleep with your weapons close. We'll take turns keeping watch. I want at least two people awake at all times. The faintest noise, the snapping of a twig, anything at all, you point and shoot. The rest of us will wake up in a hurry."

They were all going to bed hungry, but he doubted anyone would have been able to eat even if there had been food. The hits kept coming. It was enough to break even the strongest person.

39

Austin was exhausted. They had been moving for two weeks straight. Traveling on foot, taking turns riding the horses. They'd scavenged edible wilds, including some very good wild strawberries, but they were all in serious need of protein. They'd decided not to take the time to hunt, though. They wanted to keep moving, to put as much distance between themselves and the NWO as possible. It was a risk to deprive their bodies of nutrition, but as long as they ate a little something every day, including some really nasty bugs, they could survive for weeks.

Fortunately, there had been no shortage of water. They had attempted to fish, catching a few tiny ones that they'd cooked on sticks. Malachi had managed to catch a few frogs, as well, but the meat they'd offered had been negligible. They were starving in a very literal sense. The walking meant more calorie burning, too, which wasn't good for their long-term survival, but it was a necessary evil.

Austin had chosen to walk most of the time, leaving the horses for the women, like Tonya and Savannah and the doctor, who weren't as strong as the rest of them. His chivalry was wreaking havoc on his recently-healed leg. He wasn't sure how much more he could take.

He looked up, hearing the plodding of the horses' hooves coming closer and spotted Amanda atop Raven with Malachi behind her on Charlie. They had ridden out, searching for one of the elusive hunting cabins he knew had to be around.

"Found one!" Amanda said gleefully.

He looked at the dark circles under her eyes, noticing how much weight she'd lost in her face since they'd set out two weeks earlier. The physical exertion, lack of sleep, and severe lack of food was taking its toll on everyone.

"You found a cabin?" Tonya asked hopefully.

Amanda was still grinning as she slid off the horse's back. "We did. It's maybe five miles west. We can make it by nightfall."

There were sounds of muted exhilaration at the thought of finally finding a place to call home, however temporary it might be; it would be a roof, at least. Malachi helped his mother into Charlie's saddle, holding the reins and leading the way as they walked over the rocky ground. Austin guessed they were on the west side of the Rockies, probably in Utah.

"Is it a cabin?" Austin asked Amanda.

She nodded. "Yes—not big, but it is empty. We didn't take a

lot of time to scout around, but it didn't look like anyone had been in it for a long time. I think it will do for now. We'll all be very cozy."

"Anything is better than nothing at all," he muttered.

By the time they made it to the A-frame cabin, Austin felt as if he was at his wit's end. He'd pushed himself to the max of his endurance. Despite his attempts to sleep at night, nightmares had kept him awake. He constantly felt like there was someone lurking in the shadows. They were all suffering from PTSD in one way or another.

Everyone stumbled inside. There were only two chairs in the living area, and one at the tiny wood table. Tonya, Drew, who was still healing from his gunshot, and Gretchen were given the chairs while everyone else found a spot to rest on the floor. Even the good Dr. Bastani had been quiet over the last couple of days.

"Now would be a good time for you to work on that file," Austin said after they'd all had some time to rest.

She shot him a glare. "No, thank you."

It was the same fight they'd had every evening when they'd stopped to rest through the nights. For whatever reason, the doctor refused to try opening the encrypted file with the software he was keeping safe. He didn't trust her not to smash the discs, truth be told.

"Look, you might hold the answer to making all of this go away. You alone might be the only person in the world who can unlock the key that shuts this thing down," Austin said.

The others around the room were staring at her. They were all angry with the woman for her obstinance and refusal to do the one simple task. He was seriously considering leaving her behind at this point, too. She was dead weight. Only the fact that she seemed to be their only real shot against the NWO had kept him dragging her along for this long.

"I told you, I don't want to know. Whatever is in that file is bad news. I don't want to know what's to come. Ignorance is bliss," she retorted.

Austin scoffed. "Ignorance is a lame excuse. You're not an ignorant woman. You left the NSA because you knew something was coming. That was a cop-out. You ran and hid while they did their thing. Now's your chance to make a difference," he told her.

She shook her head. "It's too late. It's already happening."

"If you'd seen the death in the cities, the starving children, you wouldn't think that way," Amanda said in a quiet voice.

Dr. Bastani shrugged. "I chose to hide away. I knew I couldn't live forever in my little hideout, and I was okay with that. I was okay with dying."

"You made that choice for everyone else, though," Malachi interjected. "My dad died because you chose not to take a stand."

Dr. Bastani looked guilty, however briefly, but visibly pushed the emotion away. "I couldn't have taken a stand. You don't understand how powerful these people are. They would have killed me, just like they killed Callum."

Austin shook his head. "Callum died trying to stop it."

"And look what good that did. He died," the doctor retorted.

"You don't have to read the information. Do whatever it is you do with those discs and I'll read it. We'll let you go as soon as you unlock that file," Austin promised.

"Do you really think you're some kind of hero? Do you actually believe you can stop them?" she asked with disbelief.

Austin mulled over the question. "I don't know. I don't know because I don't know what it is I'm up against. I have to try. I'm not like you. I can't run and hide and hope someone else will do something. I can't roll over and die because trying is too hard. I have a kid to think about. I don't know if you can understand that, but I cannot give up. It's not an option."

Savannah offered him a faint smile before looking at the doctor. He couldn't understand Bastani's reluctance. His eyes drifted to Wendell, who was sitting near the doctor. Austin had been watching the guy for the last two weeks, as he tried to buddy up to the only person he hadn't made mad.

Dr. Bastani shook her head. "I can't," she replied.

"Okay, fine, so tell me this," he said with a sigh. "How much do you know about what they were planning? I mean, Callum said you figured out the plot long before he did, which is why you quit and ran. What is Blackdown? Nash tried to tell me about it before he died and I've seen it mentioned in a couple of the memos Callum stole. Have you heard about it?" he asked.

The doctor's eyes widened. "Blackdown?" she whispered.

He nodded. "Yes. It was the last thing Nash said. Amanda said he was in the lair with computers and a functioning satellite. I'm assuming that's where he heard it."

"Where's that laptop?" she asked suddenly.

Savannah looked at Austin before jumping up and grabbing the case. She delivered it to the doctor, who quickly fired up the machine.

"Is it charged?" he asked, hoping the battery was still full from when he'd put it on the solar charger the day before, in the hopes that she would use the thing.

Dr. Bastani nodded. "It is. Give me the discs," she ordered.

Austin jumped to his feet, his energy renewed at the thought of finally uncovering what it was that had gotten Callum killed. He handed her the discs and took a seat nearby. Everyone watched and waited.

She looked up, seemingly surprised to see so many eyes on her. "This isn't instant. Please don't stare at me the whole time. It's going to take some time," she muttered.

Austin burst into laughter and was soon joined by the others. Their emotional journey to find out what secrets the USB held was finally coming to an end. He knew the information was only the beginning to the next leg of their journey, but it was something. He was only sad Nash couldn't be there to see what it was that was happening, but he had a feeling Nash had already figured it out before he'd died. Now it was their turn.

END OF SURVIVE THE AFTERMATH

SMALL TOWN EMP BOOK TWO

Survive the Chaos, 11 July 2019

Survive the Aftermath, 8 August 2019

Survive the Conflict, 12 September 2019

PS: Do you love EMP post-apocalyptic fiction? Then keep reading for exclusive extracts from ***Survive the Conflict*** and ***Freezing Point.***

THANK YOU

Thank you for purchasing *Survive the Aftermath*
(Small Town EMP Book Two)

Get prepared and sign-up to Grace's mailing list and be
notified of her next release:
www.gracehamiltonbooks.com/mailing-list

If you enjoyed this book:

Share it with a friend,
www.GraceHamiltonBooks.com/books

Leave a review at:

ABOUT GRACE HAMILTON

Grace Hamilton is the prepper pen-name for a bad-ass, survivalist momma-bear of four kids, and wife to a wonderful husband. After being stuck in a mountain cabin for six days following a flash flood, she decided she never wanted to feel so powerless or have to send her kids to bed hungry again. Now she lives the prepper lifestyle and knows that if SHTF or TEOTWAWKI happens, she'll be ready to help protect and provide for her family.

Combine this survivalist mentality with a vivid imagination (as well as a slightly unhealthy day dreaming habit) and you get a prepper fiction author. Grace spends her days thinking about the worst possible survival situations that a person could be thrown into, then throwing her characters into these night-mares while trying to figure out "What SHOULD you do in this situation?"

You will find Grace on:

BLURB

The world has descended into a nightmarish hell. Death and destruction reign at every turn. Everywhere Austin Merryman has led his tightknit group of survivors has gone from bad to worse as enemies pursue them for the intelligence he possesses. Yet, his group remains steadfastly together even as the infighting continues.

It's only when the cryptologist traveling with them finally breaks through the last coded barrier, exposing the full extent of the data on the mysterious USB drive, that their luck finally seems to be turning. So many have already given their lives to secure the information, and now they know why.

Now, a small window of opportunity remains for stopping the New World Order from succeeding in their plans, but Austin and his cohorts will have to move fast. Once again, splitting up may be their only option, but at what cost? And can they really launch the countermeasures that could take down the NWO's plan for domination?

But when the enemy closes in and lives of his entire group are threatened, Austin will be forced to choose between his family and the ultimate survival of the entire world...

Grab your copy of *Survive the Conflict*
Available September 12th, 2019
www.GraceHamiltonBooks.com

EXCERPT

Austin Merryman kept his guard up as he headed inside the small convenience store, Amanda Peterson right behind him. The place had been used to serve campers staying in the nearby RV park, and he knew it wasn't likely they'd find any food, but they had to try. Months without any stores and surviving by the seat of his pants meant that just about anything he could loot from the store could be useful—anything they could carry off, anyway.

Austin double-checked behind the store's counter, but the place was empty. Most of the shelves were, too. Off to the side, he saw Amanda pick up some empty boxes from the shelves and then begin rummaging around in the counters beneath the old coffee station, looking for anything that could be useful. They'd learned a lot about improvising and repurposing regular everyday items, all to make living without electricity, running water, and even grocery stores possible.

Leaving her to it, he ducked down to the lower shelves and began searching through the spaces that other scavengers were more likely to have missed. The place was empty enough that he figured that was about their only shot.

"Transmission fluid and some oil," Austin said, standing with the bottles of car fluids that had rolled under a shelving unit.

"Good fuel," she replied. From the look on her face, she hadn't found anything to be excited about.

With their limited loot in plastic bags, they walked back to the door, waiting and listening for any signs that there were other people around. Their scavenging mission was proving to be futile, like the one yesterday and the day before that. They'd hoped the small towns would provide something worthwhile, but destruction had become widespread. The towns had been abandoned for some time, but only after being thoroughly ransacked.

"Clear," Austin finally muttered, stepping outside with the Glock in his right hand, ready for whatever popped up.

He would have killed for one of the ARs or M-4s they'd taken off the NWO back at the house, but their guns had been stolen right out of their hands days ago while they'd still been generally heading west toward a more temperate climate. Without any sure destination, that had been the fallback plan —to keep going and find somewhere they could hole up. They'd landed in an abandoned lodge that had seemed to have a lot of promise, but the nearby scavenging wasn't offering much to live from. Those guns, though—he could still taste the anger over losing them. It was the way of the new world, though. A game of Yankee Swap. They kept their weapons, food, and gear only until someone came along and took it. Then, they in turn did the same thing to another group. It was a revolving door of easy come and easy go with weapons, especially. He was ready for the tide to turn back in their favor and allow them to stumble on more weaponry, but it hadn't happened yet.

Amanda pointed off to the side, away from where they'd come from. "Let's head down that trail and see if we can find anything in the RVs. Maybe we'll get lucky."

He nodded, his eyes scanning the area. "But where is everyone, seriously? Bed, kitchen, shelter, and porta-potties... why wouldn't anyone make this their new home?" he pressed even as he followed her. Maybe this could work for their own needs.

"I don't know, but let's hurry up and get moving. This place is kind of creepy," she answered, her voice low. "Maybe that's reason enough."

The RV park was basically a parking lot with designated spaces. Not many trees, not much natural beauty. Even in the middle of nowhere, it was the park owner's way of packing in as many RVs as possible and taking advantage of the beauty of the area. Austin guessed they were in the lower west corner of Wyoming now, but he couldn't be sure. And had they been tracked? It was hard to tell, but he suspected that they had—whether that suspicion was made up more of paranoia or intelligence, he couldn't be sure.

Austin thought back to the months prior to the EMP, when he'd been living in the fifth-wheel with Savannah, traveling the country. They'd stayed in various campgrounds and parks of nearly all sorts, but this specimen of resting spot was the kind he'd avoided at all costs. There was no real privacy, and in the tenuous situation they were in now, there was no real cover. He and Amanda couldn't help being exposed as they walked along the narrow paved road that led into the park.

Scanning the grounds, Austin noted that there were only a handful of RVs remaining, and even so, the place looked junky and cramped. The EMP would have hit right at the beginning of the RV season, but occupants had disappeared fast. He imagined it had been an older crowd—people who full-time RV'd after retirement. They wouldn't have stood much of a chance against the soldiers or the hordes of people fleeing the cities.

"Let's start with the motorhome there," he said, pointing to the newer Class A with a slide-out and big sun shields placed in its front window. "I'll stand guard while you go in, and then we'll trade off on the next."

"Got it," Amanda replied, pulling open the flimsy door as Austin stepped to the side.

Almost as soon as she disappeared, he thought he saw movement near the picnic table parked under a single, lonely tree. He swung his gun up to point in the general direction, but whatever had moved was gone.

"Drop your weapon!"

Austin glanced over his shoulder, finding a man in his sixties standing on the one-way road behind him—bearded and thin, and pointing a hunting rifle at him.

"Sorry, mister. Apologies," Austin said, trying to keep his voice calm as he lowered his gun. He didn't drop it, but he pointed it at the ground as he faced the man. "I didn't know there was anyone around. Is this your place?"

The man smirked, closer now. "You already know who lives here. We've told you before: Stay out of our camp, and we'll stay out of yours!"

Austin shook his head, willing the man to believe him as he answered. "I've never met you before. I don't know who you think I am, but this is the first time I've ever been here. I didn't know it was occupied."

He'd made a point of using 'I' instead of 'we,' hoping Amanda would stay out of sight. If this was the man's place, they could figure out how to get her out once this guy lowered his hunting rifle.

The gun wavered, but remained aimed at him as the man scowled.

"We want to be left alone," he said after a minute had passed. "We're not causing you any trouble. There's plenty of hunting and water for us all to live here in peace. If you keep coming over here, we'll be forced to kill every one of you," he added, sounding almost saddened by the idea.

"Okay," Austin said. "I'm sorry. I'll go," he agreed, no longer wanting to argue about who he was or wasn't. The man seemed decent, and he clearly wasn't NWO. If he wasn't going to shoot his rifle, then Austin had no intention of killing him over what amounted, more than likely, to nothing more than a scrapyard of RVs that was all this man and his group had left.

"Your lady friend needs to go with you," the man said, jerking his head towards the RV.

Austin nodded, and he kept the surprise out of his voice when he called for her to come out.

She emerged with her hands up, still carrying the bag of things they'd picked up at the convenience store. The old man aimed the rifle at her now, silently telling her to leave what she'd found.

"Sorry," she said sheepishly. "I didn't realize anyone was still living here; I was just on the other side of the door. I didn't take anything. This is stuff I've been carrying around for a while," she told him. "Take a look and you'll see it came in with me."

"Drop it. Now. Or I'll drop it for you," the man said, no sympathy in his voice.

Austin widened his eyes at her, trying to tell her to let it go.

Amanda put the bag on the step outside the motorhome as she stepped down. "Sorry. We looked around and didn't see anybody. We didn't realize you were living here."

"Well, we are!" a woman's loud voice snapped from the other side of the park—near the RV by the tree where Austin had spotted movement earlier.

"We'll go. We're sorry," Amanda called out, her voice aimed toward the woman's.

"Go," the man ordered them, using his head to gesture them out of the park.

The man sidled out of their path to the road, and Austin slid his gun into his holster, not wanting to appear threatening in any way. It was nothing short of a miracle that they'd let him keep the gun, but he guessed this man didn't want a fight any more than they did. Reaching the road, he reached for Amanda's arm and kept his ears and eyes open as they headed away from the park, walking in silence until they passed the store and got headed back towards the two-lane highway they'd come in by.

"That was close," Amanda finally said.

"Yes, it was. They don't seem like bad people," he added after a minute had passed. Now that there was no danger to be felt from the man's rifle, sympathy was creeping in.

"Who do you think they thought we were?" she asked.

"Maybe part of the group that has the town we passed locked down, or people from that other campground we passed on the other side of the highway. There are clearly some very marked territories around here, and we stumbled right into the middle of them," he said.

She stopped in her tracks and he turned to face her, meeting her intelligent brown eyes with his—they were one of the few sights he'd enjoyed lately. "Why do you suppose none of them took over the hunting lodge?" she asked.

"Luck?" he joked, but then he shook his head as she turned to keep walking and he fell into step beside her. "I don't know. Maybe there was someone in there and they were run off by one of the other groups. Might not have been empty when they checked it out."

"So, do we keep looking or head back?"

He sighed disgustedly. "We're empty-handed."

"That tends to happen," she replied with a small laugh.

"You remember when needing milk or craving a candy bar meant running to the nearest store? I never realized how easy we had it before all this. I'll never take overpriced convenience store food for granted again—assuming it ever returns," he muttered.

She gripped his shoulder in quick understanding. "Let's head back. Maybe the others had better luck."

He nodded, knowing there was little else they could do. Hot and hungry, he felt more than ready to take off the boots that were making his feet feel like lead. They headed towards the lodge, the road making for a steady climb upwards. A trickling creek ran alongside it, almost nonexistent with the July heat drying everything out. Austin looked longingly at it as they walked, wishing he could dip his feet in for just a few minutes. Amanda drifted away from him, inspecting a car stopped dead in the middle of the left lane of the highway. He moved towards the creek instead, drawn to the crystal-clear water flowing downhill.

And then the silence around them, filled with the gurgling sounds of the creek and the few birds braving the heat over-head, was interrupted by gunfire.

Grab your copy of _Survive the Conflict_
Available September 12th, 2019
www.GraceHamiltonBooks.com

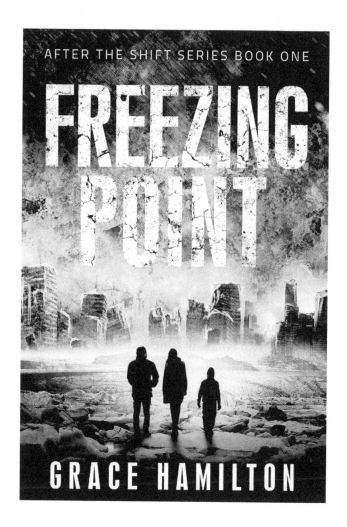

BLURB

In the dawn of a new Ice Age, families everywhere are taking to the road to escape the frigid landscape—but you can't outrun the cold.

No one could have predicted the terrifying impact of human interference in the Arctic. Shifts in the Earth's crust have led to catastrophe and now the North Pole is located in the mid-Atlantic, making much of the eastern United States an unlivable polar hellscape.

Nathan Tolley is a talented mechanic who has watched his business dry up due to gas shortages following the drastic tectonic shifts. His wife Cyndi has diligently prepped food and supplies, but it's not enough to get them through a never-ending winter. With an asthmatic young son and a new baby on the way, they'll have to find a safe place they can call home or risk freezing to death in this harsh new world.

When an old friend of Nathan's tells him that Detroit has become a paradise, with greenhouses full of food and plenty of solar energy for everyone, it sounds like the perfect place to escape. But with dangerous conditions and roving gangs, getting there seems like an impossible dream. It also seems like their only choice.

Get your copy of *Freezing Point (After the Shift Book One)* from www.GraceHamiltonBooks.com

EXCERPT

"What's that?" Freeson asked, pointing beyond the wrecker's windshield.

Nathan squinted through the swirling snowflakes peppering the glass, but the wipers were struggling to give meaningful vision beyond the red expanse of his Dodge's hood. He thought they were on the spruce-lined Ridge Road running between Lake George and Glens Falls but he couldn't be sure. The cone of light thrown out by its headlights only illuminated the blizzard itself, making it look like a messed up TV channel.

Without any real visibility, the 1981 Dodge Power Wagon W300 4x4—with driver's cab, a four-person custom-sized crew cab behind that, a wrecker boom, and a spectacle lift—grumbled deep in its engine as Nathan slowed the truck. To stop the tires fully, Nathan had to go down through the gears rather than by the application of the discs. There was a slight lateral slide before the tires bit into the fresh snow. The ice beneath was treacherous enough already without the added application of fresh flakes.

Who knows how thick the ice is over the blacktop, Nathan thought.

With the truck stopped, he tried to follow Freeson's finger out into the whirlpooling night.

For a few seconds, all he could see was the blizzard, the air filled with fat white flakes, which danced across his vision like God's dandruff. Nathan was about to ask Freeson what the hell he was playing at when he caught it. He saw taillights flicker on and the shadow of a figure move towards the truck's headlights.

Sundown for late April in Glens Falls, New York State, should have been around 7:50 p.m. The Dodge's dashboard clock said

417

the time was 5:30 p.m. and it was already full dark out on Algonquin Ridge.

The world had changed so much in the last eight years since the stars had changed position in the sky and the North Atlantic had started to freeze over. The pole star was no longer the pole star. It was thirty degrees out of whack. Couple that with the earthquakes, volcanoes, and tsunamis wrecking countries around the Pacific Rim, and the world had certainly been transformed from the one Nathan had been born into twenty-eight years before. And this year, spring hadn't come at all. Winter had spread her white skirts out in early December and had left them there. It was nearly May now, and there was still no sign of her fixing to pick them up again.

A face loomed up in the headlights, red with the cold, hair salted with snow, the flakes building up on the shoulders of the figure's parka. It was Art Simmons.

Nathan zipped his own puffy North Face Nuptse winter jacket up to his chin, opened his door, and jumped down into the powder. The snow came up to his knees and he could feel the hard ice below the chunky soles of his black Columbia Bugaboots.

Even through the thermal vest, t-shirt, and two layers of New York Jets sweatshirts, the cold bit hard into Nathan. Without the meager, volcanic-ash-diluted sun in the sky, the early evening was already steel-cold and the blizzard wind made it near murderous. He rolled his hips and galumphed through the snow towards Art.

"Nathan! Is that you?"

Art had, until recently, been a Glens Falls sheriff. He'd been a warm-hearted gregarious man whose company Nathan enjoyed a lot. But since being laid off when the local police department had shut down, he'd become sullen and distant. Seeing Art so animated now offered the most emotion Nathan had seen coming from the chubby ex-cop since before Christmas.

"What's the trouble, Art?"

Art's words tumbled in a breathless rush. Sharp and short, it was clear that the cutting air had begun constricting his throat. "Skidded. Run off the road. I couldn't even *see* the road... I'm in the ditch... Been here an hour..."

"*Run* off the road?"

Art nodded. "Glens Falls has been overrun, Nate. Scavengers tracked me. If I wasn't trying so hard to outrun 'em, I wouldn't be here now. Hadn't driven so fast, when I lost them through Selling's Bridge..."

Nathan had heard the rumors of small packs of raiders using snowmobiles to hold up residents in their cars, stealing supplies and invading homes. But he hadn't seen evidence of them himself. He'd only been told by neighbors and friends they were operating in other parts of New York State, fifty miles further south than Albany, but not until now had he gotten any notion they might be as far up in the state as Glens Falls. But now that they were here, the lack of an operational police department in town might just make them bolder and more likely to try their luck with what they could get away with.

"Where did they go?" he asked.

Art shook his head. "Guess they lost me in the blizzard when I came off the road. Maybe gone off to track some other poor bastard. They won't be far."

Freeson joined them in front of the truck, banging his arms around his own parka to put feeling into his fingers. His limp didn't help him wade through the snow and his grizzled face was grim, but Nathan knew the determination in Freeson's bones wouldn't allow his physical deficiencies to stop him doing the job Nathan paid him for. The cold might freeze and ache him, but the fire in Freeson's belly would counter the subzero conditions for sure.

Freeson hadn't been right since the accident, maybe. Quiet at times, and quick to anger at others, but he was always one hundred percent reliable.

Together, they walked the ten yards down through the snow to the roadside ditch beneath the snow-heavy trees.

An hour in the blizzard had made Art's truck almost impossible to recognize. Nathan only knew it was a white 2005 Silverado 1500 because he'd worked on it a dozen times in the past ten years. The last time had been to replace a failed water pump that had fritzed the cooling system. Nathan smiled wryly. No one needed their cooling system fixed now—not since the Earth's poles had shifted. Since that unexplained catastrophe, the Big Winter's new Arctic Circle had been smothering Florida and the eastern seaboard, all the way up to Pennsylvania and beyond. It had frozen the Atlantic clear from the U.S. to North Africa.

Art told them he'd been turning the taillights on and off every ten minutes to signal to anyone who might be passing, trying to preserve battery life at the same time. He said Nathan's wrecker had been the first vehicle to show up since his slow-motion slide into the ditch.

Nathan scratched his head through his hood and looked up the incline of Algonquin Ridge. The Silverado was trapped between two spruces on the edge of the ditch. The tail had kicked up as the front end had dropped, leaving the back wheels floating in space—or, would have done that if the snow hadn't already drifted beneath them and begun to pack in.

There was no leeway in the tree growth to get the wrecker onto the downslope of the road, either, though the easiest way out of this would have been to pull the Silverado down the thirty-degree incline. Instead, they were going to have to pull Art's truck up the slope and fight gravity all the way.

Nathan opened his mouth to tell Freeson to get back in the wrecker and start her up, but Art placed a hand on his shoulder and pointed into the trees. "Look."

Through the forest, three sets of Ski-Doo headlights were moving along two hundred yards up beyond the treeline. The blatter of two-stroke engines was dampened by the snow, but still unmistakable. This part of the ridge was well out of town and had once been a popular tourist trail. There were wide avenues between the spruce where summer people rode chunky-tired trail bikes, and winter people, Ski-Doos. They had room to maneuver.

"They're back," said Art.

Better get this show on the road.

Get your copy of *Freezing Point (After the Shift Book One)* from www.GraceHamiltonBooks.com

WANT MORE?

WWW.GRACEHAMILTONBOOKS.COM

Made in the USA
Monee, IL
25 April 2022

95372978R00243